Knitting Up a Murder

Second Edition
A Yarn Genie Knitting Mystery

CELESTE BENNETT

Island City Publishing LLC

Library of Congress Cataloging-in-Publication Data
Bennett, Celeste
Knitting Up a Murder: a Yarn Genie Knitting Mystery/Celeste Bennett—Second edition.
Pages: 247

Summary: "Imogene Dalmat, knitting agoraphobic, believes her new husband is after her billion-dollar inheritance and is willing to kill her to get it. On the run, she sheds her rich identity and navigates life without servants or money. When she chooses undercover FBI agent Frank Bachman's car to hide in, she begins the wildest journey of her life. When her husband is found murdered with her knitting needle, Imogene enlists Frank's help to find the real killer. Imogene and Frank must sidestep their growing attraction to unwind the web of deceit surrounding her. As her world unravels, Imogene learns the truth about her life, her marriage and why more than one person wants her dead."
—provided by publisher.

ISBN-10: 0-9977380-2-2
ISBN-13: 978-0-9977380-2-5
Library of Congress Control Number: 2017903003

ACKNOWLEDGMENTS

Thanks to my writers' group, Verbosity, and my editor friend, Dee Cassidy. A special thanks to my writing buddy, Lisa Ulman, and my creative children, Katharine, Christa, Allen and Emily, who inspire me every day.

CHAPTER 1

An earsplitting, soul-piercing scream cut through the middle of my Zumba workout. I dropped the one–pound weights I was hefting and eagerly streaked towards the front door. I was almost at the door when I stepped on one of my untied shoelaces and took a headlong plunge onto the entryway rug. As I laid there cursing my aunt's sense of humor in doorbells, Gordon, my aunt's butler, calmly and deliberately stepped over me, unlatched, and swung open the massive oak doors. I rolled out of the pathway so my husband could get into the house unhindered. In the course of my rolling and flopping, I caught sight of the shoes that stepped into the entrance hall.

Jorgji did not wear black stilettos.

Still prone, my gaze roamed upwards past slim ankles, graceful calves, dark blue skirt, open-throated white silk blouse, thick gold chain necklace drooping into ample cleavage, all the way up to a bronze triangular face framed with shimmering black hair. My hands flat to the floor, my arms in push-up position, I got ready to spring back up to my feet. However, I didn't. I was nonplussed that the doorbell ringer was not my husband returning from his latest business trip.

3

"Can I help you, Miss?" Gordon blandly asked the woman—as though we got strikingly beautiful women ringing our screaming doorbell every day.

"I am looking for Jorgji Dalmat. Is thes correct?" Her accent was heavier than her mascara. A queasy feeling bloomed dead center in the pit of my stomach. Beads of nervous sweat popped out on my forehead, but since there was already sufficient workout sweat there, the nervous sweat popping was unnoticeable. I got into push-up mode and shoved my upper body up. I was trembling, just a bit, but it was enough that I couldn't get my suddenly-rubber legs under me to stand up. I plopped back down to the floor.

"Mr. Dalmat is away on business. Is there someone else who might help you? Perhaps Mrs. Dalmat?" Gordon asked, looking down at my supine position on the floor. His left eyebrow arched just a minuscule amount. This was his unemotional, butler way of saying to me (without saying it) "get off the floor."

Her gaze swept down to the floor where it blanketed me with disdain from my sweat-soaked headband right down to my untied Reeboks. Her emerald eyes narrowed a fraction, and then they narrowed even narrower when I did not get to my feet. She arched her perfectly plucked brows, looked at Gordon and asked him, "Thes her?"

Gordon reached a hand down to me. I latched on and with his help, managed to get up from the floor. My legs felt like limp ropes, but for the moment, they were holding me up. I was acutely aware of my slouchy workout attire and that the short hairs falling out of my ponytail had plastered themselves to my neck and forehead. *Darn.* If I had known it wasn't Jorgji, I would have let Gordon answer the door. I wanted to shrink into the wall, but remembering my therapist's instructions for meeting new people; I swallowed, took a deep breath and opened my mouth, only to stumble over my words, unable to talk coherently to her smashing beauty.

4

Gordon, always good at sensing my panic, spoke for me. "May we ask who is inquiring?"

The woman straightened up to her full height, thrust her chest out further and said, "Mees Dalmat."

"Yes?" I responded automatically to the mention of my name.

She laughed. Not a sparkling, warm, full-bodied laugh. It was a cynical, boarding on hysterical laugh. I was glad it was short because her laugh was more annoying than the doorbell scream.

"I am Karine," she said to Gordon. "Jorgji's..." she paused, hugged the black clutch purse she was holding in front of her closer, looked up at the ceiling as though the word she is searching for was spelled out on the acoustic tiles.

Gordon remained stock-still waiting for her to continue; his gaze never left her face. I, however, could not resist the urge to look up. Seeing only the crystal chandelier attached to the center of our white ceiling, I returned my gaze back to Karine's face. She was now smiling brazenly at Gordon with one of those smiles accustomed to getting action. She continued her sentence when Gordon provided no reaction, "...Sister. From Hayasdan. I think here you call 'Albania.' I come to see him."

Ahhh. That explained her striking good looks, her difficulty with English words, her thick Albanian accent, and her action-inducing smile. Knowing she was part of my husband's family relaxed my xenophobia—a little.

I finally found my voice and invited her in. "I'm expecting Jorgji any time now. He's been away on business." I showed Karine Dalmat into the sitting room just off the foyer. My Aunt Tilly, a mystery writer with a deadline, was already there, stoking her creative fires. Seemingly unaware of our presence, her purple pen was scribbling at a steady clip on a yellow legal pad. A pot of tea covered with the tea cozy I had knitted for her was on a stand nearby. It was one of her writing rituals—purple on yellow followed up with sips of strong green tea.

Karine stepped into the spacious room. She sized up the room's contents with one sweeping glance. She observed my preoccupied aunt for a few seconds before moving on to study the bone china cups, the silver tea set, the Renaissance artwork on the walls, the hand-crocheted lace draped over the serving table. A smile began in Karine's perfectly smooth face—until her gaze returned to me. Her brow wrinkled, the smile dissipated, the nose tipped up just a fraction of an inch higher. I appeared to be the only thing in the room she was not impressed with.

Aunt Tilly was working on the latest book in her Penelope Pembrook mystery series. She punctuated a sentence with a stabbing flourish of her pen, stopped writing and contritely looked up at us. "I'm terribly sorry. I didn't mean to be so rude—jut had to get that plot twist down before the thought was lost."

"Aunt Tilly, this is Karen Dalmat, Jorgji's sister from Albania. She's stopped by to see him," I said. "He should be home any minute. I thought maybe she could wait for him in here with you while I shower and change for dinner." It was better for my aunt to entertain Karine so I wouldn't have to.

"Yes, of course. How nice of you to visit. Do come in, my dear," Aunt Tilly said setting aside her pad of paper and pen.

My aunt, accustomed to long book signings and adoring fans, was totally at ease with Karine. They began a conversation regarding the state of unrest in the Balkan states. I was happy to remove myself from the room.

Fresh out of the shower, I wrapped up in a bath sheet and riffled through my walk in closet, uncertain of what I should wear to visit with a newly discovered sister-in-law. After much deliberation, I slid on the crinkled, jacquard-weave chiffon dress with the tiny white polka dots, the dress that I had bought while surfing the internet. I blow-dried my damp hair, which refused to cooperate. The brush tangled in my hair and pulled some of it out. I gave up my illusions of what I thought my hair should do and let my hair hang limp to my shoulders. My hair was not going to resemble anything sophisticated, so I swiped on a little mascara to appear more fashionable. I blinked while swiping. My attempts to fix the small streaks of mascara that settled above my eyelids made them more smeary. I had no choice; I wiped all the makeup off both eyes with facial cream and tissues. Staring at my sallow face and too big eyes in the mirror, I decided to forget the mascara, and just gloss an orange-based blush over the 'apple' of my cheeks, an easier task. I spritzed on a light gardenia scent and decoratively arranged around my neck one of the blue and purple cotton lace scarves I had knitted for myself.

The scarf must have taken lessons from my hair because it refused to stay properly in place until I secured it to my dress with an oyster shell pin I fished out of the dark recesses of my jewelry chest.

Satisfied that I had done the best I could to measure up to the creamy bronze and glamor of Jorgji's sister, especially under short notice, I arrived back at the sitting room just as Aunt Tilly was finishing Karine's tour of the house.

"—the then governor of Illinois had this mansion built at the turn of the century to accommodate his frequent guests," my aunt explained to Karine. "I moved in 20 years ago after my first few mystery novels became bestsellers. I've done some upkeep since then and made the third floor into an apartment for our butler, but other than that, it's mostly in its original condition."

"Will there be anything else?" Gordon asked as he folded the last of the napkins on the serving table into little triangles.

The scent of the freshly baked, warm sugar cookies Gordon had set down on a silver tray near the tea service drew me in.

"No, thank you, Gordon. The afternoon tea will be plenty. Tell the cook we'll have dinner at the usual time," Aunt Tilly told him.

"Very well, Madame." Gordon glanced around the room. He straightened one of the love seat throw pillows near me before leaving. That gave him a chance to give me that look again with no one else noticing. The brief eye contact, one brow micro fraction up, it was a look I knew from childhood. It said something without saying anything.

I supposed he was right. I should have tried to be more sociable.

I went over to where my aunt and Karine are standing, conversing about an impressionist landscape painting on the wall. They did not acknowledge my presence, so I stood silently with them like the third wheel that I was.

Aunt Tilly was focused on explaining what she liked about the artist's painting technique. Karine's focus was entirely on my aunt. She was studying my aunt's face, hovering so close that they were almost physically touching, an invasion of her personal space. Uncomfortable, I moved back to sit on the loveseat, uncertain what, if anything, I could add to a conversation on art.

"Beautiful," Karine said, refocusing her attention on the thick brush strokes. She turned in time to see me sneaking a sugar cookie with pink frosting and rainbow-colored sprinkles from the cookie tray. When she came over to the tray near me, I found myself just as tongue-tied as when I was wallowing on the welcome mat. She frowned. I fidgeted. My scarf slipped, lopsided.

"Imogene, darling," my aunt said, coming over to me, sitting and looping her arm through mine, "Karine let it slip that she is here only a few days. She is going to help Jorgji with a business project he's been delaying. Don't you think it would be nice if she stayed here so you two could get acquainted?"

"Well, I..." I cleared my throat. I was already as acquainted as I wanted to be. How could I politely say I didn't think it would be nice? Not nice at all. "It would be all right with me if she—"

Before I could conclude with 'went elsewhere' my aunt said, "It's all settled then."

My aunt's arm pressed in to tighten my arm to her side. *Yup.* No escape there. I kept my lips pressed together, vexed with my aunt's old adage, "if you've nothing nice to say, then say nothing at all." Flustered, knowing my aunt orchestrated this so I would be unable to change the course of events, I wriggled my arm free of the hold my aunt had inflicted on it. I said, "Excuse me. If Karine is staying, then I guess I'd better go make arrangements." I got up and walked towards the door, taking the easy way out.

"Imogene," my aunt called after me. I stopped. Trapped. "I've already asked Maid Mary to freshen up one of the suites for Karine."

Darn it all. After living with my aunt for 20 years, she knew me too well. I would have preferred Karine to stay in the old storage pantry off the kitchen, where Mary sometimes stayed when the weather turned bad, but Karine was to be in one of the larger rooms. I turned, smiled and nodded. I had to stay and make small talk as my excuse for the leaving the room had been removed. Unable to think of something clever I fluffed my frilly scarf, which was too tightly knotted about my neck.

The doorbell screamed. I jerked the scarf, and the oyster shell pin popped loose. It dropped to the carpet and bounced under a chair. I stooped to retrieve it, and a pair of Forzier Italian leather dress shoes stepped into my line of vision. My gaze traveled up the burnished blue Brioni suit to the crisp white shirt, deep blue hand-knit silk and cashmere blend tie. The tie that took me ten hours to knit.

Jorgji!

Relieved, I stood to greet him. I pressed against him. My arms encircled his neck in an embrace. My relief turned cold when I saw his face was a blazing glare. I turned to see what he was looking at.

Karine. She was sitting on the Louis Vuitton chair sipping tea, surreptitiously sneaking glances at the yellow legal writing pad my aunt had put on the stand. Jorgji pulled my arms off him and brushed me aside. He strode into the room and stopped where Karine was smiling up sweetly at him from over the rim of her cup.

He towered. He glared. She sipped. They exchanged terse words in Albanian.

I remained close to the doorway. In addition to my agoraphobic ways, I was a self-proclaimed wimp. If there was a family fight, I was going to take flight.

After a brief, heated exchange, things between Jorgji and Karine appeared to ease up a bit, so I sat down by Jorgji on the love seat. I knew the calm he was exhibiting resided only on the surface. The pulse at his temple was visibly throbbing, and his hands were clasped so tightly together the knuckles were white.

When Jorgji learned Karine had been invited to stay with us, his neck turned a reddish haze, and the pulse at his temple did a tango. More terse foreign words flew between them. I suspected he was trying to un-invite her from the home he and I shared with my aunt. I was secretly relieved. I did not do well around strangers and Karine was definitely strange.

When the Albanian talking stopped, the broken English started. Jorgji told my aunt and me, "Karine be best comfort in hotel. I drive her there."

As she stood, Karine smiled a syrupy smile at Aunt Tilly and said, taking her hand, "It so good of you to let me stay where I be near my Jorgji. I not see him in numeral months." Karine then turned and drizzled her smile at Jorgji and said to him, "I do not want to go. It make me unhappy to be far from you." She hugged his stiff form. "My brother."

My aunt said to Jorgji, "We have two perfectly good, unoccupied guest suites. She'll be more comfortable here than in a hotel. I must insist your sister stay with us."

I wish I had inherited the resolve that came from my

father's side of the family. When my aunt made up her mind, she was not easily dissuaded.

In an effort to mitigate my discomfort, I instructed Mary to see that Karine's luggage was taken to the empty west side suite, situated nearest my aunt. The logical choice since my aunt was the one who invited Karine to stay.

Dinner was grueling. It was a good thing I ate those cookies because I was having trouble eating in front of a stranger, especially one who made chewing food look sexy. I had trouble keeping my food from spilling down my front, so I ate carefully.

Not eating much lent credence to my pleading a headache later. I took leave of the three of them to lie down in the suite of rooms I shared with Jorgji in the east wing. Upon passing what should have been an empty bedroom in the east wing, I saw Mary turning down the bed. A glass and carafe of water had been placed on the nightstand.

"Mary?" I stepped into the room. There was a closed suitcase on the bed, another on the floor.

Mary looked up while continuing to hand-smooth the turned down sheets. "Yes, Mrs. Dalmat?"

"Why did you put our guest's things in this room?"

"I didn't bring them in, Mrs. Dalmat. Her things were already here."

I didn't know when Karine found time to waylay my plans for her to stay in the west wing, but she had.

"Is there a problem with using this room?" Mary asked.

How could I tell her I didn't want my husband's sister to be in close proximity to me? I shouldn't have minded where Karine slept. It was logical for her to want to be near to him. If I had a sister, we would probably have shared a room, no matter how big the house was. "No," I responded. "I just have a bit of a headache. I'm going to go lie down."

My headache could have been from Jorgji's behavior at

11

dinner. His posture was stiff and rigid. His voice higher pitched than normal. His hands were always clenched. What he said in English seemed forced and carefully worded. His conversations with Karine in Albanian were less careful and controlled. They bordered on hostile.

I understood how it was with family. Karine and Jorgji acted just like my cousins, Mandy and Martin, and me. We had a love-hate relationship. Sometimes they made me so angry I said a bunch of terrible words in my head. As children, they were always on their best behavior when the adults were watching, but when the adults disappeared— watch out. Martin was good at doing offensive things to me behind everyone's back. Mandy was good at playing the innocent whenever she was suspected of doing something distasteful. Maybe that was where I had seen that smile of Karine's before; it was the universal symbol for a troublemaker.

CHAPTER 2

Jorgji tossed and turned all night. I doubted he got any sleep, but he insisted on going to work the next morning because Karine was accompanying him to his office at the Chicago Stock Exchange. I had never spent the day at his office with him. I wasn't hurt over her joining him; I was mostly okay with it because I do not like elevators. I am not at ease around people. And there were a lot of people at the Exchange, people who rode in elevators. I preferred to stay home, knitting.

My aunt went out to dinner with her literary agent. As her assistant, I should have gone with them to take notes, but since she was only asking for a reprieve from the latest publishing deadlines, I was off the hook.

Jorgji managed all my aunt's business investments. That gave me more time to type her manuscripts, maintain her website, take care of her correspondence, and help her with the research for her next novel, *The Lonely Heart Club Murders*, a story taken straight from the newspaper headlines of romance, deceit, and murder for money.

With everyone gone to dinner, I had some time to

enter my aunt's office and quickly log on to her website's e-mail. Her most persistent fan, who signed on as "Undercover Fan," was not on chat that evening, so I logged back off in favor of relaxing with my knitting.

I slipped a stitch when Cookie stomped into the sitting room and asked me, "How long do you expect me to keep a drying out roast warm? I need to get home to take care of my husband. Your aunt doesn't pay me enough to be sitting here all night babysitting you."

I tried to salvage the stitch, but it had already dropped down two rows. I would have to pull those two rows out and start over to fix the slip. With a sigh, I set the partially knitted sock down and looked at my watch. It was 7:30, only thirty minutes past our usual serving time. "I'm sorry, Cookie. I had not realized it was so late. If you show me what to do, I can reheat the food when my husband and his sister get home."

Cookie gave a "harrumph" and said, "Like I'd trust you with my roast. You'd burn boiling water. I'll call my husband and let him know I'll be late." She turned and stomped back out.

Cookie's husband was seriously ill; I was sure she was needed at home, so I phoned Mary to come back and take over for Cookie.

Mary, a quiet, demure girl, was doing an excellent job of keeping the roast warm and un-dry, but when Jorgji called and said, "I still talk to Karen about business. I not home until we get agreement," I ate alone.

"Can't you talk business with her here over dinner?" I asked. I last saw him when he slipped from my arms and the comfort of our bed to shower for work. I missed him.

"No. This old business I do before marry you."

"All right," I said. "But, Cookie made a roast." It was one of his favorites.

"I love you more than roast," was his only response

before disconnecting.

I snap chatted a picture of the roast to his cell. If a roast didn't entice him home in 20 minutes, then I knew all was lost.

All was lost. I just hoped that picture didn't make him so hungry that he took Karine to dinner at Everest. Everest was our special place. It was where Jorgji proposed to me. It was sacred.

I heard a bump and what I could only assume was an Albanian swear word, and I woke up from where I had fallen asleep on the divan in our bedroom suite. The lighted dials on the clock showed 10:30. Everest closed at nine. It must have been an enormous project Karine was helping Jorgji with.

The next day I responded to all the e-mails and typed up the fourteen pages my aunt provided as an introductory chapter to *The Lonely Heart Club Murders* before returning to my sock knitting. I tried to appear focused on my knitting whenever Jorgji and Karine were around me so that Jorgji didn't know I was jealous and watching him while he watched his sister.

Karine was so beautiful he was probably worried she would get involved with the wrong type of man while visiting Chicago. He just didn't need to be so vigilant in my aunt's house. The only unattached male around there was Gordon, and he was not a threat. He was old enough to be my father. Plus he was un-phased by Karine's charms.

When Jorgji kissed me awake in the morning, I felt silly for having been jealous of the close family bond and the ethnic familiarity that he shared with Karine. Family ties are strong in the Balkans, so I should have expected that.

The close personal bonds between siblings are why I begged for a sister whenever my parents left me in the care of my latest nanny. After one particularly tearful bout of begging, my father sat me on his lap and explained, "Mothers and fathers don't request babies from a catalog. They don't always have control over when or what they have. If we do have a baby, you could end up with a brother just as easily as a sister. Do you want that?"

"No. I don't want a brother. I only want a sister." I ran off to ponder on this new revelation. I did not want a brother, especially not one like my cousin, Martin, so how did I ensure I got a sister? I figured there must be some way to do that since I knew lots of children with sisters.

At my sixth birthday party, I thought I'd found the answer. I ripped off the packing tape, peeled away the pink wrapping paper with its sparkly white bow and pulled a fairy crown and wand out of the yards and yards of pretty pink and yellow tissues in the box my parents had given me. The crown was silver with scrolling. I set it aside to get to the wand nestled under it. I was positive my wish for a sister could be granted with such a wand.

The wand had a silver scrolled metal heart attached to the tip of a long sculpted wooden handle; streamers in rainbow colors flowed out from edges of the heart. The heart was coated in sparkles and glitter, a little girl's dream. There were many other prettily wrapped gifts, most with brighter paper and bigger bows, but I only had eyes for that wand. I let Mandy wear the crown and Martin open the remaining presents while I grasped that the wand tightly to keep it safe.

"Can everyone go home now?" I asked after the presents were unwrapped and Martin had broken most of the gifts he'd helped to unwrap.

"What?" asked my mother. "It would be rude to send your guests away before cake and ice cream is served, and there are still the party games to play."

I ate two of the cookies my father baked then

devoured a slab of the chocolate cake my mother made. It took me four heaping spoons to get rid of my ice cream. When I saw that everyone else was allowing their cake to languish on their plates next to their melting vanilla ice cream, I began scooping up their uneaten cake and ice cream and eating theirs, too. Until Billy Hankins squealed on me and I was told I had to stop. It was just as well. I was getting brain freeze.

It was difficult to do things one handed, but the wand had to remain with me until I was sure I could safely use it without interruption. In my rush to pin the tail on the donkey, I stuck Martin in the arm. He slugged me, but unlike other times, I didn't cry. I held fast to that wand. Not wanting to repeat my mistake at the piñata, I peeked outside the blindfold so I could take better aim when I swung. I needed to get that candy broken free, so we could get on with the next scheduled event and get everyone out of the house.

When you are holding a wand in one hand, it's hard to control a piñata stick with the other hand. At least that was the story I told my parents when Martin got a bloody nose. That effectively ended the games.

I slipped every child attending money from my piggy bank to leave quickly. I had to pay Martin double. After they had all collected their party favors and gone, my heart held so much joy I thought it would burst before I got to use my magic wand.

My chance came when my parents were packing for a flight to Asia. I went into my father's office and crawled under his massive old oak desk, my favorite spot in our Maryland house. I closed the kneehole panel that hid my scrunched up self from view and chanted, "Faithful spirit maker of babies, please grant my wish for a sister." After I had chanted this over and over, I also added, "I promise to love her. You don't have to worry about bringing food or clothes or toys or things like that. I'll share my stuff with her. Bring her tonight if you can manage it. My parents are leaving again, and I don't want to be alone with a nanny." Then after I thought about my desire to not be alone, I added for good measure so there was no way the wish could go astray, "I want a sister only. Don't bring me a brother."

I twirled that birthday wand until the streamers got so tangled in my hair I had to run to my mother for help. She laughed and patiently untangled my hair. She fixed the wand so all the streamers were flowing freely again. When she handed the wand back, she told me, "Be careful what you wish for because not all wishes come true in the way we want them to. Now find a place to put the wand where you won't lose it because it has a special kind of magic inside. Like you."

I never saw my parents again. They died in a car crash in Asia the week after my birthday party.

The wand was broken within hours of my going to live with my cousins. They revered nothing. Martin took the wand's stick and used it for his homemade sword's handle. Mandy cut the streamers off to pin in her hair. By the time I left their house to live with my Aunt Tilly, all I had left of my parent's magic was the little dented tin heart.

I wasn't liked by my cousins as a child, so it came as no surprise to me that I didn't measure up to Karine's standards for a sister-in-law. In the few days she had been there, she hadn't said that in so many words, she was just patently rude when others weren't listening. She thrived on my discomfort so much that I found it difficult to be alone in the same room with her.

Fortunately, my aunt's house was large enough that I could find plenty of places to be where Karine was not. The bay window seat in the den overlooking the rose garden was a favorite spot of mine. The window sill was broad with a comfy, thick custom-made cushion. As a child, I would get a book from one of the nearby shelves and sit lengthwise on the sill seat with my knees drawn up, sheltered from the outside world behind the drawn heavy thermal drapes.

I was there reading in reclusive peace by the light streaming in through the bay windows when I heard the door of the den open. I was almost to my favorite part of *Harper's Fairy Funerals*, one of my aunt's less popular fantasy books. I knew that chapter well because I had typed it. I knew the guy coming down the trail looking for fairies couldn't see the trip wire. I hated to stop reading, but I did when, from behind the drapes, I heard footsteps enter the room.

I thought it was Karine come to tell me again how inept I was at everything. I remained still, waiting for whomever was there to either speak up or leave.

To my relief, I heard Jogji's voice come through the thick fabric. I closed my book and prepared to slide off the seat. When he started speaking Albanian, I carefully pulled the toe of my shoe back within the confines of my shelter and didn't let on that I was in there. I know it was rude to not speak up, but I couldn't. I leaned my head against the cool of the window glass and closed my eyes. If Karine or Jorgji opened the drapery and found me there, it would look as though I had fallen asleep in the warm sunshine pouring in through the tall windows.

They were having another of their private family conversations. I listened without the slightest bit of guilt because if I didn't understand a word of what was being said it wasn't an intrusion on their privacy.

I may not have known what was being said, but I did understand the way it was being said. I didn't have to know exactly what Karine was saying to recognize that her low guttural growls and Jorgji's pleading replies meant that Karine had the upper hand.

Jorgji did not fare well in that family disagreement. I wanted to go out and defend him, but I had been sitting there too long to just peak out and say "Hi" so I continued to fake-sleep hoping my bladder would behave until they were gone. After much discussion, most of it heated, Jorgji finally agreed with Karine and said in partial Albanian accented English. "I finish plan. You get you money share."

Karine purred something to him in Albanian, and Jorgji's voice returned to the rich, sexy timbre I remembered so well from our brief dating days. He was his sweet, charming self when he said, "You leave. Go home. I finish job."

I looked out through the tiny slit where the curtains come together, curious about this change of heart. I saw them embrace, their lips touching lightly, briefly. It appeared Jorgji had pacified her. When they moved apart, I allowed the drapery material to fall back together.

There was silence in the room for a spell, but I could tell by the lessening odor of her spicy perfume and the sound of a turning doorknob that Karine had left. Jorgji sighed, a sound like despair, then I heard the door open and close. I waited a few minutes pondering the significance of what I had seen and heard. If that was about money, then it must have been about the investment work Karine was helping Jorgji with. Jorgji's work never concerned me, so I put it out of my mind and left the room.

The next day I pondered again at what I'd seen, but I didn't know how to broach the subject with Jorgji without letting him know I had been in the room, eavesdropping.

I said to him, "You and your sister are so close. It bothers me that she doesn't like me much. I'm afraid she'll try to convince you to leave me."

He plunked his coffee cup down so hard that black liquid spilled over the rim into the saucer below. "No. No. She like you fine. I like you fine. I not leave you. She go soon. I promise. Do not worry." He stood to lightly kiss my forehead and rub my upper arms as though to warm them. Despite the summer heat, they were cold, as cold as the tendril of fear that encircled my heart.

Karine didn't go back. She stayed to help Jorgji with his business. Jorgji kept telling me not to worry, but each time Karine finagled to get him alone for a family conversation my anxiety grew. I was never invited to join their conversations, but Jorgji, accustomed to speaking English for his investment business, sprinkled in an English phrase or word, even when speaking Albanian, so I caught a few phrases during their talks.

I could have heard more of what they are saying if the walls weren't so thick.

Like Penelope in *Murder Mansion*, I "borrowed" a glass from Cookie's kitchen to press against the wall so I could hear better. Even with that darned glass I still couldn't understand what they continued to talk about. But I kept trying because my name was often mentioned.

Straightening up during a long session of crouching in a choice hearing spot, I found Gordon looking vapidly at me from the doorway of the room I was in. I flushed to have been caught red-handed or rather red-eared. Gordon raised an eyebrow, cleared his throat, handed me a stethoscope, turned roundabout and quietly left the room.

After that, I could hear everything clearly, but none of it was clear to me. The only non-Albanian words I understood were, 'more time,' 'money,' 'no' and 'accounts' or 'donuts' or something like that.

I took to carrying a small pocket pad and pencil to write things down phonetically so I could use an Albanian to English dictionary to look words up. At least I did until I realized how jealous and foolish I was being and gave it up, returning the stethoscope to Gordon.

While Cookie was at the market, I went to return my spyglass to the kitchen. It would not have been good for Cookie find me in her kitchen. Once you set your *Easy Bake Oven* on fire at the age of ten, no one ever lets you forget it.

I pushed the swinging kitchen door open and was surprised to find Karine going through one of the kitchen drawers. She seemed as surprised to see me as I was to see her. She hurriedly placed the bottle she was holding back in the drawer.

I said in what I hoped was a pleasant, un-guilty

manner, "Oh, hello. I'm just returning this glass." I held the glass up for her to see and added, "This drinking glass. A glass that people only use for drinking."

"I know what glass for," she said to me.

I hoped she didn't know what I had used that glass for. I blushed pink as I rushed to the sink, eager to be done with that unavoidable encounter with her. I startled and dropped the glass when she slammed the drawer shut. It hit the stainless steel sink bottom and shattered. I should have used plastic.

"Stupid American," Karine said as she watched me.

I said nothing. I had no legitimate counter. I had to get the mess cleaned up before Cookie showed up, so I started to search through the cupboards, to find something to clean the splinters of glass out of the sink. Karine made a disgusted sound, judging me. I tried to ignore her by busying myself opening drawers and pulling things out.

I didn't know why Karine was sticking around. She wasn't helping. All she was doing was standing and scoffing as I piled an assortment of strange kitchen gadgets on the counter. Nothing in the collection looked like it could scoop, shovel or ladle glass from the sink, so I moved on to the set of drawers furthest from Karine.

She moved along with me. Not what I'd hoped for.

The next drawer contained knives that I could maybe use to scrape the pieces of glass down the sink drain. I pulled out a knife with a wide blade and ran my fingers along the flat of it to see if it could do the job. Karine, my shadow, stepped a few inches away from me, looking at me with a strange expression on her face.

I looked at the knife, the thing that just generated a look of respect from Karine and then looked back at her, but her face had returned to its usual discourteous look. That respect was short lived.

She shrugged. No longer interested in my hunt for glass salvation, she left. I would have left too, but Cookie, who caught the door on the in swing, had already discovered me with a knife in hand scraping glass pieces into her sink drain.

Jorgji was jittery and untalkative before he left again on business, but he hadn't packed a bag, so I expected him back some time that evening.

This was the one time I wished he'd taken Karine with him because she had volunteered to cook dinner for my aunt and me so Cookie could go home early to tend to her sick husband.

Before she left, Cookie replaced her plain faded house dress with a new brown and yellow dress. A sapphire and diamond bracelet adorned her wrist. Her neck and ears were jeweled in matching stones that I'd seen before on Karine. I had also noticed Mary sporting Karine's gold scroll broach. Karine was being gracious and sweet to our household help, so I thought maybe we had reached a turning point in our in-law relationship.

But we hadn't. I was having trouble eating the traditional leg of lamb, Tavë Kosi dinner that Karine prepared and set in front of me. I watched Sheri Lewis and Lamb Chop as a kid, and I didn't find it appetizing to eat puppets, especially cute ones, but Karine was Jorgji's sister. She was trying to play nice, so I chewed a little of the lamb and yogurt dish to make it look good.

Aunt Tilly complimented Karine on the delicious meal.

Karine said, "I glad you like. Eat much."

My aunt nudged me with her foot under the table.

She could have nudged me all she wanted, I was not going to compliment anything Karen did. I didn't even like the smell of the meal. The best anyone could have hoped for out of me was that I didn't complain.

While my aunt slowly chewed her food, I pushed the meat around on my plate with a fork to disguise my not eating Lamb Chop. I wished I could have accidentally dropped some on the floor to get rid of it because there are only so many times you can circle a plate before someone notices nothing is missing.

We needed a dog.

To my surprise, I heard the doorbell scream, and we were soon joined by Jorgji.

"I'm so pleased you made it home in time for dinner," I said, jumping up, brightening at the thought of him helping us eat the meal to divert attention away from my not eating.

Mary pulled open the china cabinet to bring out a full place setting for Jorgji. The conversation flowed around her as she sat the plate, utensils, and napkin in their precise spots.

"You eat already?" Karine asked Jorgji.

"No. Look good. You fix?" Jorgji responded.

"It no good. You not like. I get something from kitchen for you." Karine popped up and made as though to leave for the kitchen.

"No. I eat this."

At the door, Karine stopped dead in her tracks and turned back to look at the table where Mary was reaching for the serving utensil.

Karine ran back and wrenched the ladle handle from a confused Mary. Their eyes locked. Mary pulled her hand back as though it was scorched. Karine scooped up a minuscule helping and put a few splatters of food on Jorgji's plate. He looked at the plate questioningly, then at her.

"Not good for health to eat heavy," she told him. I looked down at the massive amount of Tavë Kosi she had heaped on my plate. No doubt about her affections for me.

Jorgji scraped up a bit from his plate and chewed it for a few seconds. He tipped his head and swished the food around in his mouth before spitting it out into his napkin. He asked Karine, "Ju vënë në kerri?"

I opened the translation book I had kept hidden in my pocket and looked up his question. He asked, 'you put in curry'?

Karine smiled at him and said, "Hesht, budalla."

I thought that was cute because I'd never had a sister to call me a 'fool' or tell me to 'shut up' like that. I also never had a sibling to fight with either, like the fight Jorgji and Karine had. There wasn't time for me to look up any of the words, so I just watched, mesmerized as my usually charming husband lost his charm. His sister never had any.

In the midst of their argument, Jorgji slammed down his fork and rose to his feet. It was clear he wasn't going to eat the rest of his meal. There was no doubt of it when he ordered Mary to take his plate, food and all and dump it in the garbage. Aunt Tilly and I looked on in horror as he foisted the plate on poor bewildered Mary. Mary looked from Jorgji to Aunt Tilly. Aunt Tilly gave Mary a nod. She took the plate. Jorgji picked up my plate and then Aunt Tilly's and stacked them on top of the plate he originally had given to Mary. Mary carried the teetering plates out.

Jorgji then summoned Gordon and demanded that we were served something Karine had not prepared.

Lamb Chop and Sherry would have been proud.

Karine wasn't proud. She was furious. Mary and Gordon pretended they lost their hearing as they cleared away the old plates during Jorgji and Karine's Albanian shouting match.

Mary shakily poured fresh tea into our cups; most of it got in. The siblings' fight roared on around us while my aunt sipped her tea. I was not drinking. It was enough for me to keep my smile under control. I had trouble not smiling as sedate Gordon served up piping hot potato and kale soup with crusty rolls.

While my aunt and I buttered our crusty rolls and spooned up our soup, Karine packed her bags.

At the door, she turned with her two suitcases and shouted at Jorgji, "This not end. You not rid of me. You owe me. Much." Then she and her black stilettos stepped across the front threshold and into the waiting taxi.

She was gone.

An upset Jorgji slammed, locked and bolted the door the second Karine was through it.

Jorgji was so angry he didn't finish his potato soup.

I was so upset I consumed all the deliciously warm sugar, butter, and flour Hallë cookies Karine had prepared for our dessert.

My aunt was so upset that she took to her bed where she later died of a coronary.

CHAPTER 3

Flowers and tears flowed freely as funeral attendees sat on plush crushed-velvet-seated pews and sniffed into fancy lace-trimmed hankies that they plucked from little wicker baskets scattered around St. Mary's Cathedral.

I sat quietly with Martin, Mandy, and Jorgji in the front pew reserved for family. People of all shapes, skin colors and sizes shuffled past my aunt's floral bedecked, bronze casket. The unbroken line of black-garbed mourners strung out interminably long as her fans, friends, and foes passed by the rows of flowers to get to the box's contents and have one last look at the mortician's handiwork before leaving for the elaborate luncheon.

In addition to the sedatives I'd been prescribed, Jorgji must have put something in my juice that morning. My arms and legs felt like lead weights. Try as I might, I was unable to stand. It was just as well. Even if I could have stood, I wouldn't have been able to force myself over to the open casket for a last farewell. I was not holding back because I was drugged and I wasn't holding back because I am allergic to flowers; I was not even immobilized by an irrational fear of the dead. It was my fear of the living—especially the ones with cameras and notebooks—that immobilized me and held me back from one final show of devotion.

My aunt always attracted attention wherever she went. Death did not lessen the draw. I recognized only a few of the mourners shuffling past. The rest were either there so they could say they were at the funeral of a famous mystery writer or were the paparazzi.

When Aunt Tilly died in her sleep of heart failure, I crashed. Hard. I fell into a hole of despair that I couldn't crawl out of. Jorgji believed prescribed sedatives would help. They didn't. Sweet Jorgji. He never complained, even though he had to take care of everything. The funeral arrangements. The luncheon arrangements. Me.

I didn't know how I could have gotten there without him.

The ribbon of black weaving past us slowed. My husband stood to escort me out of the church, dragging me up from the pew. He tried to hurry me past the throngs of reporters and photographers that were there only to get their story on the death of the late, great Matilda Imogene Warren, but I was sluggish in my movements as we pried our way through the waiting crowd. When someone stepped in front of me, and a camera light flashed in my face, Jorgji threatened all the cameras and notebooks away from me.

My cousin Mandy, her long hair swaying almost as much as her hips, sashayed over and was only too happy to provide the press with the details of my aunt's death. I didn't wait to hear her say that my aunt had a heart condition that she finally succumbed to. Mandy was too darned jovial and dressed too flashy for a woman who had already gone through a funeral for her mother earlier that year and who was now supposed to be supporting me at the death of my aunt.

I swayed on my feet when Jorgji's sister, Karine, stepped up to block our way to the Rolls. She said something to Jorgji in their native tongue and reached out as though to grab my arm. I got the impression she was offering her assistance with me. I was almost yanked off my feet when Jorgji pulled me out of her reach. I teetered even more when he pushed Karine aside. Whatever he said put a nasty expression on her face. I fumbled and stumbled forward, with Jorgji's help, to where Gordon had parked the Rolls.

Once I was safely in the Rolls with a lap afghan I'd made tucked in around me, Jorgji returned to the open church doors to express thanks to all the funeral attendees streaming out to their vehicles. Gordon looked up from his position behind the wheel; our eyes met in the rearview mirror. Sadness pervaded the interior of our space. He opened the driver door, climbed into the back of the Rolls and sat in a spot next to me. I rested my head on his shoulder. He put an arm around me. His presence gave me a quiet comfort, that and the sugar cookies he pulled from the champagne compartment.

We didn't speak. I couldn't for fear of crying. He, being the butler, wouldn't for fear of overstepping societal bounds.

Jorgji, always congenial in his handling of people, finished the last of the farewells and came back to me just as that last dose of sedative was beginning to wear off. My head had cleared a little. Jorgji looked at me and said, "You look badly." Not something a new bride of only two months wants to hear from her husband. He then told Gordon, "Do not take Imogene to grave service; take her home."

I regret that I never returned any of the condolence messages I'd received, never read any of the thousands of cards and letters of sympathy sent to me, never got close enough to the casket to tell my wonderful, kind, gracious aunt how much I appreciated everything she had done for me. It would have been great to smell the flowers, too.

CHAPTER 4

I drew in a deep breath and slowly blew all the air out of my lungs in one long exhalation, relieved the ordeal was almost over. At the conclusion of all the wherefores and whereases, Mr. Ruben Weiss finished his reading with, "That concludes the last will and testament of decedent, Matilda Imogene Warren." He sat the document he'd been reading down on the blotter that covered the top of his mahogany desk, picked up one of the photocopies, slid it into a leather folder and held it out across the desk towards me.

I didn't take it. I couldn't. My hands were entangled in the yarn I'd hidden in my suit coat pockets. The yarns were hand-sweat soggy, and I had to work to untangle my hands from the clingy strings and un-pocket them. I rubbed my hands on my skirt so as not to blot the leather cover with my perspiration. One of the red mohair yarns had wrapped itself around the diamond ring on my left hand. It took me a few seconds to get it unwound.

I ignored the sharp intakes of breath and murmurings from the occupants seated in the eight folding chairs behind me. Jorgji, upon seeing that I was delayed in accepting the folder, snatched it out of Mr. Weiss's gnarled, arthritic fingers. Mr. Weiss winced as though the effort to release the folder cost him dearly, but said only, "Imogene, all that remains is for you to sign a few documents."

Free of the yarn at last, I struggled to move the upholstered chair I was sitting in close enough to the side of the desk to sign the papers where Mr. Weiss had indicated. Jorgji didn't wait for me to finish my struggle. He shoved my chair forward so hard and quick that my knees slammed into the desk edge. My knee caps were smarting and my nylons torn, but I disregard the pain and the holes and quickly signed the papers before Jorgji decided I was not moving fast enough and tried to do it for me.

I was not going to complain to my husband about his behavior. He had been wonderfully accepting of my claustrophobia, which was flaring up in that small office crowded with people. If lawyer's offices came with a Fire Marshall's room capacity limit, I was sure we had exceeded it. It was a good thing that Jorgji preferred to stand next to me rather than sit; there wasn't room for one more chair in there. Martin and Mandy Parker, Gordon Neal, Cookie, and Mary, were all there under the belief that they would be mentioned in the will. Two more chairs were crowded into the room when my aunt's publicist, Ronald Rosenthal, and her book agent, Gerald Gildenstein, also showed up. They claimed they were only there to ensure whoever inherited would allow the Penelope Pembrooke mystery novels to live on. More likely they were there because they wanted to get an early scoop on what was in the will so they could leak it to the tabloids.

Everyone kept their feet tucked underneath their chairs and their elbows in so as not to bump one another. Mr. Weiss wanted to book a conference room, but Jorgji insisted we get the reading done as soon as possible so it wouldn't delay our move to Detroit. Jorgji, my, via me, billions richer spouse, helped me get my signature somewhere near the dotted line. The lawyer accepted my scribble as valid, and my aunt's vast wealth was added to what I had already received from my parents' trust when I was six.

The red lipsticked smile Mandy wore throughout the entire reading melted from her face. Martin's mouth became a gaping maw just before he snapped it shut. His face transfixed into a rictus of rage. I felt the red flush up my neck under his "Mr. Freeze" glare.

I needed out. I needed fresh air.

"Don't it say nothin' about me in there?" Mandy asked jumping up, startling everyone, practically knocking her chair into Mary's lap in order to get to the lawyer's desk. "That just can't be! You mean this here document says ever'thing is left to Imoooogene?"

I hated it when she made that mooing sound. I half expected her to come over and kick my shins like she did when we were kids, and I got something she wanted.

"This is the latest version of the will that we have on file. It was amended the day before Miss Warren's death. I've been her attorney for over 30 years," Mr. Weiss said in his age-induced quiver. "I'm very familiar with her signature." He pointed to the last line of the document he still had on his desk. "And, this is her signature. Additionally, this document was properly notarized by..." Mr. Weiss shoved his glasses farther up his nose and read, "March Kelley, notary for the county of Cook in the state of Illinois." He drew the paper closer to his face, squinted and said, "And it was duly witnessed by Karine Dalmat and Josephine Walker. Ms. Dalmat is not here, but I believe we have Josephine Walker with us today."

Cookie raised her hand from the back of the room. "That'd be me. I witnessed that signature."

Mr. Weiss removed his reading spectacles to peer out into the room at Cookie. She'd funneled her matronly form into a severe-styled brown dress and perched a brown hat on her head. The hat was the same color as her hair giving her head an elongated, flat-topped look. Mr. Weiss didn't allow his gaze to linger long on the field of brown before he directed it to Mandy. She had chosen to wear a red silk wraparound dress that clung to every ample curve she had, including her indignation-heaving bosom. The effect was not lost on Mr. Weiss, who told her, "I'd be happy to discuss this with you further after everyone else has gone, but I have no reason to believe this will isn't genuine."

My husband put his arm under my elbow to help me up. *Time to go.*

"This is all your doing. I'm going to find some way to break this will," Martin said to me as Jorgji threaded our way through the maze of chairs. "You won't get away with this."

"You greedy bitch," Mandy said as we squeezed past her still teetering chair.

I had no idea of why they both were so upset. Being from my mother's side of the family they weren't even blood relatives of my aunt. She let them stay with us and welch off her every summer and every holiday. *Wasn't that enough?*

Gordon, the only one not sweating from the heat of the room, though how he did it in full black suit and tie, I'll never know, reached for my hand and gave it a squeeze as I brushed past him on my way out the door. He said to Jorgji, "Miss Matilda has only been dead a week. Any chance you can delay the move for a few days to give Miss Imogene an opportunity to emotionally recover from her aunt's death?"

"We must go now," Jorgji responded in his thick Albanian accent. His hand was on my back pushing me towards the open door. "It better this way."

Gordon didn't release my hand to Jorgji's pushing. I was half in, half out of the door. "Is this what you want, Miss Imogene?" Gordon asked me.

"Of course," I said. "Jorgji is my husband. I must be with him." I stopped my forward motion to step fully back into the room and look directly at Gordon. I knew husband trumps butler, even a long-standing, close butler, but Jorgji could wait. Everyone in the room could wait. The whole darn world could wait.

I said, "Thank you for everything you've ever done for Aunt Tilly and me, Gordon. Your life-long lease on the third–floor apartment remains intact. I want you to stay on. I'd like for you to continue on in my employ. You've always taken good care of Aunt Tilly and her house. Jorgji has promised me that we'll come back to Winnetka to live as soon as this new branch of his investment business is up and running on its own."

"Very well, Miss. I'll close up the unused portions of the house until you get back and see to it that your favorite yarns are packed for the move."

The tears I'd been holding in started to leak out of my eyes.

Mandy, never one to be upstaged, saw my tears and started sobbing inconsolably.

Martin, nostrils flaring, face crimson, patted Mandy's back, trying to comfort his sister. She wailed louder with each pat. Martin glared in my direction. I averted my look elsewhere.

Cookie was wearing a vacant smile on her face, and there was an unfocused, faraway look in her eyes. Mary looked shell-shocked and bewildered. Her lower lip trembled uncontrollably, and her eyes took on a shimmer of tears. I was determined to make sure they got a huge severance package.

I mistakenly made eye contact with the publicist and agent. Each was sweating bullets. Sweat ran down their foreheads and was mopped up by the folded handkerchiefs they blotting against themselves. Their black jackets were damp under their arms. Seeing their opportunity, they jumped up and thrust their business cards towards me.

"We need to talk to you about the unfinished manuscripts," Mr. Rosenthal said, his black mustache drooping.

"Yes. We need to talk to you about those unfinished manuscripts," Mr. Gildenstein chimed in. Jorgji pocketed both cards. I promised both of my aunt's business associates

I would keep the mystery books' website up and running until I could decide what to do about publishing the unfinished novels my aunt had started prior to her death.

Jorgji, my impatient husband, continued to push at my back until I was out of that confining room, away from the crowd, away from my vitriolic cousins and into the fresh air.

CHAPTER 5

The memory of the first time Jorgji and I ate a meal at Everest as husband and wife coursed through me as we rode the Chicago Stock Exchange elevator 40 floors to the top of the building. We had just flown back from our Vegas elopement. The velvety black Chicago night skyline glittered below us. The ring I'd chosen glittered on my finger. Love, wine, and Jorgji put the sparkle in my eyes as my aunt joined us to celebrate our marriage.

That next time, in the harsh light of afternoon, after my aunt's death, nothing glittered.

Chef Jojo greeted Jorgji with a firm handshake, and then he bowed deeply to me and took my hand.

"Welcome. I am so sorry for your loss."

"Thank you so much for allowing us to dine privately before you open," I said to Chef Jojo.

"Anything for the niece of Matilda Warren. Jorgji has told me how difficult her death has been for you. I hope a lovely meal will help ease the pain." He guided Jorgji and me past the empty central dining area. The tablecloths were all freshly pressed and draped, the tables adorned with fresh flowers and small bronze sculptures. We entered one of the small, intimate private dining rooms. The table there was set for two. A private waiter was at the ready to anticipate and attend to our every need. Chef Jojo pulled out my chair, and I sat, grateful that he remembered I liked to keep my back to the broad expanse of windows. I was jittery from the elevator ride, and the western Chicago skyline from 40 stories up would have only served to feed my acrophobic tendencies, which were already on heightened alert.

In an effort to calm myself, I focused on the fresh flowers Chef Jojo had set on our table. The waiter poured French Chablis into our crystal wine goblets. I rarely drank. Even when I did, I didn't drink that early in the day, so I took a sip for nerve-calming purposes. I found it crisp and flavorful. I took a gulp. It went down smooth. I tipped the goblet up and drained it.

"Another?" the waiter asked me, bottle poised to pour.

"No," Jorgji answered him. Then to me, "Eat first."

Chef Jojo had prepared a rare seasonal truffle risotto along with a salmon soufflé, crisp greens, and cold mink chocolate soup with a pink praline floating island so beautiful that words could not even describe it. It probably tasted as delicious as it looked, but my throat refused to swallow. There was a lump remaining from the funeral, and another from the reading of the will, and another that took up residence when Jorgji told me about our impending move to Detroit.

I was suddenly hungry for a sugar cookie.

Jorgji, seeing my untouched plate, asked, "You want different?"

The waiter perked up and came to my side, ready to pull the offending plate away.

"No. No," I said grabbing the edge of the plate in front of me. "This is all lovely. Chef Jojo has outdone himself. I just remembered how much my aunt loved to eat here and it made me sad. I don't think I can eat anything." I burst into tears. The server provided me with a white hankie. Good waiters are like good butlers—magic.

"You be better in Detroit. Scenery change good," Jorgji said, resuming his meal, seemingly indifferent to my most recent bout of grief. That caused me to cry harder. Chef Jojo dashed in. The waiter tried to explain that he did nothing to cause me to cry.

Jorgji threw down his napkin, giving up on his meal. He apologized to Chef Jojo.

While Jorgji paid for a meal we didn't eat, and the waiter summoned the valet to bring our vehicle from the private underground parking garage, Chef Jojo attempted to calm me with another glass of Chablis. It wasn't a sugar cookie, but what the heck. I stopped crying, downed the whole glass, and picked up the bottle to take what was left with me. The alcohol intake hit my bloodstream as we walked through the main dining room to the elevators.

Early dinners were starting to trickle in. I tried not to stagger, but that last glass wasn't making that easy. Unaccustomed to alcohol on an empty stomach, I was unsteady on my feet. I took a misstep and almost landed in a man's lap.

"Excuse me," I said to him. Then, I looked closer at the thin gold man I almost landed on. He seemed familiar. He was already there when we came in. Jorgji pulled me away from the Virginio Ferrari sculpture I'd bumped into and went to get my coat.

I heard someone call my name. "Mrs. Dalmat?"

I heard it again, like an echo in my brain. "Mrs. Dalmat." *Was that my imagination again?*

I wished it had been. Ronald Rosenthal and Gerald Gildenstein stood up from a nearby table and advanced toward me. I stood there, wavering on my feet. Alone. Too tipsy to run.

"We're so glad we ran into you," said Mr. Gildenstein, tucking something bronze colored into his suit jacket pocket. I thought it looked like one of the small table sculptures.

"Yes. So glad," Mr. Rosenthal affirmed. He glanced

around. My guess was he was assessing where Jorgji was. When he was done looking, Mr. Rosenthal used his fingers to smooth down his mustache and smiled a big smile at me.

"I'm not glad," I said, not wanting another discussion about my aunt's unfinished manuscripts. I looked around for someplace to lean against. My head was whirling, or maybe it was the room.

"What?" Mr. Gildenstein said. "You're unhappy to see us? You've cut us to the quick."

"Yes," Mr. Rosenthal said. "To the quick. We've been trying to reach you and keep getting rebuked by your husband. We heard you were moving. It's imperative we speak to you regarding the status of your aunt's work. The publisher is most distressed."

"Most distressed," said Mr. Gildenstein. "Tilly would have wanted her legacy to continue on."

"I'm sorry," I said. "You're right. I'm not feeling well. Can we discuss this another time?" There was a river rushing in my head.

"Of course. We will call you. How soon will you be moving?"

"Tomorrow. I'll have my butler contact you with the new address." Mollified, all four of them sat back down at their double table as I drunkenly pitched forward into Mr. Gildenstein's lap. Passed out drunk on only two drinks.

CHAPTER 6

I plunked myself down in a chair near Jorgji's desk in the study. "I want to go home. I hate it here."

He had switched his computer screen to the screen saver mode when he saw me. Numbers were replaced by squares of bright colors that swirled in a black void. He looked up at me and said, "What? This nice place. Big apartment. Classic. Elegant. Has safety doorman. Underground is parking. Balcony. Nice view of river. I got maid to keep you company while I gone. We stay."

That was all territory we had been over before, so I didn't bother to point out to him that he was omitting a few minor details about the place. The Shelby Towers, that big classic, elegant apartment building he picked out, was so ancient it had only one working elevator; building security was not optional given the number of break-ins done by the not-so-rich neighbors a few blocks over and George, who wears the doorman's uniform, was too old to be an effective break-in deterrent; our rusted iron balcony was going to detach at any minute and fall the full six floors into the rushing nice-view Detroit river below; the underground parking was nothing more than a catacomb that was always burnt-out-bulb dark, and Keiko, the maid he hired for me, only spoke Japanese.

While I tried to think of a new approach for my argument, Jorgji turned his laptop so only he could see the screen and returned to his investment work, a habit that I found annoying. The turning, not the work.

"Can't you just take your laptop and do what you need to do in Chicago? You're on that thing all the time anyway. And," I then added as an enticement, "You could invite your sister, Karine, to come visit again. This time I'll try harder to get along with her. Who knows? She and I might learn to like each other—given time." Okay. I just threw in that last part for leverage. I didn't like Jorgji's sister any better than she liked me. We tolerated each other when she came for a surprise visit, but I doubted we would ever be friends.

"I do not want her near you," he said.

When I began pacing around and didn't leave the room, Jorgji decided to shut down his computer and lock it up. Another thing that annoyed me.

"You two need to bury the hatchet," I said.

At my mention of hatchet burying, Jorgji's face went ashen. I forgot that he wasn't familiar with all of our American colloquialisms, so I explained, "Not literally bury the hatchet. It's an expression. It means 'make peace'; you and your sister should stop fighting. You need to be friends again. You know—be happy together."

As the tan color returned to his face, his face morphed into a harsh look. No smile. No frown. Eyes lit with an unreadable emotion, he commanded me, with firm resolve and disdain in his voice that I hadn't here-to-fore noticed, "Karine and I not friends. I give her money to go back home." He turned from me and walked out of the study, always his way of dismissing me and my concerns. He was not getting away from me that easily.

I followed him into the living room where he opened the sliding door to the balcony and walked out onto the metal gridded deck. *Darn.* I followed behind him, gingerly stepping out. I closed the door behind me and breathed the cool September air in short, shallow breaths. Jorgji walked all the way across the deck and was leaning forward, resting his arms on the iron railing, seemingly intent on watching the river rush by below. Ignoring my distress. Ignoring me.

I cautiously put one foot out on the open grid. The decking held so I slid the other foot out. I kept sliding one foot out in front of the other until I got closer to the edge of the balcony where the love of my life stood. Once I was there, I put my hand on his arm to get his attention (and so I had something to hang onto when that crummy balcony fell.) I pressed my hand firmly to his arm, trying to get him to look at me, but he continued to stare at the river. I couldn't bring myself to look down. My acrophobia wouldn't let me see what he saw in those turbulent waters, so I turned and studied his profile. Even with a scowl creasing his forehead and the small, angry flare to his nostrils, my heart gave a little extra beat just to be looking at his handsome features. I didn't want to give up on us.

"Jorgji, we have to talk. Something has gone wrong with our marriage. I want to fix what's wrong, but I don't know how. You have to talk to me. Please, Jorgji. Tell me what's going on." He shrugged my hand off and moved a few steps away from me.

I was not good at being ignored. I was also not good at rejection. I was, however, good at crying. I could cry silently, or I could cry not so silently by adding in little whimpers. I never wailed like my cousin, Mandy; it was not dignified. I decided that a few little whimpers couldn't hurt.

He turned to face me. His countenance softened. *Score one for not so silent.*

His scowl turned into a worried frown when he saw me clinging, white-knuckled, to the iron railing of the balcony. He took hold of my hands and pried them from the railing. I no longer felt the cool steel beneath my palms, and a slight moment of panic seized me before he grabbed me and hugged me to him, kissing the few tears that I had allowed to run down my face. With his arm around my waist, he escorted me to the closed door, slid it open, released his hold on me and said, "Do not worry. Nothing wrong. Go back in where you are not afraid. You stay viable now that your aunt is dead."

I sniffed a few times, smiled at his quaint Albanian way of speaking English, and accepted my interpretation of the situation as valid. He loved me, I was sure of it. It was just that being raised in an orphanage, he had trouble showing his affections. I felt a renewed determination to make my marriage work and to stay the heck off that balcony.

I was going to read all the marriage magazines and relationship books I could download from the internet. I was going to knit every sock and scarf I have patterns for and gift them to him, but I wasn't sure if that would show Jorgji enough attention or not. Our marriage troubles seemed to have started around the time of my aunt's death. *Had my grief unknowingly derail my marriage?*

CHAPTER 7

I wanted to rekindle the flame that had blown out of our whirlwind marriage, but not only was Jorgji avoiding me, he was uncommunicative, secretive, disinterested. All the warning signs *Cosmopolite* said were sure sign your man was straying. I found a *Ladies House Journal* article on strengthening marriages that said if I took an active interest in the things my disinterested husband was interested in he would be more interested in me again.

Things were that bad. I was willing to learn the boring investment business to stitch my marriage back together. To curtail his secretive phone calls and text messages and late nights at the office, I was going to get involved in his involvements.

Try as I might I couldn't figure out his investment files, the ones I'd managed to download the previous week after I'd not so innocently spilled hot coffee in his lap. While he hurried to change his clothes, I hurried to fill my silver USB drive bracelet with what he found more interesting than me. That *Dell* went with him more places than I did and when it isn't with him, it was locked tight with a passkey system. How else was I to get closer to the things he was close to if the things he was close to were always too close to him?

I made sure the coffee was hot enough that he'd jump up in a hurry, leaving his laptop vulnerable, but not hot enough for a drive-through-burger-joint lawsuit. My plans were to strengthen our marital bonds, not make them impossible.

I wanted to decode those files and understand his business, so I could astonish him with my 32-gigabyte knowledge of his hotshot investment company when he arrived home. We were to talk shop while we ate a romantic salmon dinner I was going to have catered in. When he saw that I could do something other than knit, he was supposed to turn that Dell off to turn me on.

These darn encoded files were harder to figure out than my on-line Japanese course. I was so baffled by those financial records that when Jorgji called me from Chicago to tell me he wanted his favorite suit cleaned for a funeral, I forgot to set it out for the dry cleaning pick-up service before they closed. Being the resourceful person—that I was usually not—I located an all-night laundromat a few blocks away that had a do-it-yourself dry cleaning machine. It was Keiko's day off, so I was going to drive over to this dirty little coin-operated laundromat and clean Jorgji's suit myself.

The laundromat's decaying, seedy neighborhood was part of Detroit's inner city encroachment on our more affluent part of town. Just the thought of traversing those few blocks, even ensconced in my Bentley, gave me the queasies, but I had to chance the trip. Things hadn't been going so well with Jorgji; I was desperate not to let this suit issue upset him. *How hard was it supposed to be to put some money in a machine and stuff a suit in there? People must do that kind of thing all the time. Otherwise, why would the Yellow Pages even advertise all-night laundromats?*

My day had been going steadily downhill every since I found my cell phone dead. I thought it better to get going before something else happened. I grabbed up Jorgji's suit, my purse, the romantic-dinner-linen tablecloth, the after-the-romantic-dinner black lace underwear and a pair of frustration-release-workout socks (in case the black lace stayed on). I took an anti-anxiety pill to calm the nervous flutter in my chest and headed over to our building's lone ancient elevator to set out on a dry cleaning adventure.

I didn't know if my heart was thudding over having left the apartment for the first time in days or if I took too much medicine. *Maybe I was just excited at the prospect of Jorgji's homecoming?*

The elevator dial pointed to the third floor and stayed there. As usual. Someone was always holding up the elevator to get their fussy poodle or Yorkie in or out. Or maybe phones and elevators got the first of the month off. There wasn't a gym in our apartment, but I had read *Health Protection's* easy work-out tips for apartment dwellers and was confident in my abilities, so I was going to go down the seven flights to the underground parking rather than stay up there on the sixth floor, elevator-less, while the night continued to get scary darker.

Pressing my shoulder into the swing of the partially opened stairwell door, I gave a slight nudge. The sound of another door opening several floors down bounded off the hollow stairwell walls and echoed up to me. I was not comfortable talking to people I didn't know. Being a *Dale Carnage* course failure, I was not even comfortable talking to people I did know. Meeting people in stairwells forced you to say something. I wasn't prepared to do that. I needed time to think up potential talk points and imagine appropriate responses to conversational questions. There wasn't enough time for that so what was I to do? This Jorgji suit thing was pretty important to me, so I continued to stand frozen in indecision. When I heard a deep, raspy, echo-y voice say, "She's 'sposed to be alone, and her cell shutdown," and the sound of heavy scuffing steps mingled with lighter tapping steps reaching up to me as I held my breath and listened.

"Why'd she have to live on the sixth floor with no working elevator? After doing all this climbing it's a good thing she'll go easy," Raspy said.

"Why do you think this one will be easy?" a younger sounding masculine voice asked.

"Because she's s'posed to always be busy reading magazines, watching TV, knitting or sump'n."

Rasp. Heavy scuff. Tap. Tap. Heavy scuff.

"Maybe sometimes, but how could he know she'll stay home every night when she's got enough money to not only go out on the town but buy it, too?" asked the younger voice.

Heavy scuff step and light tappy step wedded together as they advanced slowly up the uncarpeted steps, closer to where I was standing, listening, unable to pull away from the door.

"She's gotta be," is the raspy answer punctuated with a cough. Hearing that cough, my throat started to tickle, but I squelched the urge to cough. Only 'tap, tap' echoed up for a few seconds before the man coughed again and continued, "Her car's been put outta commission. She's got no friends. She's a prissy, spoiled, pampered little rich girl with that phobia that don't let her talk to people or go nowhere alone, especially after dark."

The tap, tap and the scuff resumed. "And if she ain't there," he continued again, "we wait 'til she comes back and take care of her then. Piece of cake."

Scuff. Scuff. Tap. Tap.

"Okay. Easy money. Someone must be planning on making a bundle off insurance to pay a hundred grand for one bitch, or maybe he'd like a new toy," said the lighter, younger voice.

Their laughter must have masked the sound of my

shoulder letting the door slide shut because even though my heart and feet pounded rapidly all the way down the hall, Scuffy and Tappy don't come bursting through the stairwell door after me.

I paused in front of apartment 604 to contemplate hiding inside, but I didn't. I didn't want to be anyone's 'piece-of-cake.' I continued on down the hall and ducked into the alcove that sat the front door of a neighboring apartment back from the hallway. A sweet-looking old lady with silvery-blue permed hair and her elevator-holding mop of a dog lived there. I thought they might be able to help me, and they might of if I could have gotten my chicken finger to go anywhere near their door buzzer. Instead, I flattened myself behind her alcove potted fig tree and stayed there frozen in terror, holding my breath.

I heard the muted scuff patterns on the hall carpet stop. The scuffing was replaced by a key jingle and a Bella Lugosi door creak. *I knew that creak!* That was one of the things, besides me, Jorgji needed to take care of.

Once I heard the door close, I knew Scuffy, and Tappy had stepped into my apartment, and I had a brief moment of time to do something. I dashed down the stairwell on the opposite side of the hall and ran down all seven flights of stairs to my Bentley. Punched in the key code. Wrenched the Bentley's door open, totally out of breath, heart continuing to pound. I guess I needed to do more than just read *Health Protection's* easy work-out tips.

I slid into my beloved Bentley with relief. Locked the doors. Turned off the interior lights to not draw attention to my get away. I fumbled around, trying to start my car. I struggled in the dark. Seemed like a lifetime, or what could almost have been the rest of my lifetime. Nothing happened. Not a spark, click or grunt or anything. Just like Jorgji at breakfast that last week.

I tried, again and again, to start the Bentley with the same result every time. Like my marriage, my car was dead. I quickly come to the realization I would be following the pattern that was developing if I didn't get out of there quick, so I headed to the only local address I had directions for.

CHAPTER 8

I soon found myself on a floor, under long fluorescent tubes of light, behind a big barrel machine labeled "heavy duty extractor," whatever that was. The wadded up suit, shirt, socks, underwear, table cloth, and purse were in my lap. Too bad that table cloth wasn't an invisibility cloak because I felt pretty certain the easy-money men started looking for me when I didn't go back to my melting raspberry lemonade and episode of *Ghost Speaking*. I didn't even know what my killers-to-be looked like. I couldn't effectively hide from them if I didn't know their names or faces. They could have been anyone, and anyone could have been them.

My Aunt Tilly, God rest her spinster soul, thought I was smart enough to handle the typing of her novels, all her fan mail correspondence and, before Jorgji, her business investments. *So why wasn't I wasn't smart enough to see this betrayal coming? How could I have been so ignorant?*

I'm sure that was what my husband was counting on. *Ignorant Imogene. She'll never suspect a thing. She'll never connect the dots and figure out I'm going to kill her for her money.*

I must admit there were a lot of connections I didn't understand at the time. It took me three months, one defunct phone, one dead car, two hired killers and that one lonely, frightening night to add the connections up.

I was a post-it-note wife: easy to use, rip off and dispose of.

I never should have agreed to move to Detroit. I should have listened to Gordon.

After that night, butler trumped husband. I was going to collect up all the marbles I'd lost and go back to Winnetka where I would eat warm sugar cookies fresh and gooey from the oven and drink steaming hot Earl Grey tea and forget my therapist's advice about finding my 'quiet center' to face my fears. I was just hoping I lived through that night to enjoy them. The cookies and tea. I never enjoyed my fears.

I felt feverish. My throat was raw like someone scraped it with a knife down the inside. I must have been coming down with something from the germs in that place. Or maybe it was my hypochondria taking hold of me.

I was hungry and hated it that I left my raspberry lemonade and plain turkey on rye back at the apartment.

The mordacious apartment I'd tried unsuccessfully to get Jorgji to move out of—the first day we walked into it. A connecting dot that I didn't connect because Jorgji was so good at playing the role of loving husband. So good I almost missed his switch from planting kisses on me in Winnetka to trying to plant me in Detroit.

Jorgji moved me hours away from my home, to detach me from people who could have helped me. He had effectively isolated me from my herd, he was going in for the kill, and I had no one to turn to. My apartment-hugging ways and the not-in-the-will-induced estrangement from my cousins were about to assure my money-grubbing husband a successful planting season.

I never found the courage to make friends with anyone. I did manage to talk a little to George, the building's doorman. And I did talk to Susie, the girl who worked the counter at the *Iced Stone Creamery,* but those conversations were always a little stilted. *'Good afternoon,' 'Lovely day,'*

'Tut. Tut. Looks like rain,' *'Let me get that door for you'* or *'Would you like me to fold some extra chocolate chips into your French Toast ice cream?'*

French Toast ice cream. Ahhh, that was always worth the effort it took for me to leave my apartment; I couldn't get tasty un-melted ice cream on-line.

No friends and no meaningful contact with the outside world is why I hadn't realized my phone was dead. It took me even longer to recognize the correlation between that and my husband's plans for me.

I had accumulated hundreds of e-friends under my aunt's nom-de-plume, Penelope Pembrook, but I didn't have actual friends. At least none that would rescue me from being killed in an all-night laundromat.

Given all his e-mails, Friend Face messages, Bleets, and on-line chats 'Undercover Fan' was as close to a best friend as I'd had. No. Cancel that. When he signed into the Pembrook Detective Agency website, the backdrop for the Penelope mystery novels, he was signing in to converse with Penelope Pembrooke, the mystery novel protagonist. That made him Penelope's friend—not mine.

I didn't understand how I could have missed all of the your-husband's-buying-you-cement-overshoes-for-your-swim-in-the-Detroit-River signs. I wanted to cry, but I didn't have a clean hanky with me and blowing my nose on white linen, or black lace panties just didn't seem right.

I had to pull myself together somehow. I needed to think like Aunt Tilly's novel detective heroine, Penelope. *What would Penelope have done?*

Auntie put Penelope, teen detective extraordinaire, into a lot of tough situations; Penelope always managed to outwit her would-be assailants. But, then she had a father in the detective business who taught her the ropes, and she always knew why the killers were after her. Even in *You Have to Die* Penelope knew her attacker was trying to kill her because she had witnessed him permanently ending his association with a business partner.

I couldn't fathom why my husband wanted me dead. The hot coffee notwithstanding, I tried to be a good wife. So what if I didn't know how to do some menial wife-type things like cooking, cleaning, and laundry? My knitting kept him in sweaters and socks. If he was not happy with me or my knitted gifts, he could have just divorced me. *Or, maybe he was killing me because, upon divorce, our prenuptial agreement forced each of us to forfeit half of the wealth we accumulated during the marriage?* I didn't think that money could be the motive. His investment business was doing so well it kept him non-stop busy all the time meeting with clients and managing accounts. *If he was making a killing in the investment business, why would he want to kill me?*

I could have been mistaken about the men in the stairwell. They didn't mention me specifically by name, and all the apartments at the Shelby Towers were filled with rich, pampered people. Paranoia was one of my many micro phobias that liked hanging out with my agoraphobia. *My aunt's death could have been spiraling me into a period of vulnerability where I imagined my husband was distant and men in stairwells were coming to kill me.*

I could have been wrong about what I heard earlier. Being wrong meant I could go home and snuggle into my down comforter on my own cozy bed, and I wanted to do that, but my brain wouldn't allow me to just pick up my laundry and saunter back to my apartment, so I sat there forever waiting for something to happen.

It turned one–o'clock-dark outside, and my adrenaline began to wane. My tired body was aching, cramping and protesting my brain's indecisiveness. Those dirty clothes couldn't get any more wrinkled than they already were so I found the cleanest dirty spot on the floor, bunch the clothes into a pillow, spread the tablecloth over my floor-prone body and tried to rest. Not very Penelope-like but my brain couldn't think of anything else to do because it was used to going to sleep at 9:30.

Getting to sleep on a spilled-soap-and-dirt-encrusted

floor while evading two hired killers wasn't possible; the floor was too unyielding; the lights too bright; my bladder too full, urgently reminding me it had been a long time since I had that first glass of raspberry lemonade. I gathered up my meager belongings and dashed for the single unisex bathroom. That door creaked, too. *Couldn't anyone oil hinges?*

The barrel lock no longer lined up with the slot in the door jamb no matter how hard I tried. *Great.* Next to talking to people I don't know in stairwells, I had an even bigger phobia about people I didn't know barging in on me while using a public restroom. I crossed and uncrossed my legs, the urgency growing until I decided I had no choice. I only hoped the forty-watt bulb that was screwed into the one lonely light socket over the broken mirror would at least keep anyone from getting a great view of my bare butt perched on that cracked toilet seat.

I tried to minimize contact with the seat by sitting only on the edge. *Mistake.* The back of the seat flipped up. It was not attached to the toilet. *Great.* I had to do full contact to keep the seat in place so I stretched my right leg out so my big toe could keep the door somewhat closed. I was trying to relax enough to empty my bladder when the little tinkly bell on the laundromat's outside door tinkled it's warning that someone had entered the building. The tinkle was followed by a raspy cough.

My tinkle stopped midstream like I was in a kids' cartoon show. Only any ducks shot in this cartoon wouldn't snap their bill back on, get up and walk away.

My little ducky heart was in my throat, thudding so hard I couldn't swallow it down. I doubted that customer was there at 1:10 am to wash their undies for work the next morning. I was pretty certain I was his work. Struggling, I stood up, pulled up, and tried to keep the door shut all at the same time. I didn't want to be literally caught with my skirt down. My purse, wadded clothing, and tablecloth were lying in a heap on the floor. The door, no longer kissed by my big toe, gave a tiny squeak and returned to its original gaping state.

The opening in the doorway was just enough to give me a between-the-washers thin vertical view of a heavily jowled man. He was in a dark blue polo shirt, black dress pants and black dress shoes. He paused at the entrance door, lighted a cigarette and took a deep drag down into his lungs. He left my view when his already blackened lungs protested with a coughing spasm that doubled him over.

My previously shut-down brain jump-started into automatic Penelope Pembrook survival mode. I yanked Jorgji's suit pants up over my skirt., slipped my arms into his shirt sleeves. I shoved my purse behind the grungy plastic wastebasket.

I used the water in the stopped up sink to douse my shoulder length brown hair. I messed it up even worse than what it already was. I ran the palms of my hands over the floor until they were black. Grimacing from the smell, I rubbed my hands all over my face. The suit jacket I bundled up in the tablecloth. I shoved my dirty underwear and socks in beside the suit jacket. I looked back through the door opening, worried because the coughing had stopped.

The main entrance into the laundromat swished open, and the bell tingled again. I saw the visible edge of a second man, blond, slight of build, younger. I heard a light, energetic, nervous tapping of feet on the floor. Tappy. He said in a tight, high voice to someone off to his left.

"Any sign of her here?"

The cigaretted man scuffed back into partial view along the linoleum floor. He didn't even try to pick up his feet. Man, it must have been hard to keep soles on his shoes and cigarettes in his mouth. No wonder he needed the 100 grand.

"I can hear someone in the crapper, but otherwise, the place is empty," said the raspy voice I recognized from the stairwell.

"Let's see whose tak'n a shit and then get on with the

search. I gotta work the day shift in a few hours," said Tappy. "You know too much is going down right now for me to risk calling in. She can't have gone too far without her car or phone. She's got to be hiding some where's near her place."

I hunkered down in the far corner of the bathroom. I didn't even try to block the door. What would I have blocked it with anyway? All I had, besides my useful big toe, was a cracked, loose toilet seat and a grungy brown plastic trashcan. There weren't even any extra rolls of toilet paper to throw at them.

Scuffy and Tappy came forward. The bathroom door burst open. The door knob slammed violently into the side wall, startling me. A little sprinkle of plaster dust fell to the floor from the hole the knob made in the wall.

Shrinking into my corner of the room I kept my head down, my eyes averted. I mumbled in a gravelly voice, as deep as I could get it, without sounding too much like a woman trying to sound like a man, "This 'ere is my space. You go find yer own of the night. I ain't goin' to that flop hous' no more. They's too preachy."

I didn't know if it was the hoarseness of my throat, the smell of the place, the dingy bulb, or the late hour, but Scuffy and Tappy said nothing, turned, scuffed and tapped away. Cigarette smoke, raspy cough and all. And thus I learned that being homeless was the same as having an invisibility cloak.

Homeless. That was what I was. In the blink of an eye, my life had come unraveled. I couldn't go back to my raspberry lemonade, comfy bed and 'loving' husband. I may have been mousy and naïve, but I was not ignorant. The little bell sound as the front laundromat door swooshed shut set off an internal emergency alarm in me.

I fished around in my purse, retrieved my key chain, bank and credit cards and the suit-cleaning quarters. Burying my favorite Prada accessory in the waste paper inside the trash can, I said goodbye to my good buy. I secured the waistband of those baggy pants with the two emergency safety pins I kept clipped to my key ring. Thank you, *Sewing World.* I found your article on "Little Useful Things to Always Have with You" to be useful.

Rolling my pant cuffs up, I secured my suit jacket, panties, socks, and my invisibility cloak under one arm. I hightailed it out of that fluorescent-lighted death trap before those two goons had time to realize I was their $100,000 cupcake and came back for a piece of me.

Not knowing where was I going to hide for the rest of the night, I thought if I could find a phone, I could call Mandy to come and help me. Shuddering, I realized my chances were better with Tappy and Scuffy. At least I knew their motives. Mandy hadn't been happy about not being in the will. And when Mandy wasn't happy, she made sure I knew it.

Karine may not have gone back to Albania yet, but even if I had a phone and even if I knew her number I wouldn't have called Jorgji's sister to save me from Jorgji.

I had my credit cards but decided against using them like the fool did in my aunt's third novel, *She Didn't Get Far.* That woman found out the hard way that credit cards can be easily traced. If I wanted to lead the killers right to me, using my card to secure a room would be the best way to do it.

I had to find another way to come up with hotel funds if I didn't want to cease and be deceased. I took a few minutes to collect my thoughts, then stepped out into the back alley that ran the length of the laundromat's strip mall. I chose the one-size-serves-all dumpster to hide behind. The smell was atrocious. I gagged at the putrid smell of rotting garbage that surrounded me.

The papers and boxes that had fallen from the over-full dumpster rustled in the breeze, except I didn't feel a breeze. I looked down to the pile of debris at my feet and clamped my hand over my mouth to stifle my scream as a streak of brown raced across my sneaker. We ran full tilt towards the open back door of the Seventy–Eleven convenience store. My sneakers and I. The rat was eating a discarded Moon Cake.

I found myself near the store's back room where the beer bottle returns were stacked up taller than I was. A walk-in cooler door was on one side, a cot with a blanket and pillow were farther back in the room. I headed towards the light that was streaming from the sales area.

I gulped in a big breath of the coffee laden air when I got into the light. The rotten odor of the dumpster started to fade once I got to the Little Dottie baked goods rack. I did a double take when I saw the Moon Cakes displayed on the bottom shelf, but there were no eyes glowing out of the darkness under the rack.

To my continued relief a turbaned cashier, a teenage girl, and automatic teller machine were the only interesting things residing among all the sundries in the store.

I knew the ATM must have been broken because it wanted me to put in a 4 digit PIN number to access my eight digit savings account. I wished that at one point in my life I had an occasion to get cash from an ATM so I would have known how that sort of thing worked, but I didn't.

The turbaned man behind the counter didn't even bother to glance my way when I belligerently start punching the buttons on the money machine in hopes it would start Vegas-slot-machine money spitting. He was kept busy keeping his eye on the young girl who was eying the shelf of cough medicines. He didn't notice my predicament. He didn't know I was close to tears over the frustration I felt.

Miss Teen finally selected two bottles of NyQuell and slid them across to Mr. Turban at the counter to ring up. I heard her explain to him, fake cough included, that she was buying the bottles for a medical condition, not for the alcohol. Taking her money, he shrugged at her babble like he didn't speak English.

He didn't. At least he didn't until I approached him with my proposition that I hoped would get me through the night. I was not going to ask if I could sleep on his back room cot or anything like that. I just wanted to use my credit card to get some quick cash.

Mr. Turban patiently explained to me in very clear, Oxford-perfect English, "I am sorry, madam. I cannot give you money for your credit card. Credit cards can only be used to complete a transaction. You may make a purchase with your card, but I cannot give you cash. I am so sorry."

Darn. I should have known that because purchasing items with credit cards was what I was good at. He saw my disappointment and asked me, "Do you wish to make a purchase?"

I decided I did. Penelope never walked away from a challenge, so I was not going to either. In *The Corpse Danced in the Street*, Penelope used her credit card to buy everything she needed to duplicate the scary corpse dancing around the allegedly haunted town. She then showed her purchases to the town folks to convince them that their 'ghosts' were made by the land development company to get them to sell their 'haunted' land to them at a loss. Once the town folk knew their town wasn't haunted, she convinced them to haunt it themselves. They used the paraphernalia she'd already purchased to promote the ghost town image and set up the first 'hauntings.' The town thrived as a tourist attraction.

"No. I don't want to make a purchase," I explained to Mr. Turban. "I want you to." I told him he could use my card to pick out whatever he wanted in the store as long as he gave me 1/2 of the purchase price back in cash and disavowed all knowledge of me and my card, especially to anyone in scuffed, worn shoes buying cigarettes.

His eyes grew wide. He checked first to see if there was anyone else in the store. With the surveillance recording tape shut off, he darted around the store like a *Price is Right* contestant grabbing up bread, milk, baby food, formula and family staples which he deposited on the cot in the back room, after they were rung up on my card. When he opened his wallet to give me the cash, I glimpsed a little cellophane encased picture of a smiling woman holding a tiny baby. I was happy that someone was doing better because of my situation.

Money in hand I went out back of the store, pocketed my apartment key, minus its identifying tag. I stashed my driver's license and credit cards in the toe of one dirty workout sock. I tied the sock into a knot. It took me three tries, but I finally manage to fling that sock and everything that identified me as me into that stinking, full dumpster behind the store. At least if I was found dead that morning from the filth off that bathroom floor, they couldn't return my lifeless body to my adoring husband because they wouldn't know for sure who I was.

Mr. Turban stopped speaking English right after our deal was finished and refused to talk to me again. I wished he hadn't done that. I wasn't going to report him to the Seventy–Eleven police. I just wanted to use the phone to call a taxi. I didn't dare walk around looking for a place to stay for fear of being spotted by Tappy and Scuffy and whatever else lurked out in the darkness of the night.

What the heck was I to do? I loathed the thought of the kind of meal and hotel room my new found wealth of $175 dollars and a bunch of quarters would get me. There would be no French Riviera hotel rooms and lobster meals with white Zinfandel for me that night.

Think. Think. What would Penelope do?

In *Murder Fouled by Breath,* Penelope was able to identify the method of death by smelling the victim's mouth. Penelope knew the murdered girl couldn't have drunk herself to death because there was no odor of alcohol emanating from her mouth. Penelope found a needle mark on the girl's arm. The girl's jealous roommate confessed to murder by an intravenous dose of alcohol because she discovered she was not only sharing a room but her boyfriend with her roommate.

I doubted Scuffy and Tappy were unhappy with my

choice of roommates. I also doubted they were packing a 180-proof intravenous bag for me, but alcohol gave me an idea. It was 1:30 am. The *Detroit Uncommitted* ran a story the previous week about the local bars wanting to eliminate the '2 o'clock stop' liquor serving restrictions so they could compete for business with the all-night casinos. The bar down the street was open, and where there were drinking establishments, there were drinkers. If the drinkers were drunkards then, there would be drunkard's cars left in the drinking establishment's parking lots because law-abiding drunkards were required to take a taxi home. *Right?*

CHAPTER 9

I woke to a steady vibration under me. *Dang*. I had dozed off and was curled on the back floor of the rusty old Lincoln Town Car I'd crawled into. I was with God-knows-who going God-knows-where. I prayed the killers hadn't parked that car at the bar before going inside to continue their hunt for me. I could have been in a car with my would-be killers right then, frosting their $100,000 cake.

I peered up at the back of the front seat from my floor vantage point. The lack of good lighting made it impossible for me to see anything but dark hair above the head rest. It wasn't likely blond Tappy was my driver. It was also unlikely Scuffy was my driver because no one was hacking up a lung. I was pretty sure the other seat was empty too because the driver wasn't talking to anyone. He was either alone or with his wife. Pretty unlikely the driver was with his wife because who takes their wife with them to a bar until the wee hours of the morning? Certainly not my husband. Jorgji seldom tried to take me with him anywhere after our quick elopement in Vegas. I wondered if he had a secret lover or if I was part of an insurance job. Neither one appealed to me.

Crouched on the floor of the back seat, I contemplated my sorry situation. I wanted to stretch out and give my cramped legs a rest, but I didn't dare move for fear of discovery.

I should have just done it anyway because the 'ode-de-bathroom' odor I was wearing wafted up to my driver. I heard one definite sniff from the front seat and then another.

***

Frank was about 6 blocks from the Crow's Nest, a rundown bar on the edge of an affluent part of town, when he caught a distinct sewer order. He thought it must have been coming in from the surrounding area through the car vents. He put it out of his mind because he would soon be out of the inner city and hitting the road for the department rented suburban house his boss, Merle Hartford, setup for a cover. Frank wanted to shower, shave, and catch up on some much-needed sleep, but his overriding priority was to visit the bathroom. The castor oil he downed to keep the alcohol from being absorbed into his stomach was working its way through his system quicker than he'd intended. He rubbed the scrub of the beard on his chin and shifted his body in his seat. This latest undercover assignment was turning out to be shitty in more ways than one. He needed to hit the toilet right away when he got back to the house. If he could last that long. Why did he keep smelling that smell?

***

I felt the car slow, and then stop. The dome light flipped on. A bristly-faced man's dark piercing gaze swept the back seat and alighted on me. His mouth spit out, "Shit. What are you doing in here?"

Busted.

"Look," I stammered, assessing just how big a mess I was in while still trying to keep up my bathroom-character charade. "I needed to give some fellows the slip. I didn't intend to fall asleep in your car. It's just that I usually go to bed by 9:30 and I am really tired. You can't believe how difficult it is to keep yourself awake after always being in bed at nine, and I was really tired. Even with someone after you, eventually, your adrenaline just runs down. I couldn't sleep in the laundromat. I never ever dreamed I could sleep in a car. Much less this car. Much less the back seat of this car. Not that it's not a great car. It's very roomy, and the carpet isn't too dirty, except for a few sticky spots, but you can't imagine how uncomfortable it is to be lying on the floor of a car, but must be when your body is tired enough sleep just happens." I was rambling, but I didn't care as long as my rambling delayed any action on his part. Which it didn't.

He got out of the car. We were stopped on the expressway because I noticed the heavy Lincoln swayed each time I heard a 'womp' from a semi barreling by us. I managed to turn in these cramped quarters so I could see the driver better in the dome light.

He opened the rear door and bellowed, "Get out!" at me.

A frayed denim jacket covered his black tee shirt. His worn blue jeans had a rip running horizontally across the left knee. The frayed hem edges of the jeans bunch around the tops of his dirty, no-longer-white high tops. His short dark hair was bunched in places where it wasn't fashionable to be bunched. The entire right side of his hair was flattened and greasy looking, in total contrast to the neatly combed left side. He reeked strongly of cigarette smoke and alcohol. He looked and smelled almost as bad as I did. He was about my age or maybe a little older.

The only good observation I could come up with for that whole situation was that he was brunette, he was alone, he didn't cough, and he didn't have a coughing partner. He wasn't a killer—at least not MY killer. At least not yet. From the look of those dark-circled eyes, smoldering with close-to-murdering anger, he also wasn't drunk. Drunk's eyes can't do a good smolder.

While his eyes blazed, I took a split second to review my options. I could do my usual "follow orders" and step out onto the expressway and into the path of a semi-truck, or I could go back, possibly right into the path of Tappy and Scuffy, or I could do a third Penelope-type option and stay put, risking the wrath of Smolder. Smolder won.

"No," I said plainly, my throaty-sore throat giving me an edge in keeping up a deep and almost commanding voice. The best I could manage while staying put.

"What do you mean 'No'? I didn't invite a punky, shit head, street druggie for a ride. This is my assigned car, and you have to get out, or I'll drag you out." He shouted again for emphasis "GET OUT!"

"No," I said again, just as plainly as before, but now a little quieter and squeakier as I hunkered down on the floor even tighter and grabbed the underside of the front seat. I have never cared for being yelled at, which is why at 10:30 at night I ended up trying to dry clean the clothes I was wearing and why I didn't even try to explain to Lord Smolder that I had never taken street drugs.

I did not get a chance to give him any explanations at all because a strange look twisted his face. He kicked the side of the car and said in a tightly controlled voice, "Crap. I'll have to deal with you when I get back to the house." And he jumped into the front seat, and we took off like the proverbial speeding bullet.

I bounced around on the floor of his car at neck-breaking speeds for a few minutes before the car screeched to a jerky halt. The driver-side door swung open, and then slammed shut with so much force it should have caved in the side of the car. I waited on the back seat floor terrified of when the door next to me would open, and he would forcibly remove me from his car. And I waited. And I waited. *Well, what the heck was holding him up?* I stretched up from the car floor and plopped my fanny on the back seat to peer out into the darkness.

The car was parked in the driveway of a small bungalow that was shoved in beside other small houses with similar appearances. A shuttered light shone out from a small side window of the house to the driveway.

I didn't know what to do. I didn't recall Penelope ever being in men's clothes, in the back seat of a car waiting for a man she didn't know to come and drag her out. I didn't have a clue of how to take my life from that point to the next, so I just sat, worrying. The light from the small window of the bungalow winked out. Then the porch light came on.

Lord Smolder hauled my bottom from the back seat and out into the driveway in one smooth motion before I even realized he was at the car. "Now listen boy, I don't know what you are strung out on, but I need to get some sleep, so you need to go home."

Boy? I was often mistaken for an adolescent because of my small stature and soft, quiet voice, but not usually for a boy. Must have been the baggy men's clothes, the harsh throat, and the darkness of the night.

"No," I said, keeping my voice low, not even able to do a good shout. Had I passed the *Dale Carnage* course I would have been able to do a full shout. I would have been able to say what I really meant which was '*No. I'm not a boy. No. I'm not strung out on something. And No. I will not go home. I no longer have a home. At least not one I want to go back to. Scuffy and Tappy said they'd just wait for me until I got back. There's no place like home and no place like home I'm going to. I'll take my chances here. Thank you very much.*'

A light came on at the house next door, and a curtain parted in their front picture window. Their porch light illuminated. Lord Smolder made an exasperated sound, grabbed me by the elbow and marched me up onto the porch and into his house.

***

Frank was dead-dog tired, but the last thing he wanted was for the neighbors to call the city cops believing there to be some kind of a domestic disturbance. He was undercover for Christ sakes. It wouldn't do to have the precinct he was investigating investigating him. What was he supposed to do with a street kid? He had to report in early the next day so Merle could update the mayor's office. The office had been breathing down the bureau's back ever since the case got started. Frank didn't have time for this trouble. He was almost done with that assignment. From the length and state of his hair and the look and smell of him that kid had to have been on the street for a long time. Probably a runaway or something. He was very small and looking pretty docile, so Frank figured he could just power down, lock up his bullets and park the kid in a corner of the living room for the night.

He would take him to some homeless shelter or call some runaway hotline or something the next morning. Frank's first priority was to get some sleep before he collapsed.

***

I could see the man was so tired that he was thinking with one eye shut. I was too confused and distressed to do anything more than just stand there, knees quaking, heart thudding, my gaze darting around the room while I waited for him to make the next move.

The place didn't give me much to look at. There was a brown cloth recliner, TV stand, and small TV. No pictures on the wall. No magazines. No newspapers. No books. No glass of raspberry lemonade waiting for his return. No couch. No end tables. No lamps. To my right, I could see inside the small kitchen with a microwave, a small refrigerator and a few take-out containers and cups on the counter, nothing else. Nothing. *Goodness. Lord Smolder had either just moved in or was as broke as I appeared to be.*

While the place wasn't on par with my Georgian colonial in Winnetka or Detroit's posh Shelby Towers, there were no hired killers there, so I was pretty sure if Lord Smolder didn't kill me, I was probably safe there for the time being.

Lord Smolder must have taken my silence as a good sign that I'd behave. He yawned, then told me sternly, "Listen kid. I've got to get some sleep. You can stay until morning if you shower first. You stink, and I don't want you to stink the place up." He yawned again and walked away. I heard a little jingling of keys and a clanging of metal.

A shower started up. It ran for a few minutes. The water stopped and then the snoring started. Timid, I looked around the place. The house had a tiny utility closet that housed the furnace and hot water heater. There were four small rooms; a kitchen-dining room combination, living room, bedroom with a small closet, and a bathroom. Lord Smolder was passed out face down across the only bed in the whole darn place.

He was wearing a towel draped around his waist and nothing else. His long muscled, tan legs showed some white skin at the very top of his thighs, at the edge of the towel. His arms cradled the pillow under his head. His bare bronze back rose and fell with each light snore. He was very well-assembled and very much asleep from what I could discern.

That was just fine for him, but just where was I going to sleep in that Spartan house, and just what was I going to wear after I showered?

In his closet, I found a shelf with a little metal lock box on it. On the closet rod, I found a man's Navy suit, pressed white dress shirt, clean gray tee shirt and a waist-high pile of clothes heaped on the floor. The tee shirt had a big red English-style letter 'D' dominating the front of it. It looked comfortable enough to sleep in. On the hook next to the tee shirt was a Glock in a shoulder holster. I figured it was safe to take the thing for the night since Lord Smolder was out of commission. The shirt. I've never liked guns.

Once in the bathroom, I shed my clothes and my USB bracelet band. I rinsed out the underwear I was wearing plus the black lace pair and drapped them over the bathroom towel bar. I wrapped up in a towel to do a quick double take. After I was sure both he and the gun were out cold, I closed and locked the bathroom door for a quick, hot shower that got the grime and smell out of my hair and off my body.

Dressed in only his tee shirt, I discovered that not only was Lord Smolder on the only sleeping surface in the house but his body was on top of the only blanket in the whole place, too. There was no way I was touching that body for any purpose, so I just stretched out on the open recliner and used my invisibility-cloak tablecloth for a cover.

My invisibility cloth might have worked better if the darn tablecloth had kept me covered. I woke up to an expletive of, "Shit! You're a girl!"

I should have kept my underwear on or found a longer tee shirt.

"I am not a girl," I said, wanting to further explain. *'I'm a woman. Not a girl.'* But I didn't try to explain. I was too mortified.

He, with his eyes still fixed on where that traitorous tablecloth was before it hit the floor said, "I beg to differ. You are definitely female." I couldn't seem to get the shirt down or the table cloth up fast enough to keep the red out of my face.

He leaned over me, both hands resting on either side of the recliner. "You need to start giving me some explanations," he said in a dangerously low voice that I was not liking too well. His face was so close that I could see the little, unshaved whiskers poking out of his strong square chin. I looked down, away from those smoldering eyes, but then his sparsely haired chest muscles come into my view, so I looked straight up again. There was an intensity in those brown eyes, flecked with spots of blue, that sent a shiver through me. That probably had more to do with my state of undress than the nearness of him, but I was intimidated. Not a terrified intimidation like with Tappy and Scuffy, but my heart was beating fast, and I was feeling alarmed. Another little shiver coursed through me.

"You can start by telling me who you are and why you were in my car last night," he demanded of me in that tightly controlled voice.

With his tautly muscled arms on either side of me, his masculine face just inches away from mine and his deep male voice assaulting my ears, the man may have been intimidating, but not threatening enough for me to risk my life for. I was not going to tell him the truth. He didn't need to know who I was. Never one to think of quick, witty retorts I stalled with, "Why?"

Okay. So I was not good at stalling, but, fortunately for me, the cell phone clipped to the waistband of his trousers started jangling to the tune of *The Lion Sleeps Tonight*.

***

Frank was glad his cell phone rang because he was enjoying looking into those brown eyes too much. She wasn't drop-dead gorgeous, but she had a fresh-scrubbed, no makeup, healthy, sweet-faced look. He knew that had to be a ruse. No fresh, wholesome girl would be lodged in the back seat floor of his undercover car at 2:15 in the morning dressed like she was. Was she a druggie? His Detroit Tiger's tee hadn't covered much of her before she yanked it down. He didn't notice any needle tracks on those smooth, velvety arms or legs. Maybe she was on something else? She'd reeked the night before but not from alcohol.

Hearing the boss's ringtone he had no choice, but to stop musing. He straightened up and turned away from her to take the call.

"Did you get everything we need?"

"Yes," Frank growled, not daring to say more.

"How soon can you get here with it?" Merle asked Frank, turned back to face the girl, no, woman. She was still trying to hold the bottom of his tee shirt down as far as she could get it. For some reason, Frank found this honest modesty even more appealing than the view before. He felt a slight arousal begin before he squelched it by walking into the kitchen to focus on the call.

"I just got up." Well, he knew if he didn't get his mind off the woman and back on his work he would be. "Give me 50 minutes."

"You've got 40. The deputy mayor will be here in 60, and I need to review what you've got on their officers first."

Frank knew better than to ask for more time. He didn't know why the mayor's office was anxious to see the evidence, and he couldn't ask. It wasn't wise to discuss any of the case while on an open cell phone line. He just couldn't understand what the rush was. They had been working on the case for months. The Attorney General's office wouldn't even take incoming cases before 10:00 am. Hell, something big had to be up.

Frank was relieved that the "kid" he thought he'd have to babysit was really a full grown woman who could take care of herself. Forty minutes wasn't even enough time to include a shave and breakfast, so all that would have to wait.

***

"Look," Lord Smolder said to me as he dashed for the bedroom to grab his shirt, shoes, and gun—into which he shoved a magazine clip. "I don't know who you are and I don't care as long as you are gone within the hour. I have to be somewhere quick and can't drop you off anywhere. Here's 40 bucks." He slapped two twenties down beside the TV. "Get yourself a bus or a cab or something. Go back and make up with your parents, boyfriend or husband or whoever it is you left to roam the streets." He shoved the gun into its shoulder holster and covered it up with the navy blue suit jacket from the closet. At the front door, he turned back to me with a leer on his face and said, "You can keep the tee shirt. Looks good on you."

***

Frank backed the Lincoln out onto the street, annoyed that he didn't take the time the previous night to back the car in for a quick take-off. Then he remembered that he'd been in a rush last night, but that was okay because the castor oil worked as planned. It had kept the alcohol from being absorbed into his system and kept him sober enough to get the dope and incriminating statements from the dirty officers who were sloppy drunk while Frank was sober. Sober and clean. Through and through.

Last night's work was the bow on the evidence package he was delivering to Merle, the FBI Special Agent in Charge. The package would then go to the Attorney General's Office for review and processing. Everyone was anxious to get the arrest warrants issued for the two Detroit police officers that were involved in the drug bust thefts. No one was more anxious than Frank. He was energized at the thought of getting time off for good behavior; his likely reward for the months of sleepless nights spent sitting in crummy bars talking to off-duty police officers and for having to drive that rat-trap, rusty car.

Frank pulled into the McNamara Building's underground parking ramp. He was already two minutes late so to avoid the metal detectors he flashed his badge at the guard and dashed madly up the stairwell without another thought to the woman on the recliner in his department-rented house.

***

Once Lord Smolder and his loaded gun were out the door, I exhaled a heavy breath of air and looked at the two 20s next to the TV. I had more than enough wealth left to me by my parents and now my aunt. I had several cool billions spread out in bank accounts, stocks, bonds, and other investments that Jorgji set up for me. I didn't need to rely on the generosity of smoldery strangers. Except that pesky ATM situation kept eating away at my thoughts. I stared hungrily at the two 20s and tried to put myself in Penelope's place so I could think logically and stay alive.

I knew I had to get myself together and get out of there before Lord Smolder came back, so I grabbed my now dry underwear and put the un-sexy pair on. The black lace I decided to shove into the kitchen wastebasket. Like my Prada purse, this pair wasn't going to do me any good. I slipped my skirt over my hips and took Lord Smolder at his word, keeping the clean tee shirt on.

There was only the refrigerator hum echoing off the bare walls to fill the palpable emptiness of the stark bungalow to remind me of how alone I was in the house and the world. Mother. Father. Aunts. All gone. My cousins were mad at me. My husband was trying to kill me.

I startled when I heard a loud sound—like a door being shattered into splinters. *Had Scuffy and Tappy found me there?* I looked around for a place to hide. There wasn't enough furniture to get under or behind. I didn't want to be shut up in the utility closet. I tried to get down with the dust bunnies under the bed, but all I accomplished was to get dirty when I laid flat on the floor behind the bed, unable to get under it. Then as the house returned to an eerie silence, I heard a spray of water in the kitchen and came to the realization that the noise I heard was just the refrigerator's ice maker letting go of its load.

I needed to get a grip.

My cousin Mandy's incessant chatter about trivial fashion issues and 'hot' movie stars or her brother Martin's talk about sports cars and making it big in the stock market would have almost been preferable to the eerie quiet of that house. Almost. But not quite.

I turned on the TV, always a faithful companion for me. The local morning news broke the empty silence of the house. I turned the volume up to listen while I searched for a phone to call a cab. My search netted me a phone book but no phone. In fact, there was little in the house at all. Very few clothes and only a few personal effects. I looked through the few clothes on the floor of the closet and found nothing remarkable. They were all grubby old and needed washing.

There on the tiny shelf over the toilet was a single-edged razor blade, shaving cream, toothpaste, toothbrush, comb, body wash and dark designer-style sunglasses. Used plastic cups, plastic silverware, paper plates and take-out containers lined the counter in the kitchen. A cardboard box with a few pathetic pieces of dried left-over pizza dominated the little, ice-dropping, humming fridge.

I devoured the pizza, hoping it hadn't been in there long enough to poison me. I washed the pizza down with tap water in a paper cup with a few of the noisy ice cubes because the only other drink I could find was a lone Bud Lite in the fridge. I didn't think it was my wisest choice to consume the man's last beer—just in case I was not out of there before he got back. Which I was working on, but not very fast.

I was stalling, and I knew it. It was hard for me to be decisive beyond what to eat and what internet specialty yarns and needles to buy, but it was not my fault. I had always been taken care of. The first six years by my parents, then when they died in a car crash, my mother's sister, Selena, and her husband took me in. Luckily that lasted less than a year. My father's sister, my dear Aunt Tilly, showed up and took me home with her. Nineteen years later Jorgji came along. He assumed the role of caretaker. He wanted to take care of me all right. Right from caretaker to undertaker.

I could have called Gordon to come and get me, but what could he do except take me back to Illinois to be found by Scuffy and Tappy? I debated going to the police, but If I did what would I tell them? *'I heard two men in the stairwell, and though they didn't mention me specifically I think my husband hired them to kill me because he might be having an affair?'*

My story of two men in a stairwell talking about money and cake sounded bizarre, even to me, and I was the potential killee the killers were after. *What if I was mistaken?*

Munching on the last bite of pizza I caught the sound of my name on the morning news, so I walked until I was directly in front of the screen and turned up the volume. My picture was pasted to the corner of the screen with Jorgji's unsmiling face smack dab in the center of the screen telling the reporter's camera that he feared for my safety. My picture stayed in the corner as the female reporter flashed back on the screen saying, "Mr. Dalmat was away on business in Chicago until early this morning. He returned home to find evidence of a break-in." Here she paused and waved her right arm towards the splintered door jamb of my apartment's front door. "His wife," she continued, "the heiress billionaire niece of the late great murder mystery author, Matilda Warren, is gone. While no ransom note has yet been received Mr. Dalmat believes foul play and expects a ransom demand to be received soon. Anyone who has seen Mrs. Dalmat or knows anything about her disappearance is being asked to call the Detroit Police Telephone Crime Reporting Line at 313–267–4600." An image of me from our wedding photo in Vegas zoomed forward with a number below it. Then, "Back to you, Jeff."

What break in? Those men had a key and walked in! My gut instincts had been right. Jorgji married me for my money and would stop at nothing to get it, just like in my aunt's latest novel, *The Lonely Heart Club Murders.* I couldn't stay at my apartment, and I couldn't go back to my colonial in Winnetka. Those would be the obvious places the killers would look for me.

I, the hunted, must turn into the hunter, like Penelope in *The Stalked Strikes Back*. Penelope disguised herself as her client and used herself as bait to smoke out her client's killer husband. I needed to find a way to bring charges against my cheating, murdering husband so I could get out of the marriage. I had to find the guts for that. *What would Penelope do?*

I knew that Penelope wouldn't have been that gullible in the first place. She wouldn't have married a money-grubber who wanted to kill her for her money. If she had, she wouldn't have become a sitting duck waiting around for Elmer Fudd to show up.

She also would not have gone around hiding in the shadows, afraid of everyone and everything. She would have gone on the attack, seeking out the proof she needed to bring charges against her would-be killer husband.

Penelope always had her detective father to help her solve all of the murder mysteries she was involved in. Too bad I wasn't her.

I absentmindedly twirled my USB bracelet around and around on my wrist (a nervous habit I had) while thinking up investigative strategies on how to prove my husband was trying to kill me for my money. *How long did I realistically have before Scuffy and Tappy finally found me?*

I didn't have time to waste.

With a new sense of Penelope bravado, I seized the two 20s, snatched up the designer-style sunglasses and the beer. I launched myself out the door and over to the neighbors who were awakened last night when we first pulled in.

"Hi," I said to the older couple answering the door in my cheeriest, friendliest Penelope-voice I could muster given my aversion to talking to strangers. "I was…I was…at the house next door when…when…the guy who brought me here was called away. I need to get away from here before he comes back. Can I...can I...would you let me use your phone to call a cab?"

When the cab company answered, I had to ask the neighbor woman with the matronly-coiffed, stiff-sprayed white hair what their address is. I told the dispatcher "111 Stratford Circle."

Mrs. Stiff glanced at the beer in my hand. Her look traveled down my unmatched ensemble of a big 'D' tee shirt, and rumpled, dust covered brown skirt. Her gaze traveled up to meet mine. She told me to go out and wait on their porch for the cab. I heard two locks click into place the second their door shut behind me.

CHAPTER 10

Fifty–seven minutes later, I was in the large handicapper restroom stall at the cabbie-recommended *Rmart*. I took my newly purchased scissors and chopped, chopped, chopped. My hair was a mess, but that was what I was going for. Short and hacked. With red dye in hand, I used the stall's convenient sink and mirror to turn my mess into a big red mess. The dye instructions were easy to follow, and my hair was easy to color in its shortened state, but I was not quick or skilled enough to keep the dye drips off myself, the floor and the sink. I wiped the splotches of red up as best I could with the last of the paper towels from the emptied dispenser. The dye had stained the floor into splotches that resembled wiped up blood.

Oh, my. Rmart was going to think someone lopped off their arm in there and not that *N'Oreal* helped me dye my hair in their sink. I was not worried about discovery. I doubted Tappy and Scuffy were going to try to find me in a super-store ladies bathroom stall.

My wet red hair, red splattered clothes and I foraged in the women's department. It was fun flipping through the hanging clothes, not at all like scrolling around on a monitor screen. I loved seeing the textures and vibrant colors in person, but sadly, they were all more money than I had to spend.

How quickly a dime turned.

I found a whole section of the department with several racks labeled 'clearance.' Most of what I found there were super-size-me dresses and slacks, and maternity separates, stretchy stomach panels and billowy tops. I was not super-sized or pregnant, so I skipped the clearance rack and flung a package of new underwear into my cart. I started expanding my search so I could find something other than underwear to complete my next disguise.

I hit the men's wear isles with their zippered flies and button up shirts, wide belts, dark socks, and ties. All more expensive than the super-sized rack, so I doubled back to the women's department, discouraged.

I did still have Jorgji's pants, coat, and shirt in a plastic bag with the greeter at the front door that I could have used to hide in again. But I was thinking not. Lord Smolder easily mistook me for a boy. If I did that disguise again, I would have to use the men's bathroom to keep people from figuring out that I was a woman dressed as a man. Being in a restroom with men using urinals was way too creepy a thought, so back to the clearance rack I went. Better to be pregnant.

Final purchases in hand, forty–seven dollars poorer, I made my way back to the restroom at the front of the store; I was the proud owner of a loud, bright orange maternity top, deep purple maternity pants, a teddy bear print design diaper bag and a very firm foam pillow. With scissors in hand, I shaped the pillow to look like a pregnant stomach and slid it into my new stretchy pants and covered it with the orange top. I caught sight of myself in the full-length mirror as I stepped out of the handicap bathroom stall and gave a startled gasp.

I was a pregnant stranger. Red hair, orange top, and purple pants were way out of character for me, but so bracing. So Penelope.

But I was not Penelope. I was just scared Imogene. My situation hit me hard, and I began to cry. My wish for a husband, home and baby were in the trash can with soppy paper towels, scraps of my hair and pieces of foam. I looked like an expectant mom, but I had no expectations of ever being one. My husband didn't want a wife, at least not a live one, so he certainly didn't want a baby.

I cried even harder when a woman entered the restroom with a tiny, pink bundle nestled in a baby carrier, a toddler's hand intertwined with hers.

She looked at me sympathetically, patted my hand and said, "It's your hormones, honey. Trust me. Just try to enjoy this time with your husband before the baby gets here." Then when she noticed my engagement ring with its interlocking wedding band, she said, "Wow. That's some rock. Your husband must love you very much," I burst into fresh tears.

She didn't know I bought that big engagement ring at our Las Vegas elopement. Jorgji wanted me to have a large diamond to make up for our not having a long engagement or big wedding. I would have been happy with a plain white gold band, but I thought it was sweet the way he wanted me to have this huge diamond. It was just as well that Jorgji's money was all tied up in bonds that he couldn't liquidate before our elopement to Vegas. Having paid for that ring, I wasn't going to feel guilty about hocking it for the cash I needed to live on while I filed attempted murder charges against Jorgji and worked to find evidence of his duplicity.

***

Frank had turned on the black light and was using it to show Merle that the crack cocaine he purchased from the two off-duty police officers was the same crack they'd marked with near infrared dye, proof that the crack was the same crack stolen from a Detroit Police drug bust. It was the crack he'd finally gotten the right contacts to purchase the previous night. The tiny digital recorder Frank used to document the transaction last night was downloading the digital evidence onto Merle's computer.

"Good idea to stage a fake drug bust where we marked the crack with something that could identify it as taken from the cache confiscated during the raid. That and the rest of what you've got will clinch the case against these two dirty cops," Merle told Frank.

"I wish I could take credit for the near infrared marker, but a friend of mine suggested using it," Frank said, then added upon seeing the disapproval on Merle's face, "Don't worry. This person doesn't know anything about the case or even that I work for the FBI. It's been all hypothetical e-mails. They don't even know what I look like."

Johnny Gage, Frank's friend on the task force, poked his head into the office and asked, "Hey, Frankie, what was the address of that house you were set up in?"

"109 Stratford Circle. I'm heading back there to get my things after I swap that junker for my Jag. Why?"

"Better take your badge and talk to the couple next door. They say they saw you manhandle someone into your house late last night. She came to their house this morning to call a cab."

"Yeah, so what of it?" Frank asked.

"They were just at one of the local precincts saying their suspicious-acting neighbor of six months kidnapped that rich dame's niece. They say a woman who came to their house this morning acting all jumpy and scared was the same one as the missing person on TV." Johnny flipped a picture down on Merle's desk so Merle and Frank could both see it.

Merle's left eyebrow shot up as he picked up the picture. "You had Matilda Warren's niece as a house guest?" he asked.

"Not exactly. I didn't know who she was. She sort of came home with me and stayed the night." Then Frank's face flushed red at the memory of the scene that morning. "Well, it's not what it sounds like," Frank said, flustered. "I thought she was a boy when I went to bed. I didn't find out she was a woman until I woke up."

"Sounds interesting," Johnny said as both his eyebrows shot up and a toothy smile flashed across his face.

Frank gave Johnny a look of disgust and took the picture from Merle to study it hard. The image was a black and white copy from the fax machine, but he knew those eyes. They are soft brown velvet, doe eyes. He smiled as he pictured them looking up at him innocently while she squirmed to keep his tee shirt down covering her thighs.

"Oh, brother," Johnny said. "You must be slipping Frankie. Mistaking a woman for a boy. How drunk were you?"

"Not that drunk. I don't do boys or married women, Gage, so wipe that smirk off your face, or I'll wipe it off with my fist. And get me the info that we have on this missing person case. This woman said she was hiding from someone. If she's missing now maybe they found her."

"Hey, you're to take the next few weeks off, remember? The warrants will be issued later today for the dirty cops, and their trial won't start for a few months, AND, unless we're invited in to assist with something, this missing woman is a local case—out of our jurisdiction," Merle reminded Frank.

"I've got to go back to that house and get my things anyway. I'll talk to the neighbors. If she called a cab then I'm sure she's long gone by now, but maybe someone can tell me something about where she might have gone. If I find anything out I'll turn it over to the locals," Frank reassured Merle.

Deputy Mayor Chester Rhodes was waiting outside Merle's office. He had leafed through every magazine they had on display in the three minutes he had been waiting. All he wanted was for Merle to give him the go-ahead for entry. He started pacing back and forth across the carpeted area, not even bothering to remove his long outer coat.

Another two minutes passed. He decided he had waited long enough. As the secretary gave a loud protest of "You can't go in there," he barged into Merle's office.

Merle, hearing his secretary's warning, had thrown the micro recorder to Frank, who easily caught it from across the room. The deputy mayor brushed past Frank to get to Merle's desk. Merle had slid a handy gun magazine over the crack cocaine spread out on his desk just as the deputy mayor barged through his office door. The much larger black light wasn't so easy to conceal. It was out in plain sight on the desk. Merle decided not to touch it. He left it out, hoping the deputy mayor wouldn't know what it was or its use in the case.

Frank was put-off with the guy from the mayor's office not even waiting until Merle invited him in. Frank didn't want to stay for the meeting. He was not supposed to be giving up his undercover identity—not even for that jerk, but he didn't need to worry. The Deputy Mayor didn't even glance his way. He was focused on Merle and what was on Merle's desk.

Merle leaned forward and placed both hands on the desk. One was strategically placed on the magazine to keep it in place. There were no preliminaries or polite greetings between Merle and the deputy major.

Frank slipped his micro recorder into his pocket. Making as little noise as possible, he left through the door the deputy mayor had left open. Frank didn't even clear the doorway before he heard the deputy mayor demand of Merle, "The mayor wants to know the scope and nature of the evidence the FBI has gathered and what else we can expect before you wrap this investigation up."

***

I couldn't stay all day sobbing in an Rmart bathroom, so I wiped my eyes with toilet paper, hid their puffy redness with Lord Smolder's sunglasses, and put on my best Penelope attitude to go out and pawn my diamond ring set.

Pawning rings was not that easy. I didn't have any identification and was not a good liar. At the third pawn shop, I managed to get more Penelope-like and told the man I was a victim of domestic violence so I couldn't give him my name out of fear of being found. That was close enough to the truth to make my stomach flip around as he took pity on me and peered at my diamond ring with a jewelers loop. He looked up at me and shook his head.

"Sorry, Missy. I don't know if you are a scammer or if someone scammed you. I'll grant you; this is an excellent fake. It's worth some money as a fake because it's so good. I'll give you $300 for it."

"What!" I said. "It can't be a fake. I bought and paid for these rings myself at *Boutique Cartiler*. These rings have been in my possession since my elopement. You're the scammer. I can't believe you'd try to give me only $300 for a $250,000 ring set. I should report you to someone, like the Association of Pawn Shops' Men or the pawn police or something."

Jorgji! He had taken my rings to have them cleaned. Or maybe to clean me out.

I managed to calm down enough to realize that the nice man behind the counter wasn't responsible for my situation. I took the proffered $300 and walked out of the pawn shop crying, which seemed to be a recurring pattern.

I scrapped my plan to go to the bank and make a cash withdrawal; my picture with a sizable reward for information had been flashed all over on TV. Besides, I had gotten rid of my identification and changed my looks. The bank tellers wouldn't let me withdraw money if they didn't recognize me and I couldn't produce any identification to prove who I was.

With no other means of income to support my neophyte investigation of my husband, I headed back to my apartment, compelled by my dire circumstances to take the household money from our bedroom safe. It shouldn't have been too dangerous to go there on a Monday, even with Jorgji in town. He was the consummate workaholic who was always at the office without fail on Mondays. If my luck held, that was where he would be. I should have been safe, because Keiko, our maid, had Mondays off. That should have given me a few hours to get into the apartment and get the safe open—provided Jorgji and Keiko kept to their regular routines.

I just hoped Scuffy and Tappy weren't going to keep to their routines and wait for me to get there.

**

Frank received some incredulous looks when he flashed his former neighbors his FBI badge and I.D. Once they got over the shock that their secretive neighbor was with the FBI, they gave Frank a good description of Imogene's taxi and its driver. He tracked down the right man with no problem and then figured out where the cabbie had left her.

The Rmart cashiers had seen a lot of faces, but none was the one in the copy Frank showed them. None of the service counter clerks could remember anyone fitting her description either. *Damn.* Frank wondered, w*hy come to Rmart? Why not just go home?*

One of the floor detectives told Frank he saw a petite redhead in a gray Detroit Tigers tee shirt rummaging through the lady's section clearance rack. She looked like a punker, so he kept an eye on her. Once he was able to confirm that she was going through checkout lane two to pay for what she had in her hand, he lost interest. Upon Frank's closer questioning, the checker on lane two did recall a wild-haired red-head in a skirt and a gray tee shirt coming through her lane. She didn't remember what she bought or what time she'd been in; only that she'd paid cash and didn't buy much, just some clearance clothes or something.

Frank checked the ladies clearance rack. It was filled with plus sizes and maternity clothes—nothing that Imogene would be buying. Frank wasn't fond of redheads and this being Detroit Tiger country, he wasn't going to waste his time weeding through store video surveillance tapes to spot a Detroit Tiger's tee shirt. He felt he had taken the investigation far enough. His preliminary inquiry was over. Merle was right. She was a local problem. Not his problem anymore.

CHAPTER 11

Imogene may not have been his problem, but the memory of her eyes staring up at him from the recliner kept tugging Frank's mind back to her missing person case. The pull was strong enough that he decided to head back to the FBI office—just to check out a few things with Marion Mosier, a.k.a. Marion the Librarian.

Marion, the FBI computer records specialist, was known for her pure genius with all things written. She had been known to pull up volumes of recorded information on anyone. If the information were printed or stored somewhere in the world, Marion would work until she found it. If Marion plugged Imogene's name into the National Crime Information Center records and found a criminal record, then Frank could put the whole matter out of his mind and move on with a clear conscience, brown eyes and smooth legs be damned.

Frank didn't have to wait long. Within an hour, Marion summoned him down to her record morgue in the basement. He walked down one of the long storage aisles and stopped at one of the work tables Marion had set up in a clearing between shelves. She was there reading the newspaper she was holding in her white cotton gloved hands. Most records experts had long since switched entirely to digital storage, but Marion felt some records had to be seen in their original state to get their full import. These items she stored in archival safe storage boxes, after scanning them into her digital files for easy reference.

"Matilda Warren's popularity as a mystery writer gave me plenty of magazine and newspaper stories. There are lots of files in the data systems for her. Unfortunately, I haven't found much yet on her niece, Imogene Warren Dalmat," Marion explained.

"Most of what I found is related to Imogene being her aunt's secretary and business manager. She was interviewed a few times by the media because she was in the enviable position of knowing 'who done it' before the old woman's fans did, but Imogene said very little to the press or the fans. Appears she likes to stay out of the public eye. Way out. What she did say in those rare interviews was strictly about her aunt's books—minus the endings everyone sought from her. The Chicago society pages ran articles this past summer when she eloped with Jorgji Henry Dalmat, 32, an investment broker. You have any interest in that?"

Frank scowled at Marion and asked her to search further back and run the husband's name through the system, too.

Marion found a series of old, short news clips from years earlier when there was a bitter custody battle between Matilda Warren and Selena Parker. After the simultaneous death of both Imogene's parents in Asia's Meghri mountain range, both the paternal aunt and maternal aunt fought over guardianship for the rich, little heiress. Miss Warren was initially out of the country, having flown to Asia to identify the parent's bodies and make arrangements for final interment. There was a snag in the paperwork, so she remained there several weeks. While she was gone, Imogene was taken in by Selena and John Parker. Matilda Warren came back to the U.S. and filed suit for custody.

Mr. and Mrs. Parker testified in court that they took in Imogene so she could be raised in a family environment with her cousins. They argued that she had bonded to them and it was in her best interest to remain with them. They also stated that all of the $200,000,000 trust fund money they used was strictly to care for Imogene's needs and see to her happiness.

Miss Warren testified that the Parkers were misappropriating young Imogene's trust fund for their own personal gain; Imogene couldn't possibly need a new $175,000 sailing yacht, a $200,000 sports car, a $400,000 hunting cabin, a $100,000 home stereo surround system, oak kitchen cabinets installed in the Parker household, or size 12 woman's designer clothing. The court agreed, and Miss Warren was awarded custody of Imogene.

Frank paused his reading to look at the pictures of a young Imogene that every newspaper ran at the end of the long, protracted custody trial. Every one of the pictures showed a frightened little girl, dressed in oversized boys clothing, clinging to a ratty rag doll as a policewoman walked her down a long sidewalk towards a waiting Rolls Royce. The headlines read "Little Rag Doll's Billions Returned to Her," and "Relatives Live High Life—Little Billionairess in Rags" and "Riches to Rags to Riches again." Frank could see the girl in the pictures resemblance to the woman Imogene had grown into. In the pictures, her doe eyes looked even bigger in the small face, surrounded by her dark blond curls.

"Check this out," Marion said, interrupting Frank's reading to hand him a court copy of Matilda Warren's will. "When the old lady died suddenly of a heart attack the niece inherited the 3.9 million dollar home near Chicago and the aunt's hefty bank account along with all her book and movie royalties. The will is dated just one day before the aunt's death." Marion brought a picture up on her data screen that was nearby. "And here is a picture that ran in the *National Questioner* at the time of the aunt's funeral."

Marion printed out the article and put it down in front of Frank. She added, "Seems there were a lot of nasty tabloid innuendos of foul play surrounding the aunt's death, but nothing notable in any reputable papers and nothing proven. The medical examiner's report is clean."

Frank ignored the will and the medical examiner's report since Marion already summarized their contents, but he looked intently at the picture of a black-garbed Imogene being helped into a Rolls by a slender, handsome man. The slight upward curve of the guy's mouth gave Frank a sinking feeling in his gut. This guy looked every bit like the proverbial cat that swallowed the canary.

Imogene's husband's name wasn't in the National Crime Information Center arrest records, but Marion had found a 'Jorgji H. Dalmat' listed as a person-of-interest in the FBI Financial Crimes Investigation Section's records under 'current open investigations.'

The FCI section of the FBI worked solely to uncover corporate deceit and concealment; many of their cases had an element of physical violence. Finding Jorgji Dalmat's name as a person of interest here only confirmed Frank's suspicions of canary swallowing.

Frank wasn't assigned to the FCI section, but he sometimes helped with undercover work for them and knew a few of their agents. He contacted the only FCI agent he knew well enough to call in a favor on, Michael Stevens.

"Hey, Frank. Good to hear from you. How's Janey doing?"

"Haven't seen her yet. How's your hip?"

"It's healed up nicely and doesn't bother me much these days. What's up?"

"I think I've snagged a case that your section might already have some information on. Jorgji Dalmat."

Agent Stevens said, "I'm not familiar with the Dalmat case file, but I'll check into it and get back to you."

Frank headed to one of Marion's back corners to read the rest of the printouts on Jorgji while he waited. He didn't wait long. Agent Steven called back in just under 10 minutes with a measure of excitement in his voice, so Frank shoved the files he was reading in a folder and sat them aside to read later.

Agent Stevens summed the file up for Frank. "The case file is still preliminary. It was started because we got some computer matches on banking information. Jorgji immigrated to Chicago from Albania a few years ago, and with no visible means of support, he started a Stewart Dunnings investment franchise. That business just expanded to Detroit a few months ago. We suspect him of shady investment dealings and possible money laundering because he has known family ties to the Albanian Mafia. There isn't enough substantive evidence in what I'm seeing here in the file to get any charges going against Mr. Dalmat yet, but there have been some large deposits put into Albanian banks from the U.S. The complete Albanian bank records haven't been obtained yet. Albanian bankers don't usually process our requests or follow international banking laws. That makes a full investigation difficult. You want copies of the file?"

"Sure. Just have it sent to my office. I'll add it to what Marion's already found. Thanks, Mike. I owe you one."

"Nah, this one's on the house—if you hadn't taken down the Josini Gang I wouldn't be here to tell the tail at retirement parties."

Frank pulled Jorgji's Steward Dunnings Investment website up on one of Marion's secured computers. Jorgji's firm had an enormous market spread, with some business recommendations from some pretty recognizable names, mostly movie stars and politicians. The deputy mayor of Detroit was listed as a client and has his endorsement posted to the site. Everything looked to be on the up and up. Still, Frank didn't like the look of the guy he saw on the screen. Jorgji was a little too smooth, a little too polished, a little too clean and a little too trustworthy-looking. He was so clean he seemed slimy. Frank didn't much like the thought of slimy touching freshly scrubbed Imogene. But then that wasn't his business, so he shoved everything Marion printed for him into an expanding file folder and thanked Marion for the use of the computer.

He tucked the folder away in his office at the same time he shoved the thoughts of Imogene's graceful, curvy legs aside so he could call Janey with a clear conscience.

Janey understood that he was on a special assignment and unavailable. He hadn't expected the assignment to last six months. She must have been worried. He had been close by, but unable to risk contacting her for fear of her being tagged or his cover being blown. He managed a quick call to her on her birthday. That was when she'd told him she was pregnant.

This latest investigation was all behind him now. He was looking forward to a few weeks of R & R before his next assignment. He was going to do his rest and relaxation with Janey and a case of Bud Lite.

On the way to Janey's, Frank decided he would pay a visit to Imogene's husband to let him know his wife was alive and okay and that she would probably come back home once things cooled off between them. He knew he'd be worried sick about her if he were her husband.

***

I slunk around the corner near my apartment, not sure if I dared to just go up, unlock the door and walk inside because I didn't know if Jorgji or one of his killers was waiting for me. I could have rung the bell and ran away, like a kid playing a Halloween prank, but that would have drawn even more attention to me than my big pillow bump. My hurting throat was so dry that I was unable to generate enough saliva to wet my parched lips. It was hard to swallow properly. I looked and felt like an orange and purple python that devoured a pig.

I stepped up to the door and rang the bell—just to

make sure no one was inside. After I had heard the bell resonating inside I realized, that was not my brightest move. I would know Jorgji wasn't home when he didn't answer the door, but I was pretty sure hired killers didn't answer doorbells at their victim's houses.

After an abysmally long and short waiting period, I took out my key and unlocked my newly repaired apartment door.

Dang. That door creak was even louder than I remembered. I froze just inside the door trying to breathe while I rubbed my sweaty palms on my pillow stomach and peered into the shadows of the room.

"Hello?" *Where did that come from? Why did I say that?* Doesn't every scared woman in every murder movie ask a stupid question like 'Who's there?' Everyone watching knows who's there except for the dumb woman who is advancing into the room to meet her psychotic killer.

I flipped the light switch on. Thirty seconds. Forty seconds. Fifty.

How long would it take for a psycho to advance on a horrified woman? I dashed into my bedroom and turned on the light. No psychos anywhere that I could see; however, I was not going to tempt fate by looking under the bed or in the walk-in closet. I headed to my wall safe hidden behind a clichéd landscape picture over my dresser. This was our personal safe. It was where I kept my jewelry and my household spending money. Jorgji had his own stash of business cash hidden in another safe somewhere in the study, but he kept the exact location and combination known only to himself.

Jorgji was good with numbers and money. I was not. Good with numbers or cash. That's why he knew I'd have trouble remembering the combination of our safe. He tried to keep it simple for me so I could remember it. Except I couldn't remember it. I never could remember it.

My sweaty fingers turned the dial numbers to my birthday, 6–4–8–7. Not working. Next, I tried his birthday,

4–6–8–0. I tried various backward and forward combinations with no luck. Next, I tried our anniversary date. Those numbers came up short—just like my marriage. Next, I entered nine–oh two–one oh, one of my favorite shows. To my relief, the safe clicked open without a squeak or creak. Oh, that he oiled.

Too bad there was no money in there. There was nothing in there. It was empty. *Had the killers drained the safe when they couldn't drain me?*

Now what was I to do? I knew Jorgji's business safe was somewhere in the study—if he hadn't moved it. On more than one occasion an investor had come to the house with huge sums of money that Jorgji secured there before going to the bank. I just didn't know where he kept the safe, which he sometimes moved to other areas of the apartment. I was too nervous to do a serious look through the place. I had already been there a long time. Worried that Jorgji would come home early or the killers would come back for me I couldn't fuss around in there anymore.

Abandoning my Jorgji's-money search, I ran to my walk-in closet door and yanked it open. I stepped inside and shoved aside my winter coats and sweaters to get to the back wall of my closet. I kept a stash of my favorite yarns there on a hook that I personally twisted into the wall. I bought the self-starting screw and using a butter knife I screwed it into the back wall. All by myself, with no one's help. It was one of my favorite hiding places since no one knew about it but me.

My cloth bag was still there. I unhooked the bag that hid my latest compulsive internet purchase of specialty sock yarns. I selected and then crammed two balls of yarns into the teddy bear print diaper bag that recently served as my travel suitcase and purse. Stepping over to the other side of my closet, I slid open one of the drawers that held my blue purses. My Lois Vuitton zippy wallet was there. It had a little zippered pouch inside that held my loose spending money for those rare occasions when I left the house to go to the

Iced Stone Creamery. I nestled my little zippy into the 'diaper' bag with the comfort yarns.

That diaper bag was a useful thing to have, lots of roomy pockets. I ran my hand over the yarns a couple of times before I closed the bag. I had yarn and all the loose change I could get my hands onto, so I scurried out of my lodgings towards the elevator.

I was in luck. There were no doggy dawdlers. The elevator dial was steadily rising to the sixth floor. The bell dinged, and the door slid open.

I was out of luck. Jorgji was stepping off the elevator.

I stood rooted to the floor right in his path, my mouth open in fright. He looked straight at me and came forward. I couldn't move. *"This is it'"* my brain shouted through my dyed red hair. My heart was pounding to a Gladys Knight's *'This is it'* rhythm. My hands involuntarily came up shoulder height to defend myself as he brushed past me.

Wait a minute. He passed me. He just went passed me.

He looked directly at me, and then passed me. Okay. I understood his not recognizing the loud red hair, fatso stomach, and gaudy clothes but *"Hey buster I didn't have plastic surgery. This was the same face you kissed so sweetly a week ago. These were the same ears you whispered 'I love you' to in Vegas, and the same body you once...."* Yech! I hurried into the elevator before it left the floor.

I was so furious with hurt that my ride down the six floors was done before I realized it. I just managed to recover my composure when Lord Smolder stepped onto the red-carpeted floor of the elevator.

"Getting off?" He asked me. He put his hand on the edge of the elevator door to hold it open for me. He was looking straight at me.

I was stunned to be facing him again. Unlike Jorgji's reaction, I saw a slightly puzzled flicker of recognition cross his face. I put my head down and mumbled something about being late for my baby's doctor appointment. I sprinted past George, the doorman, and out of the building.

***

Frank shook his head to clear it. He released the elevator door and punched the circular six on the control panel. He did need a break if he thought there was something familiar about that woman getting off the elevator. That just couldn't be. He didn't know any pregnant women, except Janey. He smiled at that and wondered how big she'd be. She must hate the confinement and heavy slowness that pregnancy brought. He couldn't wait to see her. It had been so long. He just had this one last nagging detail to take care of first.

Jorgji opened the door straight away. Frank tensed. His hand moved up in alignment with his gun when he saw a hammer in Jorgji's hand.

The hammer was held loose, in a non-threatening manner, so Frank relaxed his stance but kept his hand close to his gun at the ready—just in case. Jorgji seemed unaware that he was even carrying the hammer. He seemed distracted. Frank pulled out his FBI identification in such a way that the department issued Smith and Wesson was visible to Jorgji—just in case he got a twitchy hammer hand.

Jorgji didn't display any reaction to the sight of Frank's gun. He also didn't move from the doorway to allow Frank access inside. Jorgji's reaction when he saw the FBI badge was to become agitated. He hyped more when Frank told him he had seen Imogene.

"Where? Was she with anyone? Where is she now? Can you take me to her? What she say?" The rapid fire questions came so fast that Frank didn't have time to decipher the thick accent completely before another query shot out of Jorgji's mouth.

Frank held up one hand to stop Jorgji's onslaught. Frank wanted a moment to think.

Once he thought about it, he decided he would not answer any of Jorgji's questions. It had nothing to do with

96

not following the accented English very well. Something wasn't quite right. Hadn't this guy's wife originally told Frank she had to get away from someone? Wasn't that why she was hiding in his undercover car?

Frank sometimes worked missing persons' cases. When a person was found, you went and told the family. He hated that part when the loved one was found dead. The family didn't take the news very well even when they knew in their hearts that bad news was coming. Mothers, Fathers, sisters, brothers, and husbands only want you to tell them their loved one was found safe and unharmed. Something he hadn't heard of out of this guy's mouth.

"She was at a bar over on Washington Avenue last night; The Eagle's Nest. I didn't really talk to her much. I just thought you might want to know she looked okay when I saw her." That was true. Frank hadn't talked much, and she had looked really good to him the last time he saw her. Frank figured this partial truth was good enough for this guy, whom he was starting to dislike intensely.

"Washington Ave. That not far? She must have run on her feet. Maybe she's still that area. Good. Anything else you know that help me to get her?"

Frank wasn't sure he wanted to assist this guy with 'getting her.' He needed to learn more about what was going on with this missing person case. "No. Sorry. I just thought you'd want to know that she was all right."

"Yeah. Yeah. Sure. Thanks for information. Here my number. Give me call right away you see her, so I go get her." Jorgji scribbled his cell phone number on a business card and passed it over to Frank.

"Sure thing, Mr. Dalmat. I bet you're anxious to have her back home," Frank ventured.

"Of course I want to get her," Jorgji nodded and reassured Frank. Frank didn't find that reassuring. He was disturbed. Jorgji hadn't expressed one iota of genuine concern for his missing wife.

***

The bus driver waited patiently while I fished out enough change from the bottom of the diaper bag to put into his token box. Since I'd never ridden a bus before, how was I supposed to know you had to pay to ride a city bus? Wasn't that bus *public* transportation? I had already visited three pawnbrokers. That cost me $25 in taxi fare. That taxi ride to Rmart cost me $12.50, plus I had to figure out what tips to give. I didn't have enough money or good enough math skills to keep taking taxis.

I didn't like that bus. It was full of people. People I didn't know. Like a large, long elevator, only you stayed on it longer. I looked around to find an isolated seat away from everyone. There wasn't one. Every row of seats had at least one person sitting there. I could feel little beads of sweat start on my forehead as the bus pulled away from the stop and the driver told me to sit down. I didn't want to sweat. Fear sweat did not smell pretty; it was the worst kind of odor.

I needed to get that situation under control. I saw a little old dark-skinned lady with work-worn, leathery hands clutching a big tank handbag that was parked in her lap. Her knee-high sock tops showed just below the hem of her navy blue dress. She looked harmless enough, so I settled my bottom onto the aisle seat next to her. She gave me a tired smile. Relief washed over me when I realized I was not going to offend anyone's olfactory senses.

"When's you baby due?" Ms. Navy Blue Dress asked me politely.

"Huh?" I said and then quickly recovered my surprise and said, "Uhhhh, in two months, I think."

"Must be a hard thing with no husband and no doctor. They got a shelter for single mothers over on Fifth Street if you needs a place to go. It's just down from Helga's bakery at the Langley Street crossing. Shelter's a big brick building with green shutters and a green door. They be a dry cleaners on the other side. Can't miss it."

"How do you know I don't have a husband, doctor or home?" I asked her incredulously.

"Easy," she said. "No ring. No smile. No date. Anyone expcect'in a baby usually got a smile when someone axes about they baby. Anyone big as you gotta doctor to say they date by now. And," she added, her soft, warm, worn hand patting mine, "you looks scared."

"Well, I don't need a doctor," I said, then added, "but a place to sleep tonight would sure be nice. Thank you for mentioning the shelter."

***

Frank was thinking on the incongruities of the past two days. Why would Imogene, who had a posh apartment with tons of money, end up dirty, stinky, and disguised in men's clothing in the back seat of his undercover car? She seemed so innocent when he looked into her blushing face and huge doe eyes. Those eyes held a look of fear when he'd asked her who she was. She had been genuinely scared. He thought at the time she was scared of him, but now after talking to her hammer-toting husband, he wasn't so sure. Those eyes. He couldn't get her eyes out of his brain. He had seen those eyes recently, but he couldn't remember where.

Frank backed his Jaguar into the driveway of the house he'd been set up in and took off for the house next door. He had to step off into the grass to weave his way around a woman pushing a stroller down the sidewalk. She was taking up the whole walkway while she struggled with the accessories that always come with a kid: toys, diaper bags, bottles. He smiled at the chortling baby in the stroller. He felt lighter and happier about seeing Janey after seeing that precious infant. Babies were cute and fun. That baby's mother gave him a wan, drained smile as she struggled to push the heavily laden stroller past him. Yeah, they were cute and fun to look at—from a distance.

What was it the woman in the elevator had said to him? She was late for her baby's doctor appointment. She had a diaper bag with her, so he hadn't thought anything of her statement, but since when does a pregnant woman carry a diaper bag and have a baby doctor appointment *before* the baby has been delivered and how could she have run out of the building in her heavily pregnant state without even a trace of a waddle? Frank didn't know how he could have not seen that the elevator woman was Imogene in disguise. Those eyes were the same eyes he stared into that morning. Why didn't it occur to him that she'd be concealing her identity again when she'd been disguised as a boy when he first met her? He couldn't believe he was such a sap and wondered if all his FBI surveillance training had drained down to his crotch after encountering that woman.

***

I looked around at the bustle and tussle of the police station entryway trying to find a convenient corner to shrink into. There wasn't one. There were no seats, no benches. The lobby area was a wide open space. The main entry room lead to locked and button keyed glass windowed doors in various spots along the wall. There was a bulletproof-glassed window protecting a man sitting at a reception desk, talking into a handset. There was a metal detector located just behind the glassed door to the right of the phone-talker. 'Enter' was stenciled on the glass. I could see a guy in a dark suit standing next to the detector holding out plastic trays for people to empty their pockets into. His badge was visible on his belt. I knew there was a gun hidden under his coat. It wasn't visible, but it was there.

Monstrous fear pressed in on me. I started shaking like a mad bomber within seconds. A few tiny beads of sweat popped out on my brow. I unsuccessfully tried to draw in a breath as my lungs and throat squeezed shut in anxiety.

If I couldn't breathe, then I surely couldn't talk. If I

couldn't speak, then I couldn't explain to the police that my husband was trying to kill me. I didn't even give the man behind the glass the chance to finish his conversation on the phone and ask through the metal speaker hole if he could help me. I was out the door and back on the street within two minutes of my arrival.

That had been a waste of bus fare.

What was I going to? Did I find a way to go back to Winnetka? Was it safe? I was a hunted woman. That would put Gordon and the house staff in danger to have me in close proximity. I didn't want anyone at risk just because I was at risk. That would be like going home with a loaded bomb strapped to me hoping it wouldn't go off while I was near someone I loved.

I wandered around what was left of the evening in a mental turmoil. Nothing looked or felt familiar or friendly. I couldn't sit down or rest anywhere for more than a few minutes. My fears kept driving me on.

Tired and weary I stumbled down 5th street to the woman's shelter. My arm shook violently when I raised my hand to ring the doorbell. I had to use my other hand to force my finger to push the lighted button. I took in a huge breath and held it. My breath, not the door buzzer. I didn't want my situation to get any worse by laying on the buzzer. I was having trouble keeping my knees from shaking at the thought of having to stand in front of and talk to whoever opened that door. I didn't want to talk to a stranger and yet I couldn't bear the thought of being turned away. Poised between sanctuary and perdition, my whole body was shaking just as much as my arm and knees. I contemplated just asking to use the phone to call Gordon to come and get me, but it would be morning before he got there. I could have called my cousins, Mandy and Martin, to get me, but they weren't close enough or nice enough to make that a favorable option.

Dying a quick and painless death at home at the hands of hired killers would be better than dying of fright, alone, outside a red brick green-shuttered building. At least back at my apartment I would have had the comfort of dying on my own pillow topped bed snuggled into my own fluffy white feather comforter; done in by my own Tappy and Scuffy that I had come to know so well. Sort of.

The green door swung open just as my timid, fractured mind opened to the other possibilities I could be facing. A mental picture of me with my downy white comforter spread over me—with a spreading blood red stain seeping up from my chest came unbidden to my mind. Scuffy and Tappy were there—eating cake.

I stood speechless before the nondescript woman standing just inside the wide open door. Dressed in hunter green, she was a perfect match to the green shutters hanging beside the exterior windows. My sagacious Sass shoes refused to obey my usual 'turn and run' command.

I could see by the woman's wide eyes and alarmed countenance that I must have looked at least as dreadful as I felt.

Frantically, she ushered me inside. She gave me a warm cup of tea and some crackers and cheese on a chipped white china plate. The tea was soothing to my sore throat which was starting to feel better. I started to feel better. I was seated on a threadbare sofa that was missing the wood trim from its right side corner. The worn, fuzzy granny squares afghan that previously graced the back of the sofa was wrapped around my shoulders, but I was still shaking uncontrollably as the woman explained that all their rooms have been taken for the night. She wished she could help me, but they had a waiting list that my name would have to be added to.

Then she explained, "It isn't fair to give you shelter when we have so many other names ahead of yours and some already with babies. Do you have someone you can stay with until a spot opens up? Is there someone I can call for you?"

It was one thing for me to call Jorgji so he could fill my

coffin, but it was quite another thing to let someone else make that call for me. I shook my head. I was so tired and choked with emotion that I dared not open my mouth to speak for fear the dam that was inside me would break, and I wouldn't be able to control what spilled out.

The nice lady's soothing voice continued on, "We have enough funds to give you money for a hotel for a few days. You can check back then to see if any spots have opened up. I am sure that I can get you on public assistance. I'd be happy to help you contact social services in the morning."

I was ignoring the tears, the ones that kept leaking from the corner of my right eye, under Newton's theory that falling tears couldn't possibly fall as fast as my rock bottom hopes.

"You don't understand," I wailed at the woman inside my brain. "I'm scared. I have no idea of how to take care of myself. I've never slept in a bus station or on a park bench. I've never even put gas in my own car. My aunt is dead. The only family I have left can't stand the sight of me. I'd rather face being shot by hired killers than having to go live with them again."

Her monotone droning stopped short.

I hadn't been wailing in my head. Not very Penelope-like of me to come unglued like that. I stood up and wiped my tears on the afghan. Re-energized by my embarrassment, I threw off the crocheted blanket, grabbed the last bit of cheese, swallowed the last swig of tea, thanked the woman and made a beeline towards the door.

"I'm sorry," I hiccupped as I swallowed more air trying to control my panic so I could think more like a heroine. "You're right. You can't help me. I'm sure I can find a hotel somewhere. I shouldn't have bothered you when there are so many others in need already waiting."

"Wait," the woman said and rushed forward to the door to stop my exit. "We aren't licensed to take more than 12, but it is late, and we do have a sofa. You look so cold and tired. I just don't see how I can possibly turn you out this late in the evening. You can sleep on the sofa tonight, and I'll put you in touch with a social worker in the morning."

"Thank you," I said, feeling my newly found energy flagging once I had a place to stay for the night.

Emotional exhaustion covered me like an unstained, white downy comforter. I slept so soundly that I almost didn't get up in time to avoid the shelter woman's good intentions. I slipped out at 6:00 a.m. into the crisp September air, sorry to leave the sofa and warm afghan behind. The street was quiet and slicked wet from a brief late-night rain. Thankful for having evaded the rain and my killers the previous night, I hurried to put some distance between me and any well-intended government social workers.

My pillowed stomach was a little flat from trying to sleep on my stomach on the sofa. I stopped a few hundred yards away from the shelter to 'punch it' up and re-fluff it into more of a mommy-to-be shape. Movement caught the corner of my peripheral vision as a shutter rolled up in a bakery window. A plump, woman with silvery-gray hair, the color of Aunt Tilly's, peered out at the pre-dawn sky, at me and then at my fist.

I unfurled my hand and gave my misshapen belly a loving, shoving pat so as to not get arrested for pillow abuse. I tried to put my stomach pillow and this woman's opinion of me back into perspective by making a visual, obvious effort to readjust my maternity pants.

The muffins that woman was sliding onto a cart in the bakery's wide front window put the real parts of my stomach back into perspective. I could not stop my Sass shoes from propelling me and my pillow into *Helga's Bakery*, the shop name that was declared by the brightly painted lettering on the window.

I bought a specialty marzipan muffin. It came on a small plastic plate with a big smile from Helga, who owned and ran the bakery. I was proud to have made the distinction of being her first customer that morning. I sat down on one of her eight dainty bistro chairs and plucked at the round muffin on the round plate on the round table in front of my round belly.

Helga continued to busy herself pulling cakes and pies from shelves on a rolling storage rack and putting them into a counter display. To my surprise, she and I exchanged some comfortable small talk while she worked, and I ate.

Helga told me that she got out of bed every morning at 3:00 am. to whip batter up, fry donuts and pop muffins in her ovens. Just before opening she arranged the muffins on carts in the front window and did her window shade unveiling for the early morning crowd.

I couldn't verify it for sure because I was not allowed in the kitchen back in Winnetka, but I seriously doubted that Cookie ever started working before eight.

The marzipan muffin I was devouring was a Helga specialty filled with a marzipan center. The chopped, candied pistachios on top completed the muffin with a surgery crunch. "This is fantastic," I told her. "I love unusual recipes. The *Ladies House Journal* always has great recipes that I wanted to try when Jorgji and I moved here, but he didn't want me to experiment in the kitchen. That's why we always have our maid, Keiko, fix the meals in advance, or we order a 45–minute takeout creation from *Opus One*. Jorgji's sister, Karine, is a great cook, but she doesn't like me so I doubt she'd share any of her Armenian recipes with me." I moistened the tip of my finger and dabbed up the last few nutty pistachio crumbs with it.

I probably shouldn't have mentioned Jorgji's name, or that we had a maid and ate meals from a posh restaurant like Opus One, but It just slipped out. Helga turned to the counter to write down the muffin recipe for me. While she was writing she picked up the phone from behind the counter. I couldn't hear what she was saying but since she didn't seem fazed by the word 'Jorgji' or 'Opus One' I thought my secret was safe because not everyone memorized the news headlines or knew the names of expensive restaurants. That woman had been up since 3 o'clock, so I thought she didn't have the time to listen to the news.

She must have watched the news while she was baking. She must have also been good at multitasking because she had to have made a phone call to the police station while writing her muffin recipe of:

20 oz. raw Marzipan
1 c. almonds (ground)
7 c. + a little more flour
4 t. cinnamon
8 T. cocoa powder
8 t. baking powder
2 t. baking soda
8 eggs
1 c. honey
1 c. sugar
40 oz. sour cream
1 t. almond extract

topping:
4 c. powdered sugar
6–8 T. water
candied pistachios—coarsely chopped

Knead marzipan and ground almonds until smooth. Roll into 48 balls. Combine dry ingredients. Mix in liquid ingredients just until combined. Fill greased muffin pans with 1/2 of the dough. Place one marzipan ball into *each center. Fill with remaining dough and bake at 350 degrees for 20 minutes. Let cool for 10 minutes. Combine water and powdered sugar to drizzle over muffins. Sprinkle pistachios on top of drizzle. Makes 48 muffins.*

As I was trying to figure out what the little (c)'s, little (t)s and big (T)s on the recipe card stood for when I saw a police cruiser pull to the curb in front of the big bakery display window. I slipped out the door just before two hefty officers idly extracted themselves from the vehicle to go inside the bakery shop. I probably should have run, but cops and donut shops were known to go together, so I continued to stroll down the street, hoping I looked unsuspicious.

As I strolled, I notice those two police officers, who weren't in the bakery very long, were now strolling behind me. Unnerved by how close they were I stopped my stroll. They stopped. I turned around, intending to confront them, but instead, I averted my gaze and looked off to the side as though I was window shopping at a bait and tackle store. One of the officers asked me my name. Reluctantly, I turned to face him. An old Martin and Mandy childhood joke popped into my head, but I didn't think guys with guns would find a 'Puddin' Tane' answer funny, so I lied and said, "Penny Pembrook."

"You got any I.D. Ms. Pembrook?"

"No." I took a short mental pause to psych myself to become more Penelope-like and asked, "Do I need I.D. to walk down the street? The doctor said walking would be good for my pregnancy, so I stroll every morning after my husband leaves for work." Then I added, in what I hoped was a threatening tone, "He's a lawyer."

They turned to look at each other and then both looked down at my plump belly and diaper-bag I had slung over my shoulder. They each stretched out a sheepish grin across their face like it just occurred to them that I was pregnant and that I hadn't technically or legally done anything wrong. "Sorry, Mrs. Pembrook. We were just following up on a lead about a missing person, but I guess that couldn't be you."

"Well, I guess not," I said getting into the role of Penelope Pembrook since I had her name and a lawyer for a husband on my side. "Not unless your missing person is getting ready to pop out a seven-pound muffin. Have a good day, officers," I said as I resumed walking away leaving the two officers to turn and go back into the bakery.

Where had that brazenness come from?

***

Frank didn't know how much of his own free time he was interested in using to track down this Imogene woman. He was anxious to get out and take his time off. He already wasted most of the previous day getting records and documents from Marion. He was going to the office for a bit that morning to tie up loose ends. He was back to carrying the department issued Smith and Wesson, his personal Glock being locked in his briefcase. He hadn't gotten all of his paperwork on the Detroit case completed, so he didn't have the time to read all the print-outs Marion gave him. He put them in a box intending to take them to the shredder later when he was sure he was through with the case.

As he finished typing the last of his report on the Detroit Police Department investigation, he decided he would just take a quick perusal of all the leads on Imogene's disappearance that had come into the local precincts. He wanted to know if anything looked worthwhile. After that, he was going to head out to spend some time with Janey.

Kicking back in his office chair he scrolled down through the state and local police tips displayed on the FBI data collection screen. He became engrossed in reading some of the reports. Mr. Dalmat's offer of a substantial reward had ensured there were plenty of tips flooding into the precincts. Everyone wanted the easy money. The tips were all the same crackpot stuff that flooded in with every missing person report offering a reward. Ms. Shay thought her dog was the missing person incarnate. Several people were trying to claim the husband's posted reward with generic, sketchy information that could apply to anyone, anytime and anywhere, a mess to wade through.

Frank sat upright and was about to flip off his monitor screen, but stopped when he saw one interesting report. He sat back down, pulled his chair up and read the monitor screen closely. The bakery woman's tip looked promising, especially since Frank knew the bakery was near a woman's shelter. He read the scanned on-line report filled out by the two police officers who responded to the tip.

Their follow-up left a lot to be desired. They reported the woman in question was pregnant. She was just taking a walk after her lawyer husband left for work. She didn't have positive I.D., but they identified her as Penny Pembrook, not Imogene Dalmat, and then closed the report. No further follow-up necessary.

Frank grunted in disgust. *Lawyer husband my eye.* He knew the area, knew the precinct. He bet those cops had done most of their follow-up inside the bakery checking out which roll and coffee Imogene had. She was probably long gone from the area, but it couldn't hurt to do some more investigating before he went to see Janey.

CHAPTER 12

I found a small, rundown hotel near Commerce Park. The attendants were older, unshaven men in rumpled pants and holey tee shirts. Their feet were bare. No socks. No shoes. The property didn't look too seedy from the outside, so I pulled out the $155 the two guys were asking me to pay for a week's rent. The room had good locks, a door peephole, worn-but-clean carpet and a new spread on the bed, but the mirror on the back wall of the room looked old and worn with a few areas having lost their reflective properties.

Being Penelope, I was not about to be spied on by unscrupulous, murderous hotel staff, like the hotel bell boy did to his murder victims in my aunt's fifth novel, *The Bell Boy Murders*. He used spy holes in the walls and mirrors to monitor the comings and goings of the hotel guests. I grabbed one of the two towels from the bathroom and draped it over the mirror to cover the worn spots. I began looking for other suspicious signs that the room was bugged or spied on by the hotel staff. Finding no other peepholes or obvious cameras, I slid a small piece of paper in the door jamb and closed the door while holding the paper in place until it caught in the door frame. Pocketing the door key card, I went off in search of some cheap food to fill my puffed-up pillow stomach. I also needed some toiletries to keep me from sweating like the pig I appeared to be in that costume I was wearing.

Mark of Mark's Gourmet Hot Dog Stand made me a Garden Dog, an all-beef hot dog smothered in broccoli, tomato chunks, cauliflower, mozzarella cheese, mushrooms and pesto sauce. For only a dollar fifty more, he pulled me up a can of pop out of the ice mounded in his cooler and threw in a bag of chips and a napkin.

I savored the dog, chips, and Coke more than my last lobster meal. Polishing off my food in record time, I headed down the street to the local library. Thanks to my aunt's book research excursions, I knew I could sign into a community-use computer at any library. Who would have thought that a place that lends books to people would also have computers for them to use? Seemed like a conflict of interest to me.

I felt so at home sitting in front of a keyboard again that my fingers flew over the keys as I typed in my password and gained access to the Pembrook Agency website e-mail. Aunt Tilly wanted the website for her books to have an authentic feel, so she had the site designed to look just like a real detective agency site. Three thousand hits had taken place since I'd last signed on and three hundred readers had sent e-mails to Penelope. That was me. I was the one who responded to all the correspondence related to my aunt's novels.

That library limited computer use time, so I didn't have time for lengthy responses. I scanned all the e-mails until I come to the ones 'Undercover Fan' sent me, or rather sent to my alter ego, Penelope, while I was out of circulation wandering the streets.

'Hey, Penelope,' he sent. 'I have this job I have been working on investigating some crooked cops. I need to drink a lot of booze and seem to get drunk but not get drunk. Do you think the castor oil trick used by Penelope in *Do or Die* would really work? If I drink it first before drinking alcohol will it really coat my stomach and intestines, so the alcohol doesn't absorb into my bloodstream? The boss is anxious to get this investigation wrapped up because guys that are on the take are unpredictable in their actions and crooked cops present security risks. Thanks for all your advice.'

His next day's e-mail was, 'I've been getting regular e-mails from you—even after Matilda Warren's death. You usually get back to me within hours when I have a question, so I don't understand why you didn't respond to yesterday's e-mail. What gives? You sick or something? I just wanted to let you know the castor oil trick worked. I stayed sober while the suspects got drunk enough to spill their guts. I ended up running into a snag while I was on the job. I unknowingly picked up a hitchhiker. The kid was in bad shape, so I let him stay the night. Turns out he was a she. I didn't get any details like name or contact information before I rushed out the door the next morning. Now my 'kid' has disappeared, and I can't stop wondering where she is and if she's okay or not. I know it's none of my business what a grown woman does, but I feel sort of responsible for her since I let her stay in my house. Anyway, I'm wondering why you haven't responded to me. I hope you're not shutting down the Pembrook Detective Agency website now that Miss Warren is dead. I know this site is just a book gimmick, but you've been a great resource for me with my job so I sincerely hope that we can keep in touch.'

I blinked at the monitor screen. *Lord Smolder was my 'Undercover Fan'?* He was the undercover man I had been conversing with for months. He was the guy that always wanted to know the source, details, and effectiveness of all the spy and investigation tricks Penelope used in the books.

Did he know he had been conversing with Matilda Warren's niece? The missing niece. I didn't think so. Nothing I had done on the phony Detective Agency e-mail, Jitter, Blinked-in or Friend Face accounts revealed my name or my niece-to-the-famous-author status. The fact that Undercover Fan was concerned about me, me the hitchhiker and me the e-mail correspondent, gave me an inexplicable sense of comfort.

I was never the daring persona I maintained on the computer. It was just that when I corresponded with Aunt Tilly's fans, they thought they are corresponding with Penelope Pembrook, so I tried to become the Penelope of the novels: risk-taker, smart, daring, glamorous, able to give good advice and witty retorts. However, once I left the comfort of the keyboard, I turned back into Ignorant Imogene. The girl who married a man who wanted her dead.

Was Jorgji that tired of wearing my hand-knitted creations?

I didn't want to face that truth, so I turned back to the fan emails. I had thought 'Undercover Fan' was just a 'wannabe cop' questioning whether my aunt's Penelope-techniques would work in real life, but he was an I'm-going-to-get-the-bad-guys-real-life undercover cop. That explained the gun, the beat up car and the almost empty house. He must have been pretty good at what he did if he got the bad guys in that latest assignment. If I approached him in the right way, I thought he might help me investigate my husband.

I typed to him, 'Dear Undercover Fan, Sorry about the response delay. Someone is after me. Two someones to be exact. They've made it so I can't return to my apartment without fear of bodily harm. I suspect they were hired to kill me. Until I can find out for sure why they want me dead and how to stop them, I have to stay low. Do you think you'd be able to help me? I don't have a phone, but I'm able to sign on to my e-mail account at the Detroit Public Library, so please respond via e-mail. I could really use your help.'

The 'Penelope Pembrook of Pembrook Detective Agency' was automatically added to the bottom of every e-mail I sent, but before I hit send I added, 'Glad to hear the castor oil works. Sorry about the side effects.'

Maybe it wasn't a smart idea to enlist his help, but

the message had already gone out into cyberspace. Perhaps he would send me a helpful response that I could get the next time I logged into a computer.

I composed and sent out one quick generic response of, 'Your e-mail is important to us but due to the unusually heavy number of e-mails we are unable to reply at this time,' to 150 of the fans that had been waiting for a response the longest.

My library allotted computer time had been up for five minutes, and a teen was standing right behind me wanting to use the ancient CPU I was logged into. The guy must not have thought I was moving fast enough to get my diaper bag out of his way, so he cleared his throat loudly, twice. I rushed off a short personal e-mail to Gordon to let him know I was okay. I didn't want him to worry about me when he saw the news reports of my disappearance. I heard another throat clearing, loud enough to vibrate the monitor screen in front of me. When I saw the librarian look up from her spot at the circulation desk to assess the situation at the row of computers, I vacated the seat. She returned her attention back to scanning books back into the library. The young man plopped down into that seat before my butt print even had a chance to fade from the seat cushion. No matter. I needed to get some necessity shopping done.

Arriving back at my hotel door with my bag of personal hygiene essentials, I noticed the small piece of paper was not how I had it positioned in the door jamb upon my leaving. It was lengthwise. I had placed it crosswise. Cautiously, I unlocked the door and swung it open. I was going to search the room again for any newly installed cameras or spy holes and then go give those two hotel managers a stern lecture about going into people's rooms.

I didn't expect to see him sitting in the only chair in the room, his feet propped up on the bed and a Smith & Wesson in his hand with its shoulder holster resting on the bed next to him. When he saw me, he let out a sigh, and his hand relaxed on the gun.

"Just a word of advice," Lord Smolder said in dangerously low voice. "If you're trying to run away from your husband and your high society life, you shouldn't use the name of your famous writer aunt's heroine to register at motels."

"It worked just fine for the police officers. How did you get in here? And just why are you here?" I asked, allowing my Penelope role-playing and my anger at the hotel staff that let him in motivate my tongue.

"I have a badge and a federal I.D. You'd be surprised where that gets you and, for the life of me, I don't know why I'm here. I don't even know why I started to try to find you, except that you took my Versace sunglasses, my tee shirt, my $40 and my last beer."

"You gave me the $40 and the tee shirt. The sunglasses are just cheap knock offs. And a beer gut would spoil your good looks, so get over it." *Wow.* That Penelope persona was actually working for me.

Or maybe not.

His feet swung down to the floor. He stood and walked leisurely towards me peering into my face like he was trying to get a read on me. Or maybe I had some Gourmet-Garden-Dog broccoli stuck in my teeth. He stopped a few inches short of me, close enough for me to recall staring up into those eyes from his recliner.

"Just after I bumped into you yesterday I met your husband," he said with his gaze locked tight to my face. "Charming man. I looked him up in the FBI files. Are you two in this together? Is this another one of his scams?"

"What?" I asked as I felt my brain spinning in my head. *Scams? Plural? Files? Plural? FBI? As in Federal crimes?* "Who are you? And what are you talking about?" I asked. My thoughts continued to revolve. In the ten seconds that elapsed, my brain connected more suspicious-activity-Jorgji-dots then were connected at the time they happened. I was not liking the dot-connected picture I was putting together.

"Convenient how you disappear under suspicious

circumstances," he went on as I backed up a few steps to get my personal comfort space back. He followed me. "Then your husband makes an impassioned plea on television. I go visit hubby. I find you've disguised yourself so you can stay gone for a while. I just haven't figured out what the payoff is this time. You don't need the money."

"This time?" I questioned, trying to swallow, stepping away from him. I had to give up my place next to the door to get some distance from him, but I didn't mind leaving the spot at the door. A quick retreat would have been impossible anyway. My memory of his muscled legs told me he could probably run a lot faster than I could. He would have had me tackled and handcuffed before I even got the door open.

I backed up towards the back of the room, not watching where I was going because I was watching him the whole time, not trusting what he was up to.

He followed me in my retreat. He was glaring hard at me, and I doubted it was from broccoli. He thought my disappearance was orchestrated for some fraudulent purpose because he was looking at me in a cold, hard, scornful way that said, 'You're scum.' A look that asserted he had me all figured out.

That look punched me in the stomach, without the pillow. I stared back at him in my most stern, confident look, trying hard to be Penelope. But I was not Penelope, and I couldn't stand his contempt. After a few seconds of stand-off staring, I sat down on the bed, deflated by Jorgji, fraud, scams and scorn. The lump in my heart was almost as big as the bulge of my stomach.

"The gig is up," he said towering over where I was sitting on the bed. "I'm reporting that you've been found to the local precinct so they can stop spending half their budget looking for you. Whatever money scheme you and your husband have cooked up, it won't work." He reached around to where I was sitting on the bed. I trembled as his hand brushed my side. He picked up the holster from where

I had almost sat on it on the bed. He shoved his gun in its holster, strapped it on, retrieved his jacket from the back of the chair and headed towards the door.

"If you report where I am, I'm as good as dead," I said in a whisper. "There were two men who came to my apartment to kill me two nights ago. I think my husband hired them. I'm not trying to disappear from society. I was never in society. I just want to find a way to prove that my husband is trying to kill me and get him out of my life with me still alive. If you walk out now and tell him where I am, I'll have to run again, only I don't know how. I don't have much money, and my ATM card won't work and...and..." I choked on my words and noticed a round wet splotch hit the fake orange bulge of my stomach, then another and another.

He was standing silently by the door watching me. I looked down, my fingers pleating and unpleating the hem of my orange shirt. I was trying to hide the fact that I was crying, but I couldn't stop the tears coming from my eyes. They kept leaking out until I had to sniff to keep my nose from dripping.

A white handkerchief entered my field of vision.

"Here," he said in a contrite voice. "I believe you." He sat back down in the chair by the bed. "I'm not going to tell anyone anything until I can figure out what to do with you. One thing is for sure," he continued. "You can't stay here. You're pretty good at undercover disguises, but you don't know crap about protecting yourself. You pick a motel that has no security. You choose a name that ties you right back to your real name. You barged right into this crappy room unaware I'd replaced the piece of paper you'd put in the door jamb to help you see if the door had been opened. You're right. You aren't any good at running."

CHAPTER 13

Frank wasn't certain just why he'd loaded Imogene into his Jaguar and started out for Janey's. *Her tears? His protective instinct? The fake pregnancy? Who was he trying to kid?* He glanced over at her sleeping form in the passenger seat. Her head of gory red hair was pressed against her now-removed 'baby' pillow. He knew she was innocent as hell the moment he'd seen her on that recliner trying to stretch his tee shirt to her ankles. He didn't know what Janey was going to say. He had hoped she would agree to take in this runaway woman until he could get a handle on what was going on with her scummy husband, and so he could get a handle on his runaway feelings.

***

I felt the car slow, but I didn't want to open my eyes or leave the comfort of the padded leather seat of the Jaguar. Or maybe I just didn't want the ride with Frank to be over. He seemed to be very adept at taking care of things. Once the car stopped and the hum of the engine faded, I kept on fake sleeping on my side of the car until I had the distinct impression I was being watched. I slid open one eye a tiny little slit so my lashes could cover the fact that I was awake.

Yup. I was being watched. His gorgeous mouth was turned up just a little in the corner; in the same way my one eye was open just a little bit. We were both fakers.

"What's so amusing?" I asked without twitching a muscle or opening my eye any further.

"You." He finally let out a full wide grin that made my heart leap, and my eyes flutter open to see him better. Without explaining how I was humorous, he ordered, "Come on. I don't want to make a habit of having to haul your butt out of my rides all the time."

He pulled a key ring from his pocket. He didn't knock or hesitate—just barged in the door and bellowed. "Janey, are you home?" From the racket coming from the next room, someone had just dropped a pan.

A scream of "Frank" followed. A round-bellied young woman in a smocked topped dress ran full-tilt towards us. "Frank. Frank. Frank," she kept repeating while she hugged him as tight as her rotund belly allowed and kissed his cheek. "I'm so glad you're okay. I always worry when I can't get in touch with you. Come in and let me take a look at you. My gosh, your hair is long. You'll have to let me cut it. It's so good to see you!"

I shrunk back into an area beside the sofa as my heart unexpectedly shriveled. He was happily married from the looks of it. I knew she wouldn't ever need to be on the run from a Scuffy or a Tappy because she had Frank.

He was married; I again reminded myself, surprised that I felt so glum. Until that moment, I hadn't realized how fond I'd grown of him or how heavy my heart was at losing my marriage dream.

That was how it should be with a marriage, the joy of reuniting strong enough to relegate anyone else into the background. My heart was constricting so tightly I could feel it squeeze up into my throat. Not only was he married, like me, but he had a baby on the way. A real baby. He was such a great guy that I couldn't believe I'd allowed myself to stumble down a road of attraction. I turned away from them and tried to focus on the paisley print of the wallpaper.

"Janey! How are you doin'? How's the baby business coming along? You've got quite a bump there. I'm sorry I couldn't get here more, but you know how it is on special assignment."

"Yeah, I know only too well. How long can you stay this time?"

"I can only stay a little while," he began. "It's complicated." Then both of them turned to look at me in my spot next to the sofa.

I wished that scene had been one of my aunt's book signings. I was always the best wallflower at those. A real chameleon. I'd go to help unpack, set up and make sure there were plenty of her favorite ink pens for book signing. I'd then disappear into the back of the crowd until she'd finished answering questions and signing books. There weren't usually any books left after a signing, but if there were I'd pack them up and we'd head home with no one having ever known I was there. My practical disappearing skills appeared to be lost there since the orange top didn't match the blue paisley wallpaper print sufficiently for me to blend in with it. There was no sense crying over spilled milk, especially milk that didn't come from my cow, so I politely stepped forward, dampened down the disappointment in my heart and in my best Penelope-voice said, "Hello. I'm sorry to be ruining your family reunion."

"Janey," Frank said as he took hold of my arm and pulled me away from the wall and closer to his pot-bellied wife. "This is a friend of mine. Her name is...err...Genie. She's in a difficult situation and needs a safe place to stay for a few days while I see if I can get things straightened out for her. Can she stay with you? No questions asked?"

Janey agreed to let me sleep on an inflatable air mattress in the second bedroom that had already been set up as a baby nursery. We all ate stew and biscuits while Frank regaled Janey with his latest undercover career exploits, minus how we met or what had occurred since then.

I heard Janey tell Frank that she had to take her maternity leave early because 'they' didn't think she was able to keep up with the physical activity requirements so she would be able to be home with me for as long as he needed for me to stay.

The issue of me settled—at least for them—they started to get caught up on the rest of what had been happening in both their lives since they saw each other last.

Everything Frank and Janey said was just white background noise to me. The *'He's married'* mantra kept drumming in my head. I managed to swallow some of my food despite the tightness in my throat. Every time Frank and Janie shared a laugh or a special moment I felt split open with grief over losing something I never had with Jorgji.

Their closeness accentuated my alone-ness until I just couldn't bear it another second. I stacked the bowls, spoons, and plates under the pretense of cleaning up. The dishes and I went into the kitchen to find the dishwasher.

Nothing that resembled a dishwasher was anywhere in sight. I started searching through bottom cupboards for hideaway appliances that some kitchens have. Not that kitchen.

The more I searched, the more ridiculous it got. *How did they get their dishes clean?* My search not being fruitful, I gave up and put the dirty dishes in the sink for Janey's maid to take care of when she came in to work. I walked back into the dining room where Janey was showing Frank baby ultrasound pictures. Both heads were bent close together over two black and white thermal paper shots that in no way resembled the baby they were both carrying on over.

Oh, God. How could I ever stay there?

"Excuse me," I murmured. When there was no response, I cleared my nonworking throat and said a little louder, "Excuse me." Two faces turned to me in unison. Two 'alike' faces. Same color and texture hair, same color and shape eyes, same cheekbones, same sensual mouth. Only one face was male—the other a female version. I had inexplicably lost my voice and had to clear my now open throat again. "I couldn't find the dishwasher, so I stacked the dishes in the sink for when the maid comes in."

Their laughs were the same too.

"You're looking at the maid." Janey laughed again. "Frank won't get near the sink if he can help it. He used to pay me to do his kitchen chores when we were kids."

"I did my fair share of chores after mom found out I was paying you to do them. In fact, I did more than my share," Frank said. "I remember you not liking to mow the lawn. You were constantly complaining about the stains on your shoes until dad made me mow all the time."

My smile couldn't have been any wider. Siblings. Not spouses. That didn't change the fact that I was married, to a man trying to kill me, but somehow I felt a relief I shouldn't have.

It would have been better if Frank were married. At least that way we would both have been unavailable. Of course, just because he was not married to Janey didn't mean he wasn't married, but I doubted it. It seemed like he wouldn't have been imposing on his pregnant sister if he had a wife and his own home to take me to.

I went skipping my way back to the kitchen to find the bottle of green liquid they told me would clean the dishes in place of a dishwasher.

That bottle was barely enough to cover all the dishes, and it took a lot of water to rinse all that green stuff off, but I got the dishes done.

One bottle of green liquid and one bowl of ice cream later Frank and I were sitting at Janey's kitchen table. I told him all the details of what had transpired with my would-be killers. I didn't think the police would believe my story when it was all happening, but spilling it all out about my phone being dead, my car not starting, two men having a key to my apartment, hiding out in Frank's car, my getting the taxi, dying my hair and cutting up the pillow, it sounded even more made up.

The story kept pouring out of me. All of it. Every last detail, right down to the fake diamond ring that fooled me just as much as Jorgji had.

Frank listened noncommittally. At my pauses, he nodded to encourage me to continue, but he wasn't saying anything one way or the other. *Did he believe me?* I searched his face and found no comfort in his darkening eyes. He wasn't giving his emotions away, but those brown-and-blue-flecked eyes began to smolder when I told him about Jorgji not recognizing me at our apartment building. His eyes were completely darkened when I reached the end of the story and said as lightly as I could, "and that's my life for the past two days. And how I ended up here at your sister's house." I needed to know that he wasn't going to correct my assumption about Janey being his sister. I wanted my assumption to be right.

He didn't correct me, and my heart fluttered again. *Maybe I was coming down with something?*

"You've got some imagination, kid," he said. "I think your aunt would be proud of you."

My mind jarred to a halt. *Imagination? Is that what he thought all of that was? A kid's imagination?* Too much had happened to me for all of it to be my imagination. *What was wrong with him that he couldn't see that? How could he have sat there and listened to me pour out everything that had transpired for the past few days and not believe me? Couldn't he see the terror in my eyes and the wringing of my hands when I told him about my fleeing down the stairwell to my poor dead Bentley? How could he have sat there so calmly, so heartless while I was reliving my nightmare?*

I lay awake on the air mattress while Frank and Janey talked about me in hushed tones in the living room. I could hear enough of what they were saying to know they were discussing what to do with me. I fumed in indignation. I wished I were back in my own kitchen drinking a cup of chamomile tea. I made up my mind while lying there. Frank didn't believe me so I wouldn't ask him to help me. I had to go it alone. I was going to spend the night there and then go back to my apartment in the morning when I knew Jorgji would be out. I was determined to find that stash of business cash he had hidden somewhere in the apartment and use that money to hire a private investigator to find out why Jorgji wanted me dead. Then I was going to see that Jorgji was put away for what he had done. The irony of using Jorgji's money against him caused me some measure of embarrassment. I wasn't sure stealing money from the man who was stealing from me made me any better than him.

I yawned and tried to get to sleep. I knew it will be tough going it alone, but I didn't see that I had any choice. I had always relied on my aunt. When she was gone, I'd relied on my husband, but he was unreliable. My cousins hated me. If Frank didn't believe me, then I was totally alone. When I finally got myself out of the mess I was in, I decided I would consider paying Martin and Mandy a visit and trying to make up with them so I wouldn't be alone in the world, but then decided I was not that desperate.

***

Frank listened intently to everything Imogene said. He liked the expressions of emotion that showed on her face, emotions she had never learned to hide or cover up. He liked the way her eyes misted over when she told the hurtful parts of her story. She was so honest. So innocent. He liked looking at the way her mouth moved when she talked. She pronounced each word distinctly, and each sound shaped her delicate mouth into a perfect pitch. He was wondering what the mouth would feel like pressed against his. He let his thoughts carry him a little further until she started explaining how she'd run into her husband just as he was getting off the elevator at the Shelby Towers. *That bastard didn't even recognize his own wife. But, then she had quite an imagination. Who would have figured she'd take a memory foam pillow and carve out a pregnancy? She was really something. So small and fragile, but gutsy and smart.*

Frank had no doubt her creep of a husband had married her for her money, with or without a prenuptial agreement. She thought her husband wasn't after her money because she had that prenup, but Frank knew there was more than one way to get around prenups. The fact the creep hocked her diamond ring spoke volumes about his character. Frank had to use every trick he had ever learned in training with the FBI to keep his face neutral while Imogene was telling him her tale of betrayal. He was furious that someone, anyone wanted to hurt her. If his sister weren't right there making up a bed for him on the couch, he would have wrapped Imogene in his arms and not let anything happen to her, except for things they both would enjoy.

After Imogene had laid down in the baby's room, he had a quiet conversation with Janey about the need for him to continue to stay with Imogene until the guys who were after her were caught. Janey didn't see the need since no one knew Imogene was there; then, seeing his determination, she reluctantly agreed. They had done all they could for the night. If he was going to Imogene, he needed to get his sleep so he could dig deeper into her case early the next morning.

Before Janey turned in for the night, she gave Frank access to her computer so he could check his e-mails. He laughed to himself when he discovered the e-mail from Imogene asking for his help.

She was the smart Penelope of the novels he'd been dying to meet? He'd gladly help her with anything she wanted, especially anything she might like to do undercover. But, he reminded himself, she was married. He shut the computer off and tried to switch his thoughts over to just getting a good night's sleep on Janey's lumpy couch. He didn't covet other men's wives no matter how screwed up their marriage was. Sleep was all he was going to try to get that night.

CHAPTER 14

Full daylight streaming in through the little-yellow-curtained window hit my still-groggy-from-need-of-sleep eyelids. I rolled over and almost rolled off the air mattress. My hands reached the floor just in time to catch my head from smacking it. I unglued my eyelids, yawned and stretched, trying to shake off my lethargy. I should have just wadded myself into the baby bed in the corner. I'd have gotten more sleep.

Except, it was not the air mattress's fault. It was surprisingly comfortable—just not as comfortable as I imagined crawling onto the sofa with Frank would have been. I had gotten over my indignation at him for not believing me when I'd seen him in a pair of sleep shorts and nothing else. Those shorts were almost as becoming as the damp towel I'd seen him in that first night I'd spent at his rental house.

Both Frank and his sister left me notes while I was sleeping in.

Her note said, "I hope you slept well. I am out of dish soap, so I'm going to the store. I also need to telegraph my husband to tell him my exact due date so he can request shore leave. Be back soon. Help yourself to anything in the house you need."

His note said, "Genie, I have some more things to check out. Stay here. I'll be back as soon as I can." And then in bold letters, he had scribbled and underlined at the bottom of the note,"STAY PUT." That seemed even bossier than his yelling "GET OUT" back beside the highway.

I snapped on my bracelet and dressed in the navy blue pin-striped shirt and navy skirt I found in the back of Janey's closet. She did say to help myself to anything in the house and judging from the slim waistline of the skirt it was going to be a while before she wore it again.

"STAY PUT" indeed.

Penelope wouldn't have. She went to great lengths to track down criminals. In *Murderer on the Moon,* she'd gone up in a space shuttle to catch the jilted-astronaut murderer. My first course of action was not to get accepted into space camp, but that might have been easier than getting my prenup papers and finding Jorgji's cash-on-hand at the apartment. I was going to clear out of Janey's while she was out buying a bottle of that green soap and Frank was off doing his I'm-in-charge checking, because I didn't intend to come back there ever or to ever see Frank again.

I pulled the soft cashmere sock yarn out of the diaper bag. I rubbed it against my cheek, then worked to shove it, and everything I could possibly fit in that diaper bag turned purse-suitcase. I had no way of knowing if Jorgji would keep his usual schedule, or what was going on with Keiko, but if my luck held the apartment would be empty until that afternoon. I just needed to get in and out quickly.

I had the taxi driver drop me off near the garage entrance. I got on the elevators in the garage and rode them up to the sixth floor to avoid the doorman stationed at the main entrance. I didn't want to be seen in case someone reported me to Jorgji in an effort to collect the reward money.

Despite my case of nerves, everything was going smoothly. I got off the elevator into an empty hallway.

***

When Frank read her e-mails and realized that Imogene was Penelope, he was relieved that she wasn't involved in her husband's shady dealings. He had known she was innocent, but it was nice to have it confirmed.

When he got back to Janey's and found the note she'd written, he was furious. He had told her to stay where she was safe, and she had left. Her response at the bottom of his note said, "Maybe you're right about everything being my imagination, but I don't think so. I'm going back to my apartment. I need to get money so I can hire a private investigator." The dismissive ending of "thanks for all you've done for me" hurt him. The fact that mere flowery script from her could hurt him like that made the hurt flat-out worse.

She'd helped him when he was a newly hired FBI agent and needed investigative advice. As Penelope, she'd unknowingly provided that help—without his having to compromise his job or his identity. Some of his best cases have been solved because of the techniques she shared with him. He was a good agent because of her. He owed her something for that, but what he was feeling went beyond that. He cared about what might happen to her. He knew good agents couldn't get emotionally attached to people in their cases. Attachments were a distraction, a vulnerability. Maybe it made him a bad agent with a distracting vulnerability, but all he wanted to do right then was to find a way to help Imogene.

***

I paused in front of my front door. I drew a quick breath and held it, not knowing if I was ready. Then, yes, I was ready. I rang my apartment doorbell.

No. Wait. I was not ready for that.

What if someone was in there? Very un-Penelope like I ran down the hall and hid behind my neighbor's potted fig. Keiko didn't come to the door. When Jorgji didn't open the door either, I felt confident both he and Keiko weren't in so I stepped out of hiding, put on my Penelope persona and mustered the courage I needed to get the job done.

Penelope always used a hairpin to pick open locked doors, but I had no such skills or bobby pins, so I dug my keys out of the diaper bag's side pocket.

The key turned easily in the lock, but when I tried to push the door open, it wouldn't budge. I turned the key the other way and shoved, and the door gave its customary opening creak as I pushed on it. I pushed it just wide enough to enter, and then gently, slowly closed the door so it won't make that creepy creaking sound again.

I was not sure of how long I had before my distraught-at-my-wife-being-missing husband showed up, so I passed through the living room and headed straight for the study. That was where I kept all of our household records and where Jorgji did all his business transactions when he was not staying late at the office for his late night flings.

I walked swiftly past my darkened, now scummy glass of tea and stale sandwich on the coffee table, right where I had left them days ago to go learn the dry cleaning business. My knitting magazines were strewn around the room. My potted plants were tipped upside down, their dark contents scattered on the light carpet amongst barbecue sauce splotches. Keiko had not been there as she would never have left the place like that.

There, amongst the black of the plant soil, were my brightly colored bamboo yarns that I always kept hidden under the towels in the linen closet. I wondered how they got out there, but I stepped over the riot of color and dirt. I already had the cashmere and couldn't fit any more yarns into my already bulging purse, so I didn't waste time picking up those bamboo yarns.

However, my eyes caught sight of one of my long

Blackwood knitting needles lying on the living room floor. Those needles were irreplaceable. I stooped down and scooped up the lone needle without breaking stride. The top knob stuck out, but the majority of the pointed end of the needle easily slid down the inside corner of my bag-purse. I glanced around for the needle's mate. I didn't see it. One knitting needle was useless without its mate, but it was more important that I get the papers I needed, find some money, and get out, so I moved on.

I found that the desk in the study had been ransacked. Jorgji's laptop was on the floor, smashed apart, the insides broken into tiny pieces. Most probably from the hammer next to it. I rummaged through the mess of papers on the floor and at the bottom of the pile, I found the orange blossom folder that held our prenup agreement. I managed to stuff the papers Jorgji had drawn up, at my insistence, into my growing-heavier bag. I straightened up and away from my focused search of the desk and file area to start my search to locate the money.

An audible creak came from the living room. An 'uh oh' moment hit me. I was not alone in the apartment. Looking around the study, I saw nothing but the hammer to use as a weapon. I knelt down beside it. Grasping the handle, I hefted the weight of it. I couldn't use a hammer any better than I could use a gun, so I relinquished my grip on the handle, and it slid soundlessly back to its place beside the smashed laptop bits.

A series of shuffles and muffled sounds came in from the living room. I could only hope it was Keiko coming in to clean up the mess.

I tiptoed to the door of the study to peer out and saw two men dressed in navy and gold police uniforms searching my living room. One was crouched low, riffling through the scattered debris on the floor. One was standing. He picked up items from the coffee table and peered under the plate my sandwich sat on. I could clearly see their gun belts. I could also see the handcuffs swinging from those gun belts.

Their faces were partially in shadow as they continued to search through the things strewn about the floor. After a few minutes, they stood to glance around.

Getting a better look, I could see they were an unmatched set. One tall, pale, slender and blond, the other short, dark skinned with lots of muscle and closely cropped black hair; uniforms were the only common denominator.

"Looks like someone beat us to it," the blond one said.

"I doubt it. We'd have heard if it was found," the dark one said. He looked up directly in my direction just then. Our eyes met. He saw me seeing him. His eyes caught sight of my teddy bear bag with its yarns, papers, and needle sticking out of the top of it.

"Look what we have here," he announced to his partner.

Sweat began to bead up on my forehead as I stared at the guns and dangling handcuffs. A few seconds passed in quiet assessment of each other. I considered picking the hammer back up but discard that idea because paper wraps hammer, but does hammer beat gun? Not likely.

"Looks like we don't need to search after all," Officer Blond said. "We can just get it from the person who has it." He held out his left hand and said to me while pulling his gun out with his right. "Hand it over." I hesitated. He tapped his right foot, impatient.

Impatient for what? I racked my brain trying to figure out what he was expecting me to give him. I began a back step towards the study door. "Hand it over" referred to my bag. I didn't know why I was not complying with his request. He had a gun. He was an officer of the law. There wasn't anything I couldn't bear to part with in that bag, so I did not know why I didn't just give it to him, except that I was confused by the familiar sound of his voice.

He urged me again, "We know you've found it. We've got instructions to not leave here without it."

I focused on his voice. I wanted to comply, but I couldn't un-weld my feet from the floor. My trembling sweat-damp hands stuck like glue to the straps of my bag as I gripped it ever closer to my body. I stooped down and picked up the hammer at my feet.

His "don't do that" stopped me but only for a second. I picked the hammer up anyway.

Asking for identification wasn't an unreasonable request. Police officers were always asking to see identification. Except he hadn't asked me for identification. He asked for my bag.

I was pretty sure that Officer Blond didn't just draw his gun on me because I had committed a fashion faux pa of using a diaper bag for a purse.

What did they believe was in that bag? Didn't they know I lived there? Didn't they realize that was my apartment? Or did they think I broke in? Were they under the assumption I was the one who vandalized the place? Did they think I smashed the laptop? Think I was the one who cleared out the safe? Is that what they were expecting me to hand over? Money from the safe?

I started to open my mouth to explain to them that I lived there. I had a right to be there. Something about Officer Blond stopped the words from coming out. Something about his voice and his feet.

"What do you want with this bag?" I asked. I tried to get a better look at him under the shadow of his visor. He pulled his hat down further.

I clutched the hammer, keeping a good grip on my bag strap, stood up, puffed up—Penelope style, and said with authority I didn't feel, "I live here. There are only clothes, papers, and knitting supplies in my bag. I didn't call for police assistance. You both need to leave now."

Officer Blond and his gun weren't good listeners. He said, "We're here to take care of some loose ends" and started walking towards me. His buddy was right behind him.

I backed into the study continuing to back away from them. They entered behind me, but since I was walking backward, they were in front of me. I gripped the hammer tighter. I was not sure I could use it, even if forced to.

What would Penelope do?

In *Murdered by Death,* Penelope was trapped by a rogue CIA agent who'd faked his own death. Being believed dead, no one thought he was the killer. No one sought him out, so he had free rein to kill off the bad guys with impunity. When Penelope confronted him in a warehouse, he drew his gun to shoot her. She shoved a barrel over at him. The barrel top popped off. Out rolled a pungent dead body. The villain agent was overcome by the smell. While he was gagging, Penelope got the drop on him.

I needed a startling event, but I was fresh out of barrels. Just as well. If there had been rotting bodies, I would have been the one incapacitated. Given the cool September breeze I could feel coming in from the open balcony door, a decaying, odoriferous body wouldn't be an effective deterrent anyway.

Officer Blond was now directly in front of me, his partner behind him. I swung the hammer wildly at them. Officer Blond backed up to avoid my swing. I ran past him almost into his buddy's arms in my quest to get to the open front door. His buddy lunged after me.

I dropped the hammer. It landed on my assailant's foot. He hopped around while I continued my race toward the door. Officer Blond was close behind me. He grabbed the strap of my bag. We tussled. He didn't let go. I didn't let go. I looked up at his face and spontaneously decided to let go of the heavy bag.

I couldn't stop the screams that were erupting out of me. Officer Blond was stairwell Tappy.

Unprepared for the sudden release of the bag, he stumbled backward trying to regain his footing. The bag flew out of his grasp and dropped heavily to the floor. Papers, yarns, clothes and personal effects scattered in a wide arc around the living room.

If Tappy could have tripped over a ball of yarn, I could

have gotten away. Just my luck those tappy feet were nimble. He was back upright in a flash. I was as good as caught.

CHAPTER 15

Imogene's scream sparked a primeval instinct in Frank that he didn't know he had. He rushed through the open front door of her apartment, gun drawn.

Imogene was in her living room squared off against two locals. One had a grip on her right arm, a gun in his free hand. The other was hopping around holding his left foot. Under ordinary circumstances, the police were the good guys. Having just investigated two corrupt locals Frank was not so sure. He was not trusting anyone he didn't know with Imogene.

"What seems to be the problem here officers?" Frank asked. He had his FBI badge wallet flipped out almost as quickly as was his gun.

Upon seeing Frank with the gun and badge, both officers backed up like they had stepped in dog turds. The blond officer loosened his grip on Imogene. She scrambled away from him and ran to a large bag lying on the floor. The other officer released his hold on his throbbing foot and sat it carefully down to the floor while backing away.

The heavier man looked to the thinner one for guidance. The thinner officer looked around at the mess and said slowly and deliberately to Frank, "We got a 4–12, a domestic dispute call. When we arrived here, we found signs of an obvious struggle."

Frank looked around noticing that the place was strewn with all kinds of stuff. It could have been from a struggle. Imogene was picking up things and shoving them into the bag decorated with teddy bears. Both officers were wearing the Detroit blue and gold uniforms. The chest badges and sleeve patches appeared legitimate, but neither of these legits could take their eyes off Genie for very long. *Correction.* They didn't take their eyes off the goofy oversized bag she was stuffing things into. Very peculiar. He couldn't ever take his eyes off her whenever she was around so why were the local yokels eyeballing her bag?

"Did you make a call to the police?" Frank asked Imogene.

"No. They just showed up," she said. Huffing with the exertion of the past few minutes, she clutched her bag to her and came to stand next to Frank.

"Look. We were just trying to close out a complaint call," the blond officer said.

A groan emanated from down the hall. Frank motioned for Imogene to get back out of the way of the hallway. He and the officers spanned out and flanked either side of the hall. Guns were drawn. Opposition forgotten as they worked in unison to start down the hall advancing towards the sound.

* * *

Frank was a great startling event that caused Tappy to let go of me. I picked up my things and put them back in my bag. Frank was right about a Federal badge getting you into a lot of places. I wanted to hug him. I would have too except it was my job as the chicken of the group to shiver and cower off to the side.

Everyone else had their guns out. They were advancing

down the hall towards that horrible mummy-being-released-from-the-crypt moaning sound. I stayed put where Frank had directed me without hesitation. I didn't have a gun. The hammer was across the room near the study, so all I had available was a diaper bag and my knitting. I didn't even have both knitting needles with me.

That could have been because the other needle was sticking out of the chest of the man advancing towards the guns. His face was distorted into a horrible grimace.

That was Jorgji's face! Jorgji was trying to talk, but he was only managing to gurgle blood bubbles because there was a knitting needle rammed up into his chest. There was red blood dribbling down his starched white shirt. That was blood on the carpet—not sauce. I breathed in a sharp breath. Blood was not my thing. I went face down, or the floor came up to meet me. Either way, I was out.

"Hey, my dreaming Genie. Wake up." I heard Frank's voice, but I didn't comply. Something cold was lying across my throbbing right eye, and my nose was pulsating with pain.

"I can't," I said keeping my eyes shut tight. "And the show was titled 'I Dream of Genie.' Not 'My Dreaming Genie.'" My stomach was rolling and churning at the remembered sight of the knitting needling protruding from Jorgji's bloody chest. My husband's chest. My knitting needle.

My nose was probably broken. Given the pain from under my right eye compress, I figured I was going to have a fat shiner there also. There would probably be even more bruises when my body assessed the damage from my fall and figured out which parts of me it wanted to color black and blue. I opened my left eye just a little to see Frank peering at me.

"Now is not the time to be dreaming, so show me those big brown eyes, so I know you're okay," he said.

"I don't want to," I said, not believing one of my favorite knitting needles could have been capable of such horror. Lying on my bed, I held my throbbing nose while pressing a cold, wet cloth against my right eye. I kept my left eye shut so I wouldn't have to peep at any other creepy scenes that might be in my apartment. "Is he still out there?"

"Nah, the ambulance guys took him away already," said Frank, knowing instinctively that I was referring to Jorgji.

Hearing Jorgji was gone, I finally put the cloth down and opened my eyes. I stood up on shaky legs. Frank asked me, "Should I get an ambulance for you?"

"No. I just fainted. Blood makes me sick, especially when it comes out of people I'm married to." I closed my eyes briefly and then opened them. Frank was doing his thing of peering at me up close and personal. He hooked a finger under my chin and moved my head to one side to check out my shiner, or maybe he was assessing whether I was telling the truth or not.

"Do you want to tell me what happened here?" Frank asked. His finger was withdrawn. He must have been satisfied I didn't need brain surgery.

"I don't want to, but I will," I said, sitting down on the bed and then deciding to stand up and then sitting down again. A new brain would have been in order if the old one couldn't stop the room from spinning. I stood again and started pacing the room so I could get my brain reoriented and shake the shakes that kept coming at me. "I came back to get my prenuptial papers to take to a divorce attorney and some money for a private investigator."

Frank's frown deepened, but he stayed silent as I continued, "I was coming out of the study and the next thing I knew two police officers were in my apartment. The one guy, the one who looks like one of the guys I was running from the other night, told me to hand over my bag. Then you showed up, and then Jorgji showed up..." I paused, not wanting to give into the belief of it. "He...he...he came down the hall. Like...like...that." I couldn't repress a violent shudder as I closed my eyes again to shut out the scene replaying in my head. It wasn't working.

Maybe that wasn't the knitting needle I'd purchased on the internet from some destitute Kenyan, who barely eked out a living using a whittling knife, foot-pump lathe, and a scrap of sandpaper. Maybe both needles were in my bag. That had happened before. I would hunt everywhere looking for a pair of needles and end up finding they were right under my nose all along.

Well, not under my nose just then; that nose was most assuredly broken.

"You think you recognized one of the officers?"

When I affirmed this and told Frank my suspicions that the officer was one of the men hunting me down, he got out his cell phone. He talked to someone while I began to rummage through the mess on my dresser to find the aspirin bottle I kept there. Frank flipped the phone closed and told me, "Both officers left when the crime scene technicians showed up, but we'll have that officer picked up for questioning."

He took hold of my hands and pulled me away from my search for the painkillers. "Sorry, Genie. You aren't allowed to tamper with the crime scene."

Crime scene? Technicians? What did he mean? My bedroom was a crime scene? How could that be? It hadn't seen any action since we had moved there.

"Did your husband attack you? Were you defending yourself?" Frank asked me, still holding my hands while I pondered this whole crime scene business.

"No. I didn't even know he was here," I told Frank, puzzled by his questions and even more puzzled by how good the warmth of his hands holding mine felt. My hands must have been very cold from the compress.

"Was he the only one here? Did you look? This is a massive place. Could there have been someone else? Was the door locked when you got here?" Frank asked.

I was beginning to grow concerned about his repeatedly questioning who was in the apartment. "I thought I was alone when no one answered the door buzzer. I put the key in the lock and turned it, but it didn't open. I turned it back, and it opened so I suppose it's possible the door was unlocked, and I'd locked it rather than unlock it. I was in a hurry. I didn't think to look around. When I found my yarns scattered all over and the place a disaster, I figured either Keiko had quit, or Jorgji had replaced me with a cat."

"Are you sure you were alone?"

"I don't know," I repeated again, frustrated. I pulled my hands away from his, irritated at his persistent questions about who was there and self-conscious that the warmth I was feeling had nothing to do with the compress.

"As I've already said, I had some trouble with the door. I came in. I didn't take the time to go through the whole apartment. I was upset that my yarns were scattered all over. I wanted to pick them up, but I couldn't. It was too big a mess, and there just wasn't time. I needed to get my prenuptial papers and some money so I could get a restraining order—and a divorce. I was in the study when I realized I wasn't alone. I looked into the living room, and the police were there. I don't know when they came in or if they were already there. They wanted my bag." I looked around trying to see where the diaper bag had ended up. I still needed those papers.

"Did you bring your crochet needles with you?"

"No. I don't crochet. Most of my knitting stuff was already here," I said with a heavy emphasis on the word 'knitting.' Puzzled, I said, "Those officers wanted my bag. You're asking about my needles. Why is everyone so interested in my knitting habits?"

"Your bag and knitting have been bagged as evidence," Frank told me, with an emphasis on 'knitting.'

I stopped in disbelief and turned to look at him."Why

would they bag my bag?"

"Because the police responded to a domestic disturbance fight at your apartment. Because the responding officers found you here with only one needle. Because the mate to that needle was found residing in your husband's chest. Because you are their prime suspect. That's why."

"I am? How could I be? I didn't even know Jorgji was here. He didn't answer the doorbell. Look, I wasn't the one who needled him. It had to be someone else. Or he fell on my needle or something. The worst I've ever done is spill hot coffee on him. How can they suspect me of stabbing him when he's the one who has been trying to kill me!" I said in a rush of words.

I should have gotten up the nerve to file an attempted murder charge to back up my attempted murder claims so it was more than just my word against Jorgji's.

Then I asked the only person I'd ever told my attempted-murder-by-my-husband story to, "How is it that you just happened to show up here?"

We were interrupted by a man in a dark suit and sunglasses showing up at my bedroom door. Frank seemed to know him as they stepped outside the room into the hall. The man whispered a few quick words to Frank. Frank nodded. The man left. Frank came back and picked up our conversation without missing a beat. *What had that been about?*

"I came to help you. I told you to stay put while I checked out who your husband had been dealing with. Once I found out what he was up to, I knew you didn't know about his dealings. I knew you were walking blind into a dangerous situation. I didn't want you to face whatever you were coming back to alone."

"Technically you wrote 'STAY PUT.' You didn't mention that you were checking my husband out. What could you possibly have found that would lead you to believe I'd be coming back to this?" I shut my eyes again and swallowed

142

painfully hard, thinking about the 'this' I'd walked into.

"I found out that your husband's relocation to the U.S. was sponsored by one of the biggest Albanian crime rings in New York. But I'll explain it all in detail later. Right now, there are two uniforms in your living room. They've been waiting for you to come to so they can to take you into custody and book you for attempted murder."

Blacking out again, I felt my body being held up and pressed against a warm shirt while the blood pounded in my ears. I could hear Frank's voice sounding very tiny, tinny and far away as he said, "You have got to stop doing this."

Unlike at the Department of Motor Vehicles, no one at Detroit's Dickerson Detention Facility allowed me to approve my swollen-nose-and-black-eye picture before they finalized it as my arresting mug shot. But then the DMV never strip searched me, dressed me in a hideous florescent orange jumpsuit, and shoved me into a small cell to cry myself to sleep while waiting for a bail bond to be arranged.

That wasn't the worst of what I'd suffered; that barrel-chested Police-woman took my silver USB bracelet from my wrist and wouldn't give it back.

Bracelet back on, dressed again in the navy pinstripes—minus my diaper bag, I was feeling a little more human, confident the worst was over. I stepped out of the jail house's Lysol-smelling restroom trying to rub fingerprinting ink from my fingers—like Lady Macbeth.

Frank found me an alcohol swab for the ink. He introduced me to the woman with him, my criminal defense attorney, Samantha Simpson. She was dressed in a dark brown business suit that must have come from the 'big and tall' girls' section of Bloomingdale's for the skirt to even begin to come down to her knees the way it did. She had on an I-can-still-be-a-woman-in-a-man's-job light pink blouse

143

with lace trim peeking out of the top of her closed and buttoned double-breasted jacket. The severe bun that she had pulled her light blond hair back into proclaimed to every doubter: don't mess with me because I'm tougher than you.

Frank covered my head with his jacket, and he and Ms. Simpson flanked either side of me and like guide dogs they lead me from the station into the blinding sunlight. The warmth of the sunshine brightened my spirits, but when I heard Ms. Simpson remark, "No Comment" over and over to the camera-clicking reporters my spirits turned cold and dark. I kept looking down at my feet and walked unsteadily to the car they had waiting at the curb. A cold gray dread seized me as I slipped into a mental fog.

I was facing attempted murder charges.

I heard a car door open. I felt the cold leather of the back seat as I was guided in. I sensed the motion as I was driven away from the diminishing camera clicks, but I could see nothing with my wide open eyes.

The jacket was gone, but the fog was still my best friend as I stepped into the crystal-chandeliered lobby of the Crumby, Lawton, Simpson and Dewy Law Offices. Me and my fog, and Frank and Ms. Simpson, floated up to the third-floor offices in a glass encased elevator.

Nothing Frank or Ms. Simpson said penetrated the haze that glazed my thoughts. My knitting needle protruding from Jorgji's chest was the only thing I could focus on. I continually pictured Jorgji stumbling down the hall. That mental image overlayed everything they said, and it just wouldn't stop.

Frank roughly grabbed both of my shoulders and shook me hard, which hurt my nose.

"Listen to me, Imogene Warren," he said. "I'm sorry for all that's happened. You've been through a lot. Maybe we should give you some time to grieve, but there isn't time to wallow in sorrow. You have got to get a hold of yourself and snap out of this stupor you're in. You are facing some very serious charges. Sam can't help you if you're off somewhere that neither of us can reach you."

"All right. All right," I said so he wouldn't shake me again and dislocate my nose or give me a concussion or worse.

I knew he was right. I needed to stop being the mousey me I had always been. I needed to be stronger. I found the strength to be Penelope for a little while longer.

I pulled my shoulders back, put my chin up. I straightened my torso up in the designer leather chair I was sitting on in that huge designer conference room with its expensive Slava Posudvsky landscape paintings. "Tell me what evidence the police have against me," I demand in a firm Penelope voice.

Both Frank and Ms. Simpson blinked in rapid succession. My attorney cleared her throat. She spoke first. "Number 1. You buy a place in the Cayman Islands, a country noted for its lack of accountability in international banking," she began.

"Number 2. The bank records show your bank accounts have been systemically cleared out over the past two months."

"But," I sputtered, beginning to protest that I didn't have that money. "I didn't clear out anything. My butler had to post my bail. I don't even own the clothes I'm wearing."

Frank's hand came up to caution me. "Just listen," he said.

"Number 3," resumed Ms. Simpson. "Your husband didn't know you were leaving him. He thought you were kidnapped. You say he hired a police officer and another man to kill you, but there is no proof of this. The officer you identified denies all of it."

Well, of course, he would. I remained still. Just listening. And fuming.

"Number 4. You came back and cleared out your apartment safe.

"Number 5. The police received a call reporting a domestic dispute going on between you and your husband.

Your neighbor claims it was so ugly she had to call the police before someone got killed.

"Number 6. Your husband's laptop was found smashed. Your prints are all over the hammer used. The police believe you did this in a rage during the fight.

"Number 7. The responding officers found you holding a bag with one ornate, very sturdy needle.

"Number 8. Everyone, including you, sees your husband with the mate to said ornate, sturdy needle planted into his aorta."

"Okay," I said trying to reign in my anger and remain impassive and failing. "Number 1. I didn't buy that place in the Cayman Islands. Jorgji did. Numbers 2 and 4." I began to take on a very defensive, disrespectful tone that I was not caring sounded rude. "If I cleared out my bank accounts where did I put the money? If I cleared out the safe why wasn't any of it with me? Number 3. Of course, that tappy-footed guy will deny all of it. He's a police officer. He knows what trouble he'll be in if he confesses he was trying to kill me. My prints are on the hammer because I had to use it for self-defense against him and his partner, who were coming after me. And, numbers 5, 7 and 8 are just ridiculous. I typed all of my aunt's books on murders. If I was trying to kill my husband, I know of numerous, almost indiscernible killing techniques from her books so why would I mess up my favorite knitting needle by pushing it into my husband?" *Oops.* I probably shouldn't have mentioned I knew several ways to kill people.

"The police figure you read the prenup they found in your bag. When you found out Jorgji would get half of your inheritance in a divorce, you killed him rather than let him have any of it." Frank said in his calm, neutral, respectful-of-my-feelings voice.

"What?" I said in an escalating voice. "My prenup keeps Jorgji from getting any of the wealth I brought into the marriage with me. Oh." My voice trailed off as I realized what a fool I had been. It was Jorgji who had the prenup drawn up at my insistence. I only skimmed the agreement before signing it. I should have seen the loopholes he'd hidden. "My inheritance from my aunt came at the time of her death. I'd been married to Jorgji one month by then. The prenup allows for equal sharing of anything accumulated more than 10 days after the marriage."

"Bingo," Frank said when I finally got it. "The police figure you started clearing everything out and putting it in offshore accounts so you could flee to the Cayman Islands and keep Jorgji from getting any of your money. When he found out you were leaving him and taking all the money, he confronted you. You argued. Then you stabbed him with your knitting needle. You trashed the place and the computer to make it look like a robbery, but they came in and caught you before you could leave."

"That's absurd!" I said dropping my Penelope persona for my own indignation. "I don't have any offshore accounts. I've never even set foot in the Cayman Islands. I barely ever leave my house, except for yarn and ice cream. Besides," I said, confident of the final piece of my exoneration. "Jorgji has to know who stabbed him. He can't possibly have told the police that it was me because he knows it wasn't."

The look on Frank's face as he takes both my hands in his and crouches down in front of me at eye level puts a massive lump of cold, hard stone in my chest. I had not been told everything yet.

Frank said softly, "Imogene. I'm so sorry. I thought you'd been told at the jail last night. Jorgji wasn't able to tell the police anything. He died soon after arriving at the hospital. The needle shredded his aortic valve so badly they couldn't keep him stabilized long enough to get it repaired. He wasn't able to tell anyone anything."

I was not out-of-control-inconsolable crying. That was just my trying-not-to-cry crying. I was able to talk between sobs and hiccups, so I didn't know why Frank stopped our defense strategy meeting to load me into his car.

I continued my trying-not-to-cry crying all the way back

to Janey's, where she put her arm around me and told me how sorry she was for my loss. Then, I didn't try-not-to-cry cry. I cried like my world had been shattered because it had.

I guess it was fitting that they put me back in the baby's room.

My parents were gone. My aunt was gone. My cousins hated me because I was rich and they weren't. My gold digger husband wanted me for my money, which was the only interesting thing about me, but he was gone, and it appeared my money was gone, too. Everyone thought I was smart enough to have electronically spirited my fortune away to some obscure account on some obscure island; they didn't know I couldn't even operate a simple ATM. It was Jorgji who had bled me dry. No one else had access to all my accounts. There was no one else I trusted. He was so capable. So responsible. He seemed like such a nice guy.

Only, Jorgji wasn't the nice guy I thought he was. He was planning to divorce me and get half my money. Except he wasn't even that nice. He was going to have me killed so he could get all of my money.

If I had known my husband's intentions to kill me, I wouldn't have bothered to buy a sock yarn that matched his favorite sapphire blue silk tie. The tie he was buried in.

CHAPTER 16

I wanted to run away from all that murder mess, but I couldn't. Gordon would have been out the bail money if I did. I couldn't do that to him. He had been more than just a perfect butler every since he came to work for my aunt 19 years before. Normal butlers managed every aspect of the household they work in, the contents, the staff, the budget, and vehicles. Premium butlers, like Gordon, went the extra mile and then around the block again.

Gordon did everything he could to ensure my aunt had plenty of free, uninterrupted time to write best-selling novels. He monitored my childhood activities, bandaged my scraped knees, and fixed my broken toys and when necessary refereed my bouts with Martin and Mandy. In exchange for his allegiance, my aunt provided Gordon with liberal vacation time, a huge salary, his own car, and a lifelong lease on her house's third-floor apartment.

I remember one day while playing as children, Martin became distraught that neither Mandy nor I would play cowboys and Indians so he could use his newly acquired BB gun. Mandy had my newest china doll with its dress of yards and yards of lace ruffles. I was playing with a cloth rag doll Gordon had given to me. In truth, I preferred the cloth doll with its simple print dress and bonnet, but I had to protest somewhat over the established caste system to keep Mandy from finding out my preference and thus making it hers.

When Mandy and I refused to play guns, Martin stomped off, muttering something about not playing with dumb girls. Martin decided that if we wouldn't play, he'd use our dolls for target practice. He leveled his toy gun at my doll sitting on her little chair awaiting tea. Seeing this, I let out a scream. I put my doll safely behind my back but neglected to move out of the line of fire.

A surprised Martin let out a yelp as Gordon hefted the gun away before it could be fired. There was a second yelp as Martin's behind was swatted and Gordon told him, "Master Martin, all guns are considered weapons and must never be aimed at people."

Martin's face erupted red as he bellowed, "I didn't aim it at her. She stepped in the way. Give me back my gun. It's mine. You have no right to take it."

"It is your gun," said Gordon, "But, you'll not be getting it back until you leave for home, and I must ask you to never bring it back with you again."

"You give me that back or I'm telling my mother." Martin didn't wait for a response; he ran crying to his mother. I followed behind, curious to see how Aunt Selena would handle an imposing man like Gordon.

Upon hearing the embellished tale told by Martin, Aunt Selena's face turned as red as his. She promptly turned to my Aunt Tilly and told her, "A servant must not be allowed to take such liberties. I demand you make him return Martin's property and then fire that man at once for what he's done to Martin."

"Martin was trying to shoot my doll. He would have torn her," I said in a quiet voice to Aunt Tilly holding up my cloth doll, which I thought was the injured party in that event.

My aunt gave me a soft pat on the head and told me to go back outside and play, she'd take care of it. I started to leave but turned back around when I heard Aunt Tilly say, "Selena, Gordon is an expert marksman. He knows a lot about weapons. Guns are not toys. Imogene could have been injured. Besides, Gordon is like family to me." Here Aunt Tilly paused and looked directly and pointedly at Aunt Selena. "No matter how much you might want to, you can't easily get rid of family."

Aunt Tilly was right about Gordon and Gordon was always right. I should have paid closer attention to his advice.

The first time Gordon handed me my banking mail, I handed it back to him unopened telling him "Jorgji takes care of our personal banking now. You need to give these to him."

Gordon took the mail back. He raised one eyebrow and advised me, "Miss Imogene, one must always remain aware of what is happening around them. It is in your own best interest to review your personal mail and finances."

Gordon never gave me that advice again even when I repeatedly gave him back the banking letters he handed to me. Gordon never stopped offering me the mail, and I never stopped handing it back, refusing to open it. That became our ritual, passing envelopes back and forth. I never called him out on his act of disobedience. I didn't think Gordon, being single, understood about spousal trust. Jorgji had handled all my money as my investment broker before we got married. It seemed natural to add his name to my bank accounts after we got married. I trusted him completely.

When a quiet man like Gordon speaks up, it's because he has something important to say. I should have listened because every joint account I had with Jorgji was frozen solid while the Federal government banking investigators went over the books for irregularities. I couldn't even chip off enough to afford that decrepit run-down motel room near Commerce Park.

I was grateful for Janey's air-mattress hospitality. So grateful that when she vehemently turned down my offer to wash her dirty dishes, I offered to vacuum her floors instead. She got the vacuum machinery out of her closet and showed me how to unwrap the cord, plug it in, and turn it on. She adjusted the height and showed me how to push it around and how to unclip the canister to empty it. She then left to go to her doctor's appointment leaving me to proudly push that piece of loud-sounding machinery around the house.

The vacuum had a see-through smokey plastic canister body that allowed the operator to see the tornado of dirt and dust that whirled around in its belly. It was fun to watch the dirt being forced into a swirling dervish. I vacuumed every floor in the house three times before I ran out of dirt to watch. With no more dirt to suck up inside the house, I took the vacuum outside to the driveway. There was a lot of dirt in the outdoors to watch spin around and around.

I loved helping Janey. I just hoped my assets would get unfrozen in time to buy her a new vacuum before her floors needed to be cleaned again.

I went with her to help at the laundromat to make up for ruining her vacuum. The first time I went to a laundromat didn't go so well, so I was a little anxious about doing this as vacuum cleaner payment. *What if I messed the laundry thing up, too?*

As we walked in through the laundromat door, my arms quivered slightly. The quivering was caused by carrying a heavy clothes basket for Janey and not because I was scared witless thinking there might be more hired killers hunting me down. The clothes in the basket were piled so high it was hard for me to maneuver through the door and up to the washers without dropping everything. I left a trail of socks and bras strung out behind me, but I finally found the washers Janey had set her soap and fabric softener bottles on. I sat the heavy basket down and ran back to retrieve the articles I had dropped on my journey to the washer.

The laundromat was crowded for a Saturday. People were coming in with baskets heaped up with dirty clothes while others were leaving with baskets piled up with folded clothes. No clothes were spilling from their baskets so they must have been pros at the laundromat business.

I was starting to feel a little nauseous. It was nothing big, just a little panic attack from being around that many people. I needed to keep some distance from people until the nausea subsided. I needed to get away from everyone, so they didn't touch me or talk to me, two things I was not good at with strangers.

I sidled up close to Janey, who was taking clothing items from the overloaded laundry basket, wadding them into loose balls and arranging them around the center posts of the washing machine's belly.

"I think it's so cool that Frank met you. He was such a huge fan of your aunt," Janey said to me.

"He was? But my aunt wrote for teenage girls."

Janey laughed. "I know. That's what made it so embarrassing for Frank. He'd sneak and read her books under the covers at night with a flashlight. Like we didn't all know he read them. When one of my books was missing, I'd find it under his mattress. Honestly, I have no idea why it was so un-macho for him to read about crimes that were solved by a teenage girl. Whenever a new Penelope Pembrook novel would come out if I didn't go out and get it right away, Frank would buy me a 'present.'" She laughed her wonderful warm laugh again and added, "All my gifts from Frank were books written by Matilda Warren that he wanted to read, but didn't want his tough, lummox friends to know he liked them."

This put a new twist on an old theme. Frank was a closet reader. Instead of stashing *Playguy* magazines under his mattress as a boy, he hid Penelope Pembrook mystery novels.

"Why, that closet faker," I said. "He conversed with me

on-line and knew all about my aunt, but he didn't say it was because he read and loved her books."

"That doesn't surprise me. He even skipped school once to secretly go to her Friday book signing at the Horned Owl bookstore. When dad found out Frank skipped school, he was furious and grounded Frank for a month. When Frank wouldn't tell dad why he'd skipped school, he was grounded for another month.

"But why didn't he just tell your dad where he was?"

"Same reason he went during school and didn't go on Saturday. He didn't want anyone to know he was meeting with an author who wrote exclusively for young women. He went when none of his friends would see him and took the extra punishment rather than divulge where he was." Janey slammed down the washer lids, and we walked over to two empty seats along the windows.

I shuddered a bit when I sat down in plain sight by the front windows. That was too close to resembling the night I ran from my would-be killers and ended up crawling on a dirty floor to keep out of sight. I'd worn that floor dirt on my face and hands until I hit the hot water of Frank's shower.

I had to remind myself over and over again that I was not at that laundromat. The floor under me was clean. An attendant was busy wiping off the unused counter areas. There was a comfortable hum of clothes spinning around in dryers and washers, and there were people milling comfortably around the place. Nice people. People were reading books and using their phones, their little kids playing in full sight of the windows. Just like us, everyone was waiting for their clothes to stop turning around in a tub. I figured the toilet seat there was fully intact, also.

"If Frank didn't tell anyone back when it happened then how do you know he was at the book signing?" I asked trying to keep our conversation going to distract my overactive imagination.

"Book signings require a book to sign. All of his books were secreted into the house under the pretense of being mine. When I picked out a favorite Penelope book from my shelf to take to the signing on Saturday, I saw it had already been signed by Matilda Warren, and it said 'To my Undercover Fan, Frank.' I didn't have to be a genius to realize where he'd been on Friday with 'my' book. It's just one of those things we've always kept to ourselves. I think covertly hiding those books and sneaking around was just the start of Frank's interest in being an undercover agent. He seems to thrive on covert operations, never telling anyone where he is going or what he is doing."

Janey got up to grab a rolling cart. She sat her fabric softener, soap box, and basket inside. She seemed at ease rolling it over to her row of machines. After she'd opened every one of her three washer lids to peer into their swishing contents, she headed for the snack machine at the back of the building. I wanted to follow her, but it seemed rude to always be dogging her heels.

I didn't know what else to do to help. Gordon always sent our clothes out. They came back on hangers covered in plastic or neatly folded into plastic totes. Mary, the maid, placed the hangers and totes into our walk-in closets. They went from hamper to walk-in closet with no help from me so I didn't think I would be particularly helpful to Janey with that laundry business. I looked around, trying to see what other people in the laundromat were doing. They all seemed to know what they are doing or were sitting down waiting for the people that knew what they were doing to finish. I was not ready to sit back down, so I just observed for a while, hoping to learn something about doing laundry.

A woman perched two small squirming boys on the closed lid of one of the washing machines. She stripped off their clothes—right down to their underwear, then threw them into the washer—the recently removed garments— not the kids. The kids she freed from their perch to play with a Nerf ball she pulled out of her large purse.

Two young women in short skirts and tight shirts were sitting in a row of chairs by the dryers fiddling with their iPhones, trying to surreptitiously spy on a handsome young man who was folding his clothes. He worked diligently at one of the Formica-topped tables provided around the building, unaware that he was being watched as he folded his jeans, socks, shirts, and underwear. The two young women and I continued to watch as he carefully matched each clothing piece seam to seam, then doubled each over in half, then in half again before smoothing and stacking each onto a neat pile on the table. As he picked up the last pair of underwear, his eyes glanced over the top of the waistband. He noticed one of the girls noticing him holding his underwear. He plopped the offending article of clothing on top of his pile, unfolded. Red-faced, he gathered his arms around the entire pile of his clothing, scooped the whole thing into a large knapsack and hurried out the door.

The giggling girls returned to their iPhones, and I sought other entertainment. Drama over.

I watched in fascination when an elderly lady pulled her hot, dry clothes out of an enormous dryer. Each shirt, pants, and dress she laid flat on a table top and sprinkled with a clear liquid from a clear glass bottle. The bottle had a metal top with holes in it to allow the liquid to be released with each shake like a salt shaker pop bottle. After each garment had its sprinkle shower, she rolled it up and placed it in an oval wicker basket.

There was a tuft of gray hair showing above a *Woman's Daily* magazine held up close to a reader's face at the end of the row of chairs the two girls had recently vacated. The face wasn't visible, but a man's shirt, man's pants, and man's scuffed up shoes were. I believe him to be the mate to Mrs. Sprinkler, both holdovers from a time when husbands drove their wives to the laundromat and sat waiting for them to finish wetting down their recently dried clothes. He hadn't moved from his chair or put his magazine down even once since I noticed him because it was her job to do the laundry and his job to wait for her to do the laundry.

I should have seen if I could have helped Janey with pouring the milky blue liquid into each washer, but I thought maybe I would be better at the seam-to-seam folding part of doing laundry, so I didn't. Instead, I headed over to ask Mrs. Sprinkler why the clothes have to be dry before she re-wets them so maybe I could do that wetting part for Janey. It looked like fun. I hesitantly advanced towards Mrs. Sprinkler and mentally started rehearsing what my first few words of greeting to her would be—just like my *Dale Carnage* on-line course suggested when faced with difficult social interactions.

Right in the middle of my mental rehearsal, I felt a hard object poke into the center of my back.

"Don't turn around or make a sound. I have a gun. Just start walking toward the door. You wouldn't want your pregnant friend, grandma or any of these little kids to get hurt would you?" A raspy, harsh voice whispered into my ear.

I tried to find the 'cucumber' cool that everyone talked about, but I knew I was in a pickle. "What do you want with me?" I whispered over my shoulder as I started moving forward in slow motion, trying to think of something to do to protect myself without anyone getting hurt.

"I have a client who wants your husband's records. Now be a good little girl and head towards the door so we can go get them from where you hid them," he said, then he coughed a phlegmy cough. I hoped he covered it or coughed into his shoulder because I had just gotten over a sore throat.

"The FBI took my husband's records from his office," I said.

"I don't want those. I want the real records. Then we're going to take a little walk afterward," said the nasty, raspy whisper as the poke in my back nudged me forward again.

My walking partner was not Mr. Sprinkler. Based on his voice, cough and the shuffling of his feet, I knew he was

Scuffy from my previous laundromat experience. I had hoped he had been found and arrested when they questioned Officer Tappy about his involvement in the attempt to murder me. Officer Tappy must not have been a squealer, or he was so afraid of Scuffy that he didn't dare squeal. That meant Scuffy wasn't bluffing about people getting hurt. I started scuff walking with him towards the door, trying to steer us in the direction of the old lady's table. It was a route to the door that lead us the farthest from Janey.

Sorry, Mrs. Sprinkler. It wasn't that I wanted her in harm's way, I just didn't want Janey, or her baby harmed.

One of the little BVD boys shrieked. I turned to see him racing toward us. He was trying to catch the Nerf ball. The ball that was flying towards Scuffy's head. Little BVD's brother was chasing after the ball, too. Both mindless of where they were going. The first little BVD streaker bumped into Scuffy. The second little streaker was right behind the first. Scuffy wobbled, off-balanced from the two-boy pile-up. The boys' mother saw them bump into Scuffy. She jumped up, screaming at them to be quiet and quit running then she sat back down, her job as an inattentive mother done.

I took advantage of the distraction to grab Mrs. Sprinkler's glass bottle. I swung it up to smash Scuffy's hand.

Too bad for Scuffy my aim wasn't very good. It wasn't exactly his hand I hit.

Scuffy swore, grabbing his groin, he doubled forward in pain while he tried to regain control of the situation and his balance.

Pandemonium broke loose. The boys fought and shrieked over their captured ball, oblivious to Scuffy's pain, my poor aim and their mother's shouting from across the room. I was oblivious to Mrs. Sprinkler's screaming at me to return her sprinkler bottle. I turned, and when I confirmed for sure that my kidnapper was Scuffy, killer-for-hire, I screamed. No one within earshot was oblivious to my volume or intensity.

My intensity lessened, but I found I was unable to stop screaming for a few seconds. It all happened so fast I couldn't even conceive of how a pregnant Janey got my hired killer up against a scorching hot dryer with her concealed Smith & Wesson shoved tightly to his back.

When the Troy police arrived, I told them my version of what had happened, but I was too shaken to be of much help. Even though the police hauled Scuffy and his gun away and took everyone's statements, including the recently dressed two smallest someones, it was a while before I stopped quaking in my footwear.

I didn't care how useful those white, square Maylag machines were, I was never coming to a laundromat again. Not even with an on-maternity-leave FBI agent who always carried her department-issued Smith & Wesson with her. Laundromats were just not worth it.

I would just throw away my clothes when they get dirty and buy new ones.

CHAPTER 17

Scuffy was ex-Detroit Police officer Mario Miller. He had worked in several Detroit precincts before he was forced to take an early medical retirement. He had obtained a private investigator's license to supplement his reduced retirement benefits. When his chronic medical conditions left him with little energy to pursue legitimate investigative assignments, he began seeking easy, quick money jobs. Most of his assignments were roughing up gamblers who owed money, repossessing unpaid-for merchandise or intimidating ex-wives into dropping requests for more alimony. He wasn't in favor of taking on a termination assignment, but killing Imogene would net him enough money to finish up his cancer treatments. He wasn't sure he could kill someone in cold blood, but if he didn't take this job and get the money he needed there would be a dead body either way.

Jason Bellman, a Detroit officer still on the force, was known for moonlighting on jobs outside of the law. Bellman agreed to help Miller for a part of the take as long as he didn't have to be the one doing the killing.

Miller's familiarity with the judicial system was hindering the Troy police department's investigation of the potential kidnapping of Imogene. Miller refused to tell the investigating officer what records he was after, why he thought Imogene had them or why he wanted her to take a 'little walk.'

When the investigating officer got nowhere with his questioning, Frank told him he wanted to interrogate Miller privately: no video, no recording, no observers. Since Miller was going to be charged with attempted kidnapping, a crime that would eventually be turned over to the FBI anyway, the Troy police reluctantly agreed to Frank's request.

"Look, Miller. You are facing federal kidnapping charges. I doubt you wanted Imogene or her husband's files for yourself. Who are you working for? Why are they after those records?"

"What records? I haven't done anything. I just bumped into that dame at the laundromat. She's so afraid of her own shadow that she imagined it all. When she started screaming her fool head off, everyone just assumed I'd done something. I don't even know her. She just came unglued."

"Well, I know her. If she came unglued, I know you were the cause of it," Frank said, sneering within inches of Miller's face. Frank's fists were knuckle down on the table that separated the two men. Frank knew Imogene had an imagination, so he didn't even try to deny it. Instead, he told Miller, "You can bet I'm going to make damn sure you cooperate in this attempted kidnapping investigation—or wish you had."

Miller didn't back up, flinch or twitch when Frank purposefully inched forward in a deliberate attempt to intimidate him. The smolder in Frank's eyes was so close it almost ignited Miller's face. Miller took a hot wheezy breath in through his mouth and said, "You can't get kidnapping charges to stick. No one was kidnapped."

"Oh?" Frank backed off a few inches though his eyes remained locked on Miller's face. "You just happened to be at the laundromat to wash your gun? And while you were drying it off it accidentally got jammed into Miss Warren's back?"

"Hey. This is all just a misunderstanding. I didn't have my gun out. It was in my jacket pocket." Miller choked back a cough into his hand and continued. "I'm licensed to carry a concealed weapon. I just happened to bump into that broad when those kids knocked into me."

"Well. You can count on me 'knocking" into you if you ever happen to be anywhere near Miss Warren again," Frank threatened, clenching his fists hard then slamming them down on the table in front of Miller.

Frank knew the guy was probably right about the charges not sticking. No one else heard Genie threatened. The courts might not give any credence to a woman who was considered unbalanced and had been charged with murder, especially since she was the only one who heard his threats to her and no one saw the gun. Genie only felt the gun. No one was hurt or kidnapped. "I don't know who hired you or just what you were after, but I'm damn sure going to find out."

"Well, you won't get anything from me," said Miller, leaning back, so only two legs of the chair were on the floor, trying to make his actions appear natural rather than an avoidance of Frank's escalating anger. A coughing fit seized Miller for several seconds, and his chair legs slammed back down to the floor. Taking a puff from an inhaler he pulled out of his pants pocket, Miller shook his head slightly while he studied Frank's tiger pacing around the room.

Miller continued to watch Frank pace, trying to gauge just how much he wanted to divulge to a federal agent, who just might be working with the local precincts. After a few minutes, knowing it is just the two of them in the room, Miller said, "You feds think you know it all. You got it all figured out. You don't know shit when it's right under your nose."

"I know your story stinks."

"Life stinks. When I first became a cop, I never hurt no one unless it was them or me. Long hours filled with danger around every corner, unpaid furlough days, cuts in pay and being dissed by the people you work for changes you. You think 'cause you're a fed you're above it all? You're still wet behind the ears," Miller continued while Frank kept silent, hoping Miller would spill something useful in his rant. "Try sitting on the other side of a forced early retirement scrapin' pennies and takin' whatever jobs you can find to pay your uncovered medical expenses. You'd take on some pretty dicey clients too if you had to."

Frank couldn't keep silent any longer. "So you think your situation justifies what you do? You think you've figured out how to beat an attempted kidnapping charge?" Then, looking at the pathetic lump of a man in front of him who was after Imogene, Frank leaned his fisted knuckles back on the table again and said directly to Miller's flushed face, "Maybe you will get off and walk outta here, but rest assured you won't be able to take a leak without me knowing about it. I'll be on you like glue if you even scrape the dirt you're walking around in off the bottom of your shoe."

Miller knew the FBI was too busy to get involved in an unsubstantiated attempted kidnapping charge and all his other petty crimes that don't fall under their jurisdiction, but he also knew that Frank wasn't representing the FBI right then and Frank didn't seem worried about jurisdictional issues when it came to that woman.

Miller decided that the payout promised him wouldn't be high enough to protect him from a rogue FBI agent with a personal vendetta. Fearful of being alone with Frank in light of his increasing anger, Miller shoved his chair back— away from Frank's ire. Miller began shouting to the uniformed officer waiting outside the room. "Get me outta here. I'm all done talkin'. You get me outta here right now or get me a lawyer."

Miller thought it had seemed like a good deal to kill two birds with one stone, so he'd taken both jobs involving Imogene when they'd been offered to him by two different customers. He'd get the wife; get her to give him the missing husband files then get rid of the wife. After being in the room with Frank, Miller decided he was giving both retainers back. Just as soon as he got cut loose, he was going to try to step out of the dirt he had been walking around in—if the guys he was dealing with would let him.

"You're going to find out this thing goes deeper than just your little girlfriend. So I'd be careful who I threaten if I were you," Miller advised Frank as the guard came in to escort Miller back to his cell.

Frank stepped up and blocked their path momentarily. He said directly into Miller's face. "It's not a threat. It's a fact. And I don't care how deep this shit goes. I'll find the bottom of it, and I bet I'll find you there when I do."

***

Frank told Special Agent Stevens, "I think Jorgji's murder and the kidnapping attempt on Genie have got to be somehow related to his shady business dealings. If we can get to the bottom of what he was involved in then maybe we can figure out who had motive to kill him."

Agent Stevens rubbed the top of his balding head and then his smoothly shaved chin before he scooted his office chair closer to his desk. He peered across the desk directly at me and asked, "You say your husband was also your investment manager?"

"Yes, he managed both my aunt's and my investments."

"For how long?"

"About six months now," I said and started to rifle through the papers in the manila folders I'd brought. "It was all on the up-and-up. I've got the statements right here to show a return on our investments. They were all safe investments. They paid off fairly well."

"Every time?" he asked.

"Yes. They performed just the way he promised they

would. Right down to the letter." I handed him the investment statements Jorgji provided me with every month. Each one showed a substantial 10% return on the money invested.

Agent Stevens looked over the computer printouts for several minutes before he asked, "You ever physically see any of this money you made?"

"Of course. Jorgji hand delivered the checks to me personally. It's how we first started dating."

"You cashed the checks yourself?"

"Well, no. My aunt and I didn't need the money, so I endorsed the checks and returned them to Jorgji to reinvest. He said it was the best way to watch our initial investment grow."

"And you say he was doing so well in Chicago that he opened up shop in Detroit?" The chin rubbing got more vigorous.

"Yes. That's why we moved here. He worked very hard. Night and day sometimes. So I doubt he ever had time to be involved in shady business dealings."

Agent Stevens switched from rubbing his chin to his head and then switched back to lightly rubbing his chin again. "It's highly unusual to have investments consistently pay off as much as 10% even over a short period. The market naturally has ups and downs. Have you ever heard of a Ponzi scheme?"

I didn't like pop quizzes, but I also didn't like appearing stupid, so I answered, "Yes. A Ponzi investment broker entices investors with a once-in-a-lifetime business venture. He takes the early investors' money and uses that to wine and dine other investors. Once he has new investors he takes a slice off the top for himself then uses the rest of the new money to pay dividends to the old investors, so they don't get suspicious and ask for their investment money back. The perpetrator pockets and spends most of the money. Nothing gets invested, and in the end, everything falls apart leaving the investors cheated out of their life savings."

"That's right." Agent Stevens cleared his throat before continuing. "As the cycle goes on, it gets more and more complicated. The crook err... felon has to continually appease everyone with regular returns, so he has to continuously keep adding new investors to pay all the previous rungs."

In Penelope mode, I absorbed every word he said and repeated to him, "So you're saying that my husband was working so hard because he had to keep convincing people to invest money that wasn't actually being invested?"

"I'm pretty sure that's what happened. Albania had various Ponzi schemes in '96 and '97. Two billion dollars was swindled from the public. A lot of people were caught and put in prison, but not all and not before riots broke out and several people were hurt and killed."

Now it was my turn to be obsessive-compulsive as I ran my fingers through my short hair, over and over, not liking what I was hearing. *Hurt and killed.* "So the FBI thinks my husband was involved in Ponzi schemes in Albania and brought those talents with him to the United States?"

Agent Stevens cleared his throat, rubbed his head then rubbed his chin using both hands and said, "We don't have a lot of proof yet. Just a few transactions that set off some detection algorithms we run on our computers. We think it is highly likely that his involvement in the global financial market and his ties to the Albanian mafia could have incubated into fraudulent investment schemes and global money laundering here in the states."

"Global laundering of money?" I asked in disbelief at this new revelation. I pictured a little world globe with stick arms and legs wadding money around the center post of a Maylag washer bowl. "You don't have any more proof than an algorithm? You just think he was laundering and stealing money because my husband was Albanian and lived there during their Ponzi outbreaks?"

"Countries with bank-secrecy laws like Albania make it

possible to anonymously deposit 'dirty' money there, have it 'washed' through non-existent investment schemes. Your husband handled a lot of money for global investment corporations. One of which was recently found to exist only on paper. The company name was being used to transfer money back to the U.S. under the guise of a return on an investment. Those investment fund returns were being used as 'clean' money by drug dealers who wanted no ties to the original source of their money."

Even after that explanation, I had a hard time believing that my little mentally fabricated globe needed to clean his money. "Doesn't money obtained illegally spend just as well as laundered money? Who would need to clean money before they use it?"

"Drug traffickers, embezzlers, corrupt public officials, mobsters, terrorists, con artists." Agent Stevens stopped rubbing his head long enough to tick off each of kind of crook on a bony finger. Then he threw up his hands and said, "All unscrupulous operations deal almost exclusively in cash to avoid records and receipts. Cash weighs a lot and takes up a lot of space—not very easy to hide from law enforcement officials, like Frank here." He pointed a drug-trafficking finger towards Frank for emphasis. "And it's not very safe to keep it lying around when you can't trust your clientele."

"Then why not secure it in a bank where it's safely locked up?" *Why was Frank's mouth turning up at the corners and the crinkles at the corners of his eyes starting?* I was not asking a naive question. Not everyone with a lot of money buried it in their backyard. The majority of my money, minus my ice cream and yarn stash, was kept safe in the bank. Or it was until it was cleaned out by Jorgji.

"U.S. banks have to report deposits over $10,000 to the authorities, like me, who then check up on how the money was made. To avoid detection, crooks hire money launderers who have to do a lot of bank-to-bank transfers into different accounts, in different names, in different countries to avoid detection."

"So laundering makes the money hard to trace back to the original owner, but it isn't 'clean.' It's still dirty money—only guys like *you* can't find the dirt," I stated. Frank didn't try to hide his smile as Agent Stevens frowned.

"Unfortunately, yes," Agent Stevens admitted. "But that's because people with a whole lot of illegally gained money can hire the best financial experts, like your late husband, to hide their dirty money, and the countries they use profit from allowing anonymous banking, so they don't cooperate with our request for banking records."

"Like the Cayman Islands?" Frank asked, his smile gone.

"Yeah. Also, the Bahamas, Hong Kong, Panama, Singapore." There went the finger ticking again. "Any of the major offshore financial centers will do," Mr. Stevens confirmed for Frank while I mentally kicked myself for being so stupid as to allow Jorgji to invest in property in the Cayman Islands. Mr. Stevens continued, "Once that money re-enters the mainstream economy in a legitimate-looking form, it has the appearance of a legal transaction. It's very difficult for us to detect dirty money once it hits this stage of the laundering process."

"Then how do you ever catch anyone?" I asked, angry that Jorgji was able to get away with so much for so long. Angry at myself for being so trusting. So stupid. I was so 'needy' that I accepted the first phony story told to me by the first phony guy who expressed a phony romantic interest in me.

"If we can get documentation in the early stages of the game before it's gone through too many transactions, we've got 'em. That's why felons keep two sets of books. A doctored-up set that makes everything look legit on paper or computer. They show that to the authorities and innocent bystanders." Mr. Stevens looked straight at me over the rim of his reading glasses but had the good sense to not say 'like you.' I didn't need to be reminded of my part in Jorgji's scams. "The other set, with the real information, is necessary for them to keep track of what is actually going on with the money, where they got it from and how much they got so they can get the money back to the original owner once it's clean—minus the launderer's profit, of course. It's a complicated process to launder money. Your husband couldn't have operated without having the real transaction information stored somewhere."

"Someone tried to force Genie to go with them at gun point to get files they thought she had. Her apartment was also ransacked. Could that mean Jorgji's records of who owns the money he was scrubbing is still out there somewhere?" Frank asked Agent Stevens.

Another quick head rub and his chair scooted closer to his already close desk. "Could be someone knows their name is in those missing records and wants to get to those files before someone finds their name and knows what they'd done. The crooks know that once we have the names of who in truth owns the money we could figure out what illegal activity they did to get that much money." Then he said to Frank, "Then guys like you could stop those illegal operators dead in their tracks and cart them off to jail."

"Right now I just want to find the real killer of Mr. Dalmat," said Frank.

"Do you know where Jorgji kept his files and records?" I was asked.

I shook my head no, chagrined that I knew so little about a man I had married.

Since Jorgji was so good at laundering things, I should have made his clean his own darn suits.

CHAPTER 18

Frank knew he shouldn't stare, but he couldn't help it. Imogene's hair was dyed back to its original rich golden brown color. The hacked strands had been shaped and cut so they feathered around her oval face. Her nose remained slightly swollen, but the white medical tape was gone, and the dark bruises had almost faded from around her right eye. Her tan suede suit was accented by a cream blouse with a string of pearls dipping slightly into the hollow of her neck. The tiny pearl earrings were so elegant. So her. She crossed her legs, and he caught a flash of thigh before she smoothed her skirt back down. From where he was sitting off to the side of the courtroom, he could see one of Imogene's dainty, brown open-toed shoes come into view, and he watched as that shoe did a nervous wiggle.

Sam was droning on and on. Frank knew from working with her before, she was letting the judge know that Imogene was a well-respected member of society whose integrity should not even be held in question. Imogene was sitting ram-rod straight staring ahead, sometimes looking down at a notebook on the table in front of her, only that little wiggle in her foot was betraying the extreme anxiety she was feeling. Frank could look at her all day and not get tired of it, but he forced himself to look away to try to clear his head before he was called to the stand to give testimony at her preliminary exam.

He hadn't been sleeping well. Most nights he lay awake thinking about Imogene's case or about Imogene. The least favorite part of his work as an FBI agent was when he has to sit in a courtroom, and this session was the worst because he was personally invested in the case. He rolled his shoulders to get them loosened up and moved his head from side to side to relax the cramp starting in his neck. He saw the brown suit he had bumped into at Merle's office wedged in among the gallery of spectators and wondered what the Deputy Mayor was doing there. *Why did anyone from the Mayor's office have an interest in the outcome of that court proceeding? They should have been more worried about why one of their police officers was moonlighting as a hit man.*

Frank looked around at the observers that had crowded into the very public courtroom and wondered how many of them, like the brown suit, were there for the sensational media story.

What the heck? He turned his head to the right again and did a quick double take at the woman sitting at the end of one of the isles. The nose, chin line, and forehead resembled Imogene's, but her nose wasn't swollen, and the shape of the eyes was a little different, less doe-like, more slanted. The clothes were definitely different. The low-cut ruffled edging of the purple blouse was showing a lot of cleavage. The short black skirt showed a lot of leg, and those mile-high high-heeled strappy red sandals weren't Imogene-ish at all. The hair was also longer and a shade lighter.

Frank whispered to Janey, who was sitting next to him, "Is it my imagination or does that woman look like Genie?" Then he asked himself, *'Or am I seeing Genie everywhere because I want to?'*

Janey, who saw a slight resemblance to Imogene, shrugged and said to Frank in a returned quiet whisper,

"Same build, similar facial features, but about 15 pounds heavier."

At recess, Frank noticed the 15–pounds-heavier woman might also be a little taller, but it was hard to tell her exact height in her ridiculously high high-heels. She kept hanging on to the arm of the man she was with. The man seemed a little put out by her constant attachment as he disengaged to walk to the drinking fountain, leaving her teetering in the courtroom doorway.

***

With the courtroom cleared, I could finally stand up and stretch, glad the inquisitive eyes were now in the hall and grateful the judge had offered us his conference room to hide in for a while. As we headed in that direction, I caught sight of a blond just outside the courtroom entry door, flailing her arms about, teetering and shouting "You hoo, Imooo, we're here."

Good Lord. Not her.

I nodded the tiniest bit of acknowledgment to my cousin, Mandy, before Samantha closed the judge's conference room door.

***

News reporters always disgusted Frank. They were admonished by the judge to leave Imogene and her attorney alone within the confines of the courtroom. When Imogene didn't leave the courtroom for the break, Frank thought the reporters would lose interest and move on to the next story, but that waving, noisy blond had gotten their attention and they seized upon the opportunity to enhance their murder trial story by crowding around this newly-discovered acquaintance—sharks drawn to fresh meat.

"Oh! Miss. Are you a friend of Mrs. Dalmat's?" one of the reporters asked the blond as all camera lenses turned towards her.

"Oh no," says the puffy-lipped, red, pouting mouth. "I'm her cousin, Mandy Parker. That's Mandy with a 'y' not an 'i.'"

Not to be outdone, the drinking-fountain man she was with scurried over to get in on the action. "I'm Martin Parker. I'm Imogene Dalmat's other cousin," the man said, puffing up to his full height as he squished himself into the inner circle of reporters. Mandy again latched on to Martin's arm as soon as he was within grabbing reach. Looking at her stiletto heels, Frank wasn't sure if her latch was from fondness for her brother or just to keep from falling off her perch.

Mandy brought the cameras back to focus on her by saying, "She came to live with us in Georgia after her parents both died tragically in a car accident in south'rn Asia. Her and I were soooo close as kids."

Martin quickly added, "WE were all close—until her mystery writer aunt got her moved in with her and tried to shut us outta Imogene's life."

Mandy interjected, so as not to minimize the importance of her relationship with the accused, "Miss Warren just wanted our cousin as a ready-made assistant for her growing writing career so she said a lot of lies about my parents so the court would give Imoo to her. My Imoo may have been force-ably moved away, but she didn't wanna leave me. I visited her often. She and I have always remained close—like sisters." The reporters started firing more questions at the pair, asking them what else they knew about the famous mystery writer, Miss Warren, and her relationship with Imogene.

"I don't know 'xactly what happened with the aunt to make her turn Imooogene against us. She see-quest-ured her up in her old creepy mansion and never let her out. But," Mandy added, holding up one cautioning hand for dramatic effect to silence the reporters' questions, "we are willing to forget the past. Imoo's famous mystery-writer

173

aunt has died under suspicious circumstances, and her husband has been horribly murdered. That leaves us, as her only living relatives, obliged to be here to support her in her hour of need—now that she's gone and killed her husband, too."

Frank quickly got out of earshot before his rage exploded.

***

I was trying to sit impassively as the prosecution called Karine Dalmat to the witness stand. Her dark, hunter green dress complimented her shining black hair and dark-mascara-ed, emerald eyes perfectly.

Cool and aloof, Karine runway-model walked her way to the witness stand as every male eye in the place followed her swaying hips. She didn't look at or even acknowledge me. No surprise, given how close she was to her brother, whom I was supposed to have killed. Jorgji had said he was raised in an orphanage. I didn't know he had a sister until she showed up unexpectedly one day: bold, stunningly beautiful and foreign.

My sister-in-law may have hated me, but that woman could make a mean sugar cookie.

CHAPTER 19

Her cookies may have been good, but there was nothing warm or sugary about Karine's testimony. She testified that when she stayed with us, I behaved suspiciously. I was always nervous. I acted paranoid. I spied on Jorgji all the time. She said I had mental problems, and she saw me go into the kitchen and search for sharp implements, even though I never cooked. Most of what she said was true, but the way she said it made me appear menacing and psychotic.

She ended her testimony with, "After aunt die of heart attack sudden, I fear Jorgji be next. After they move Detroit, he tell me his wife burn him with hot liquid. I beg him to leave for fear she do worse. Now he dead. Fears true."

Most of what she said was hearsay, but Judge Rombell allowed it for the preliminary proceedings, especially since my husband was deceased and couldn't testify for himself.

My wizened, shriveled-up neighbor, Mrs. Grugel, fidgeted and squirmed next in the witness seat. I felt sorry for her until she started to give her testimony; then I realized why it was only her and her dog that resided in her luxurious apartment.

"Mrs. Grugel, can you describe what you heard from

apartment 604 on the afternoon of September 4th?" asked the prosecutor, David Quinn.

"Well, of course, I can. My hearing is fine," Mrs. Grugel declared, and then leaned forward to peer at him through the thick lenses of her glasses and launched into, "It's my eyesight that's not so good 'cause I have these floaters that float around inside my eyeball. They are these tiny flecks that drift around inside my eye. It's from stuff that breaks loose from the back of my eye. Darned annoying—"

"Thank you, Mrs. Grugel," the prosecutor interrupted when he was able to finally get a word in. "We're happy to hear your hearing is fine."

"What's that you say?" asked Mrs. Grugel. Then she leaned way back in the witness seat and chuckled a hardy chuckle, "Just a little old-age humor."

"Please just stick to the question at hand," said the prosecutor. "Now, you say you were in the hall outside of apartment 604 on the afternoon of September 4th."

"Already told you that last week. Miffy and I were going for a walk." Then Mrs. Grugel turned to the judge and added, "Miffy has to have a set schedule. She has to go out every morning at 6 and 10, every afternoon at 2 and 5 and every evening at 7 and 10. Miffy's bladder is the size of a pea so—"

"Thank you, Mrs. Grugel," the prosecutor interrupted again. "If you could just describe what you heard from Apartment 604 on that occasion."

"It wasn't an occasion. It was an argument," said Mrs. Grugel, emphatically to the judge. She then turned back to the prosecutor.

"If you could just tell us, please, what you heard."

"Well, when I went out to walk Miffy at 2 o'clock I heard that man and woman having a terrible row in apartment 604. Miffy's name is Princess Queesha Moondust Natasha on her pedigree papers. I call her "Miffy" for short because she used to miff my husband so much when he was alive. She's a Lhasa Apso. I got her when she was —"

"Thank you, Mrs. Grugel," interrupted Judge Rombell. "Miffy is not on the witness stand, so we don't need to establish her credibility." Then he admonished Mrs. Grugel, "Please just answer the questions Mr. Quinn asks."

Mr. Quinn flinched a little when Mrs. Grugel 'harrumphed' loudly, but asked her anyway, "Where you able to hear anything that was being said in apartment 604?"

"Like I told you last week. I heard the man yell 'You can't have the money.' The rest of their shouting was totally unrecognizable." She waved her right hand in the air in a dismissive motion. "Nothing but gibberish. I couldn't understand a word they were saying, but I know yelling and fighting when I hear it, so after Miffy and I got back from our walk I called the police. We can't have tenants causing a ruckus like that in our building. I pay good money to live in a place that's kept free of riff-raff. That's why we have a doorman at the front door to monitor the comings and goings of visitors. That's why we've got a big lobby people can wait in while the guard checks out their credentials. That's why all the side doors are kept locked and can't be opened unless you have a key, like this one."

Judge Rombell gave Mr. Quinn a glare as Mrs. Grugel reached into the front of her dress and pulled out a long black cord that had a key dangling from it. Twirling the key, she continued, "Why, back in—"

"Mrs. Grugel!" said Judge Rombell loudly. The key twirling stopped. Then in a tolerant, kinder voice, he said, "I will only remind you one more time to stick to the question asked. I believe the subject of the question was what you heard last week—not your building's security or your doorman's occupational duties."

"Well, I'm trying to answer the question by explaining why I called the police." She pulled the front of her dress out, looked down it then dangled the key on the string back to where it came from. "If I lived in a different building without security and if I lived in a building without a doorman to keep out riff-raff I might have expected my neighbors to be having fights all time, but I don't live in a building without security, and I do have a doorman to keep out riff-raff, so I called the police."

Judge Rombell sighed. Mr. Quinn tugged at his buttoned-down shirt collar and said, "Thank you" and immediately launched into his next question before Mrs. Grugel had a chance to expound upon her previous soliloquy or pull any more objects out of her dress. "Did you recognize any of the voices you heard from the hallway?"

"Of course I did. One was that dark, good looking man that lived there. He was a real looker, that one." She looked like she wanted to expound upon Jorgji's appeal to her, but she looked at Judge Rombell, paused and said only, "The other was his stuck up wife. Her." Mrs. Grugel pointed her crooked arthritic, swollen-knuckled finger at me.

"Let the record show the witness is pointing to the defendant."

Charming.

Once the prosecutor was done with his questioning of Mrs. Grugel, my attorney, Samantha, started her cross-examination by asking Mrs. Grugel, "Did you talk to Mr. and Mrs. Dalmat much, Mrs. Grugel?"

"Well. He always said 'hello' to me whenever we met in the hall or the elevator. We only spoke at length just the one time. After that, he always seemed to be in a hurry and couldn't stop to talk. He had a lovely accent and he was a real hunk. Why, if I was 40 years younger—"

"Mrs. Grugel," Samantha's sharp tone brought Mrs. Grugel back to the line of questioning, "Did you ever speak to Mrs. Dalmat?"

"I told you. She's stuck up. She never speaks to anyone."

"If she never speaks to anyone then how is it you knew it was her voice you heard from the hallway?"

Mrs. Grugel got a puzzled look on her face. She opened her mouth to speak, but Samantha didn't give her a chance before she said, "Mrs. Grugel, you can't positively identify the other voice as Mrs. Dalmat's can you?"

Mrs. Grugel's mouth remained open, but she didn't have even a split second before Samantha continued, "You can't identify the other voice as being Mrs. Dalmat's because you've never heard her voice. Did you? Not today, not last week, not ever."

I think I didn't need that *Dale Carnage* program after all.

Then my attorney asked a flustered Mrs. Grugel, "If this was a heated argument, as you claim, Mrs. Grugel, and you're so concerned about riff-raff being in your apartment building, why did you wait so long to call the police?"

"Well," said an indigent Mrs. Grugel, "I already told everyone. Miffy has a small bladder. I had to take her out first. She shouldn't have to suffer because that woman and her husband didn't get along."

The huge Detroit police officer from my apartment fiasco was called to the stand next. He testified that he and his partner responded within minutes to Mrs. Grugel's call about a domestic dispute. They entered my apartment and found me with a knitting bag and a dying, stabbed husband stumbling down the hall.

The diaper bag was brought out and the officer identified it as being the one they'd found me with just before my husband stumbled out and collapsed.

The second officer, Tappy, wasn't called to the witness stand. I guess corroboration of the first officer's testimony by a possible for-hire killer wasn't needed.

I jumped a little when I heard, "The state calls Frances Jonathan Bachman to the stand."

***

"Mr. Bachman, do you know the defendant, Imogene Warren Dalmat?" the prosecutor asked.

Did he know her? Frank thought about everything he

knew about her and everything more he wanted to know, but simply said, "Yes."

"Would you please describe for the court the events that took place on the afternoon of September 4."

Frank knew that date very well even without the prior testimony. It was the only day he had ever held a fainting angel in his arms. It also happened to be the day that angel was found in her apartment with a dying, stabbed husband and two local cops as witnesses. Frank told his story in as undamaging a manner as possible, but Imogene's huge brown eyes staring at him split him open and bore into his soul every time he looked in her direction. Her eyes were wide and unflinching as she attentively listened to him recount what happened from his perspective. Those eyes, ever watchful, didn't seem to accuse or condemn him for telling the truth, but he condemned himself because he knew the truth could very well be sending her down a road to life in prison. He never hated his morals and principles more than at that moment.

CHAPTER 20

I had never seen a man look more handsome, even if the words coming out of his mouth were ensuring I was held over for murder. The suit was well cut, and the crisp white shirt contrasted nicely with his tan complexion. He was drop-dead gorgeous. I forgot about what he was saying and just listened to his soothing, masculine voice talking. *How could something so dripping with testosterone be my undoing?*

He was in a navy blue suit and a red tie that had thin blue and white stripes running diagonally to keep the red from being too bold, but it was still bold enough to make a statement. The whole package screamed 'I'm a federal law enforcement officer on the witness stand—so you have to believe me.'

That closely-shaven, chiseled face showed no emotion as he told the tale of my leaving a note saying I was returning to my apartment for money and how he found me there with two police officers and Jorgji dying from a knitting needle to his chest.

It was all very factual. Very clinical. Very accurate. The only part I would have added to his story was that my yarn was strung out all over a messy, dirt and blood covered apartment. It drove me crazy when my yarns were not neatly wound into balls and stored in all their little hiding spots by color and texture.

After Frank had identified the bag, already tagged by previous testimony as Exhibit A, as the one he saw me with, he left the stand. Once he was seated behind me, I was forced to stop staring at him, and my attention returned to my surroundings again.

I could see the diaper bag on the exhibit table. I knew it was mine because it had teddy bears printed all over it, and it had the little fluffy yarn fringe I tied to the zip pull on the side pocket. The prosecutor shook out the bag's contents, and the yarns, the zippy purse, my comb, my toothbrush, my clothes, a few pair of white underwear, the prenup papers and the lone needle settled across the table.

I was glad I had ditched the black lace panties at Frank's rented house. It would have been embarrassing to have everyone in the courtroom see them.

Thankfully, the prosecutor ignored the underwear on the table and picked up the long wooden needle. He held it up and told the judge, "This needle is made from Blackwood, a dense, lustrous wood that takes 60 years to grow into maturity. Mrs. Dalmat specially ordered this needle from Kenya with special, customized instructions. We have obtained the order form, your honor." Mr. Quinn picked up a piece of paper from a file and placed it before the judge before he continued. "Notice that the order requests extra sharp points on the needles and that it is requested to be made from Blackwood." Then to ensure the judge knew what a criminal I was, Mr. Quinn said, "Blackwood is an endangered species of wood in Kenya making this purchase an illegal transaction."

That was only the arraignment to determine if there was sufficient evidence for me to stand trial for the murder of my husband. Samantha explained to me that she didn't want me to take the witness stand. There was no need for me to explain to the judge that I knit very tightly when I'm nervous or scared, which was all the time and that a sharp point helped me get my needle in to start the stitches when they were too tight.

I was also not allowed to say that I was very aware of the plight of the Blackwood trees in Kenya. It was one of the reasons I bought from Mr. Kifimbo, who practiced sustainable harvesting and planting. But the judge didn't hear any of this. He only listened to the prosecutor make a big deal about the fact that just one needle was found in my bag.

The coroner identified the second knitting needle introduced in a plastic bag as the one that killed Jorgji by puncturing his aorta.

The fingerprint expert testified that no full prints were able to be lifted off the needle because of its small, circular size, but three or four of the partial prints matched my fingerprints.

No surprise there. I have to grip my needle pretty tight to get into the stitches to knit and purl. I knit so tightly I needed a needle sharp enough to kill my husband.

The prosecutor called someone else to the stand next to talk about the odds of a needle being able to be placed correctly to do the damage it did. Next was a needle expert or closet knitter or someone or other, who testified that the needle found in Jorgji matched the one in my bag.

I did not like being the focus of that murder-suspect business. I did not like sitting on display in the front of the courtroom where everyone could see me, but I couldn't see them unless I got up the nerve to turn around. Which I did not. I did not like that the only unobstructed view I had was of the stern judge, the Michigan state flag on one side of him, the United States flag on the other, his court stenographer at her little table, the evidence table, the prosecutor and his parade of witnesses.

I couldn't stand sitting there listening to a bank official confirm all the internet withdrawals I was supposed to have made from the joint bank accounts Jorgji and I held. He said my accounts have been drawn down to about one–fifth of their pre-Detroit amounts.

Since I couldn't testify, I didn't really need to see and hear all that. I didn't really need to hear the testimony being given next by the doctor who was describing how Jorgji was injured and the length of time it took for him to bleed to death.

I needed to get up. I needed to get out. I needed fresh air. I wanted to get up and run. Run from that room. Run from that judge. Run from those charges.

I felt the sweat beading up on my brow. I needed to get out of there.

I didn't want to hear any of that. I didn't want to hear the angle of entry the needle took. I didn't want to hear that Jorgji stumbled around and went into shock almost immediately and that he was alive but probably unconscious for several minutes before he rallied up and came out into the hall dying of blood loss.

In *Chiller Killer,* Penelope used transcendental meditation to focus her gaze on something calming so she could go into a hypnotic trance and survive the sub-zero cold of the freezer she'd been shoved into by the killer.

That courtroom was my freezer. I needed to survive.

Samantha wouldn't let me cram my pockets with yarn that morning because it seemed bulges in pockets didn't look good on defendants. Bulging pockets made the court guards a little nervous, too. She told me just to maintain my focus and do deep breathing to get through. She was sitting to the left of me. Too close for me to focus my attention on her face. Frank and Janey were behind me. I couldn't focus on them because I had to turn around to do that and too many people were behind me.

The judge's scowl was in front of me. Not particularly calming to see the prosecutor either.

My beautiful yarns, however, were spread out on the exhibit table at the front of the courtroom. It would have been nice if I could have picked them up and knitted away my cares. I decided to pretend knit. I would knit an Exhibit A scarf in my mind. Knitting always gave me my inner peace and calm, my own personal meditation.

While people talked to the judge, I mentally began casting on 42 stitches of navy blue yarn onto a size 5 needle. I worked in an off-set knit seven, purl seven pattern until I completed seven rows. I then attached forest fern green yarn and reversed the off-set for another seven rows.

I continued to 'mind' knit the scarf while people around me talked or listened to people talking. I mentally picked up the navy, sapphire and green yarn balls from the table, alternating them, being careful to not tangle them when I switched colors. Nothing worse than having to unravel a tangled mess.

The soft cashmere blend I had put in the teddy print bag on my first visit to the apartment would have been an excellent addition to the scarf I was knitting. I looked at the evidence table. That yarn wasn't there. I didn't recall that yarn being part of the riot of color that was strung out on my living room floor that fateful day. It must have rolled out of my bag and away when I clumsily dropped my bag to the floor.

It didn't matter. The judge had just declared that there was sufficient evidence to try me on murder charges. The cashmere and silk blend would have to stay missing. I doubted they would have let me have my knitting needles in prison—now that the judge thought they were lethal weapons. It didn't matter.

Nothing mattered.

Released to await trial, Frank was taking me to Winnetka to search my aunt's house for Jorgji's hidden second set of records. I was apprehensive—more than usual. I hadn't been back to the house that was my home since Jorgji moved me to Detroit. Gordon agreed to look after the house. Aside from Gordon's apartment and our bedroom suite, where Jorgji sometimes stayed while on business in Chicago, the house had been closed up. The cook and the maid were given severance pay and dismissed, unneeded.

Frank handled his Jaguar XK so smoothly that I slumbered most of the way to Chicago. I awoke to the cityscape enveloping us on all sides until all we could see were tall buildings looming above us and traffic all around us. Frank battled the traffic by gliding effortlessly around pokey drivers and even pokier construction workers. When orange and white barrels stalled the traffic to a dead stop, he turned the country music up a little louder and sang. I found my lungs, too, and sang "On the Road Again" right along with him.

I love Chicago.

The heels of my sling backs clicked loudly on the pavement with each step I took on the pathway to the house. I was overwhelmed with feelings of happiness and dread.

I had fond memories of growing up there. The tree swing Gordon hung for me in the back yard. The roses he planted outside the bay window where I read. The cookies and cold milk my aunt and I would have for an afternoon snack in the little alcove off the kitchen.

Those fond memories were commingling with memories of my aunt being rushed out on a gurney into a waiting ambulance. She went out through that very same front door I was standing at. Unlike me, she never returned.

My eyesight blurred and tears begin dripping down my cheeks. With my hand trembling, I rang the bell to summon Gordon. I probably had my key in my purse, but I preferred to have a friendly face welcome me home, rather than barge in cold.

Frank lightly touched my elbow and asked, "Are you

okay? I can do the search alone if you aren't up to it."

"It's okay. I want to do this. I want to help you find the real killer," I said as I sniffled, force myself to stop crying, straightened myself up to my full five feet two and one–quarter inches and pushed the doorbell again.

Gordon didn't answer right away. Unusual for him, but then the house had been empty, and his leg wound from his military service sometimes slowed him down. Maybe he was struggling down from the third floor?

Impatient, Frank stepped up to the door and pushed the button I had already pushed twice. That action put him closer to me. I felt his sleeve brush my right breast through the thin material of my blouse. Uncomfortable, I stepped to the side of the doorway to maintain a personal distance between us. A thunderous 'bang' ripped through the air. The door jamb, where I was just standing, splintered.

The door swung open. Frank shoved me hard. We fell into the house. I hit the floor. Frank fell on top of me. Gordon slammed the door shut and locked it.

"Welcome home, Miss Imogene," said Gordon, unflappable. His hand extended to Frank. Frank's weight lifted off me. "Your life appears to have gotten more exciting since you left," Gordon said to me as Frank disentangled himself from on top of me to stand upright. Frank was over to a side window in a flash and parting the curtains with his Smith and Wesson before I could even get my feet under me.

"So exciting it's getting hard for me to keep a hold on it," I responded to Gordon's comment, taking his proffered hand to stand up and smooth myself out of my rattled state.

"So I see," Gordon said, calm, quiet and buttle-cool, with his left eyebrow raised ever so slightly, imperceptible emotion to someone who didn't know him well.

To Frank, he said, "Sir. There was a vehicle noise behind the house, on the service drive. I went to investigate, but I found no one there. The shooter could have hidden in the small grove at the front of the house and then moved back to his vehicle to escape. You can get to the back door through the kitchen off in that direction." Gordon pointed to the side hallway and said to me, "With your permission, I will phone the police."

Frank headed towards the back of the house with his gun out. Gordon headed to the phone stand in the foyer, saying with an acknowledging nod of his head as he passed me, "I'm glad your home, Miss Imogene."

I smiled, in spite of myself and the circumstances.

The police arrived within five minutes, but, unfortunately, so did my cousin, Mandy. I didn't know which was worse, being missed by a bullet or hit with a Mandy.

"Oh, Imoo. I'm so sorry I was upset with you. I've been so worried about you ever since I heard about the attempted kidnapping," she said. "I'm so glad you decided to come home where you'll be safe." She put her cheek to mine and then put her pouty, puckered mouth to the side of my face in a fake kissing motion. Seeing the flashing lights on the top of the police cruisers she asked, "Why are the cops here? Have they come for you? What else have you done, besides murdering your husband?"

"I did not murder my husband, Mandy. Someone just took a shot at me. That's what the police are here for, and stop calling me 'Imoo.' My name is Imogene. It always has been." *There.* I did it. I told her not to call me that stupid cow name.

"Well," she said, a little putout, "I thought you liked it when I called you 'Imoo.' I think it sounds kinda cute." She would. She was in a silk, clingy pink dress and had on stark white ballet-like flats. Her long blond hair was swept back to one side and pinned with a pink hibiscus flower, the same color as her pouty lips. Good thing she could stand up without help in this outfit because I didn't see Martin anywhere.

Frank came back to the front of the house to work with the police officers on a second search of the grounds. "I think the shooter is gone," Frank told me.

A trickle of a smile started on Frank's face when I tell Mandy, "There is nothing cute about calling me Imooo, Man-Dee with a 'y' or should I say A Man DUH with a Duhhh. So stop it. And just why are you here? How did you know I'd be home?"

Gordon stepped up to Mandy, put an arm protectively around her shoulders and said, "Miss Mandy has come to the house inquiring after you every day since the attempted kidnapping incident at the laundromat." His tone was his everyday butler's voice, and there was nothing about his demeanor to give me a clue, but I swear from the lilt in his voice that man was tickled to convey this bit of news to me.

The shooter left nothing behind but a bullet casing and shoe print impressions in the dirt. Mandy arrived too late to be an actual witness to the shooting, but ever one to crave the action and attention she remained outside for the second sweep of the grounds, dogging Frank's heels every step of the way.

Her amateur sleuthing was obliterating the shooter's footprints and muddying her white shoes. Frank finally managed to shoo her inside to the parlor where I was huddled under a ripple afghan waiting for Frank to be done with the search of the grounds.

Mandy was exhausting me with all her rapid-fire questions about the whole affair. *No. I didn't see who it was. No. I'm not hurt. No. No one else was hurt. Yes. Frank and I will stay here a few days before heading back. Yes. I am still facing murder charges.*

Gordon served Mandy and me hot tea and warm sugar cookies. Mandy prattled on about my needing an armed bodyguard until I thought my head was going to explode. I didn't hear most of what she was saying. My mind stayed on the shooter. That was not a warning shot. The shooter had aimed for me specifically.

After the hundredth time of hearing how I needed to get a body guard, I couldn't take it anymore. I had a splitting headache. I left my headache inducer alone with our tea and cookies and went searching for headache-reducing painkillers.

When Martin rang the doorbell Gordon politely maneuvered Mandy to the front door. He thanked both of my cousins for calling on me and not so politely informed them that I needed to rest. I heard the lock snap into place.

Grateful for this respite from them, I did as Gordon stated and went to my room to rest.

I knew I should have been more gracious to my cousins because their mother and my mother were sisters. We were all motherless, me when my mother died in an auto accident on a mountain road, them when their mother succumbed to cancer earlier in the year.

My tolerance was always put to the test with Martin, but I was not dealing with Mandy any better. If only she weren't so irritating. In my heart, I knew I was rankled because I've always been jealous of her. She's three months older than me but always wore the clothing, vigor, and vitality of a teenager. I will admit I was jealous of her bold, sexy clothing, her feminine ways, and her long blond hair that men always went for and I couldn't stand the flirty way she talked to Frank.

It wasn't that I thought of Frank as anything more than a friend. I just thought he was too good for the likes of her, and I didn't want her to destroy the friendship with Frank that I had come to know.

CHAPTER 21

I was sneezing and sniffling prolifically while Gordon and Frank shuffled through papers in the small upper attic that sat above Gordon's third–floor suite. I was tired and wishing we didn't still have the basement to search. There was that and, of course, Gordon's rooms to search, but I didn't dare suggest invading his space. Staying off Gordon's floor was the unwritten rule that had been in existence since Gordon was first hired by my aunt. She agreed to keep his quarters sacrosanct in exchange for his loyal service. Even the maid wasn't allowed to clean in there. Given Gordon's neat habits, I doubted cleaning was even necessary.

Gordon, Frank, and I had already sifted through every room on all the main floors, even the bathrooms. Frank showed me some of the more common spots that criminals used to hide things. I couldn't believe that anyone would put something in the back of a toilet, or down a sink drain but Frank assured me they did. He even loosened all the switch plates and wall sockets in the house to look inside. In the library Jorgji used as his quasi-office, we pulled out every book on the shelves and came up empty-handed. There wasn't even a suspicious scrap of paper in one of the novels that lined the shelves. Nothing.

I was almost certain that Jorgji never came up to the attic, but we came up to that dust haven out of desperation to find something, anything to clear my name.

I paused from my sorting through a box of old clothing and looked around at the small, hot attic. It was mostly crowded with paper-stuffed boxes that I carried up there during every spring cleaning season. Aunt Tilly had a writer's aversion to throwing away writing of any kind. She felt that any written thought could be pulled back out and used to spark something and fire up her imagination for another book. When she was busy during the height of her writing career, her office would quickly develop dangerous levels of teetering paper stacks. Once a year I'd gather all her saved papers up, put them in cardboard boxes and truck them up there, safely out of the way, but within reach if she asked me for them.

As her typist and assistant, I abhorred handling all that printed material. It dried my hands out and cracked my fingertips. When anthrax scares forced publishers to request only electronic submissions, I was probably the only one in the book business who didn't mourn the passing of the mailed paper manuscript. I also didn't miss the cobwebs and spiders that lurked up there.

"What's this?" Frank asked, holding up an old metal file box he had pulled out of a hump-topped chest shoved under the eaves.

Gordon stumbled a little on one of the floorboards as he swiftly crossed the expanse of the attic to get to the file box Frank was trying to open. Gordon said smoothly, "That is a private correspondence file given to Miss Warren. I'm surprised she kept it. It's only letters from long ago from people long since passed on. It hasn't been opened in ages. There can't be anything recent in that box," Gordon casually took the box from Frank and sat it back into the chest and closed the lid. Case closed.

I was suddenly not so tired as I picked up on the

quickness of Gordon's dismissal of the box 'from long ago.' As my aunt's correspondence secretary I thought it would be appropriate for me to look at her correspondence. Gordon must have read my mind. I recognized that set look to Gordon's face from when I was a child. He was not going to discuss it. His mind was made up. Once Gordon decided on something, there was no changing his mind. It didn't matter how much you pleaded he wouldn't give in, not even if you begged 'pretty please with a sugar cookie on top.'

That's why I didn't bother him about that file box just then. I would just venture back to the attic after he had retired for the night, pry open the box and take a glance at what was inside. I looked longingly again at the chest shoved back under the dark, cobweb covered eves. I would have to be careful and not turn on a light until the attic door was closed because the light might alert Gordon that someone was up there. I would also have to make sure I avoided the spiders and bats that might be lurking in the rafters of the old house attic at night.

It was a creepy attic, so I planned on enlisting Frank's help to come back up with me later.

The sunlight shining through the tiny attic window had long since grown dim. The day had worn itself out, and I could no longer hold my eyes open. We were finally done with the attic when Gordon suggested we stop, get some rest and start out fresh for the basement search tomorrow morning. We trudged single file down the narrow stairs that left the confines of the attic. Frank and I paused at the third–floor door to Gordon's suite to bid him good-night. Gordon didn't look tired, but he did seem weary.

I may have looked tired, but I was not planning on sleeping. Not when there was a chest with a locked metal file box awaiting me in the upper attic. I did an exaggerated yawn and stretched my arms up over my head in a manner that would have made Jack McLane proud. After we had finished our good nights, Frank and I headed for our respective rooms on the second floor.

Once back in my room, I quickly brushed my teeth and brushed the cobwebs out of my hair. When I thought enough time had passed for Gordon to be settled in his third–floor sanctuary, I tiptoed down the hall from my room and very softly tapped on Frank's bedroom door.

Janey was right. Frank thrived on clandestine operations. He was wide awake and lept at my offer to sneak into the attic. We used the fire escape stairs at the back of the house so we could bypass Gordon's lower attic suite and get to the upper attic undetected.

Frank was pretty good at picking locks, but disappointingly everything in the file box was faded, and yellowed old. Nothing new, just like Gordon had said.

I stifled a sneeze and said quietly to Frank, "Sorry, looks like a lot of this stuff is from before I was even born. I doubt Jorgji even knew this attic was here. I've brought you up here for nothing."

"It was worth a try. Felons have been known to hide things in weirder places than this. With digital storage devices getting smaller and smaller, the hiding places get smaller and smaller, too. I've found files hidden in unlighted light sockets, false heels in boots, hollowed out door knobs, the seams of books, furnace filters..." He paused his recitations to brush a stray hair back from my face before softly continuing, "hair clips, lipsticks..." His mouth drew a little closer to mine, and I noticed he hadn't removed his hand from my face. I was cognizant of the fingers of his other hand weaving through my hair as he slid his hand to the back of my head. His palm cupped my head as if to keep it steady for his next actions. I closed my eyes and waited in breathless wonder at what his next action would be.

I could feel his soft breath on my face; I knew his lips were imminent. His palm urged my head forward as his breathing quickened. My grip on the letters in my hand faltered. They all fell from my grasp to the floor making a little 'flump' sound.

I felt a shift in the warmth around me. I opened my

eyes to see Frank turning his face away from mine. He stepped back a step and concluded his list with a rushed, "Any place small enough to hold a microchip."

His hand was absent from my hair. His voice was husky. My face felt chilled without his warm breath.

I stood there, like an idiot, wondering what I should do.

He knelt down to pick up the letters that had scattered themselves on the floor around me. Embarrassed at how long I had been just standing there and how far I had let things go between us, I returned to my senses and hurriedly knelt down to help. We lightly bumped heads. Off balance, in more ways than one, I plopped backward onto my derriere.

He laughed gently and said, as he took ahold of my arm to help me up, "For a Genie, you aren't good at this domestic stuff, are you?"

"If I could blink my eyes, set everything right and get what I wanted, I would," I said softly. I picked up a picture that had fallen out from a torn envelope.

I stared at the old black and white. All laughter gone. The Polaroid was of a man dressed only in trousers. A coiled snake tattoo was visible on the arm he had placed around the waist of a pretty blond in a sun dress. She looked to be my age. From the shape of the man's face, the nose, the eyes, the curve of his jaw line, the way he was standing I realized that was my dad when he was much younger. From the build of the blond and the way she was holding herself back tight against the front of the man with a huge smile and her arms folded over his protective embrace, I could tell theirs was no casual relationship.

Frank glanced at the picture after he finished doing all the picking up that I left for him to do while I stared blankly at the photo.

"Your parents?" he asked.

"No. It's my dad and my Aunt Selena."

CHAPTER 22

I was grumpily tromping around in the basement, flinging old chairs and lamps aside. I should have gotten more sleep, but I didn't because I stayed up all night reading that bunch of old love letters that my mother's sister wrote to my father. That, and being angry with myself over the effect Frank's near kiss had on me put me in an appalling mood that next morning.

Why didn't he kiss me? Did he have a girlfriend? Had she written him steamy love letters? Did he have a 'Selena' waiting for him? Did she ever write 'I can't wait to lie in your arms again and share this joy I have inside me with you? Hurry back to me my love?' Was there a 'Selena' waiting for him?

I was unspeakably atrocious to Frank, who seemed to be in just as bad a mood as I was, but he continued to work stalwartly, reaching up to search top shelves, pulling down stored, framed art to check their backs and pulling gunked up old bottles out of forgotten wine cellar racks, swearing almost non-stop.

"Must you do that?" I asked him after a particularly foul-mouthed episode during which he did battle with an old upright piano's interior.

"Do what?" he shouted, slamming the lid shut so hard that all the keys jangled a mismatched tune.

"Use that language," I shouted back.

There was one more round of vulgar expletives for his response. He remained in a foul mood, but the swearing stopped after that last defiant outburst.

Gordon remained Gordon. Unhurried. Un-irritated. Unfazed. Undeniably Gordon. Which irritated me even more than Frank's foul profanity.

I kicked a box of glass canning jars that sat against one wall to vent some of my anger and frustration. The old box split open at a weakly glued seam. One of the jars rolled out and broke when it reached the cement floor.

"Why keep a bunch of jars in the basement?" I asked as I bent to help Gordon clean the glass up. "Why hang on to a bunch of old jars anyway? Why keep old pianos, old lamps, and old furniture? Why keep a bunch of old love letters? What are we keeping all this old junk for anyway?" I was not expecting an answer, so I continued to admonish Gordon. "We should get rid of all this old stuff before someone gets hurt by it."

I was tired. I was cold. I was frustrated. I was crying. Just a tiny bit.

I cried more than a tiny bit when Frank tried to comfort me by putting his arms around me. I let him hold me to the warmth of him. I let him stroke my hair while I cried into his chest.

"It's all right, Genie," he said to me, mistaking my anguish for concern over my attempted-murder case. "We'll find those records. We'll find the real killer. I won't let you go to jail for a murder you didn't commit. I won't let anything bad happen to you."

Gordon looked at me knowingly and said to Frank, "Something bad has already happened to Miss Imogene. I fear she has read the letters stored in the attic."

I pulled away from Frank, wiped my tears on my sleeve

and asked Gordon, "How could he have done that to my mother?"

"Who's done what?" asked Frank.

I walked away from Frank. Men were not my friends just then. Not men like my father. "He cheated on her."

When I saw Frank had no comprehension of what I was saying, I said, annoyed that he was being so dense, "My father cheated on my mother with her sister."

Gordon blinked heavily before he said, "Miss Imogene, things are not always what they seem. Your father's liaison with Miss Selena was a long time ago before your parents were married. Before you were born. You must stay focused on the present. It does no good to dwell on something that happened so long ago. You must stay focused on your future and let the past remain in the past."

Our search of the entire house, basement to attic, had proven futile. Sitting in the kitchen, I looked across the empty cookie plate at the basement dirt and dust coating Frank's blue cotton work shirt. That warm, cotton shirt felt soft and comforting against my skin. He had rolled the sleeves past his elbows and had undone the top buttons far enough that a light dusting of chest hair showed. His brow was furrowed; the corners of his mouth were turned down. I subconsciously rubbed at the corner of my mouth with my fingers when I observed that he had a little bit of cookie mustache at the corner of his mouth. He saw me looking at him and quickly looked away.

I couldn't blame him for not holding my gaze. I must have looked like Frankenstein's bride. I didn't need a mirror to know that my short hair was standing straight up—cobwebs, dirt, and all. I had kept my sleeves down, cuffs buttoned for the search. No basement spiders were going to crawl up my sleeves.

After Frank's consoling embrace, I did get warm enough to undo a couple of my top buttons for a little air—

no chest hair showing though. My denim jeans were dirty at the knees from kneeling on the floor to peer under storage bins and pick up broken glass. I should have gone to tidy myself up, but I was too exhausted from our search of every fissure, gap, and fracture of that old 21–room house to worry a whole lot about what anybody thought of my looks.

***

It was killing Frank to see her like that. Imogene had worked right alongside him and Gordon for two days refusing to give up the search for files that would free her from murder charges. She had moved heavy boxes, stacked papers, stood on ladders to open cupboards she probably never knew she had in rooms she'd probably never been in. She also held it together when she read those torrid love letters her aunt wrote to her dad describing all the things they'd done and all the things they were going to do when they got together again. He could see the pain and confusion in her eyes when they'd discovered the contents of the box. The life drained out of her. She'd said nothing when they'd left the attic, but she looked so tired and defeated he wanted to take away the pain he knew she was feeling, if only for a little while.

He hadn't meant to try to kiss her. He didn't know why he came so close. It just happened without his being aware it was happening. He would have to be more careful in the future. He didn't want to do anything to hurt or take advantage of her emotional state. He couldn't do that to her.

She had discovered her husband wasn't the man she thought he was and lost him all at the same time. Then she was wrongfully accused of his murder. That would make anyone off-balanced for a while. She might even still be mourning his passing, though only God would know why anyone would be sorry to lose that jackass.

Frank wanted to get to know Imogene better, but he

knew it was best for him to keep his distance until she had time to heal. His 'if only for a little whiles' would have to wait a little while longer.

Sitting with her at her kitchen table, Frank fought down the urge to kiss away the little cookie crumbs next to her mouth. *Would she taste like a sugar cookie? Or something sweeter?* Her fingertips came up to her mouth. Worried that this Genie could read his thoughts, Frank looked quickly away from her delectable mouth and tried to focus on Gordon's activities instead.

Gordon, across the room at the counter, was pouring freshly squeezed lemon juice and sugar into a glass pitcher filled to the brim with ice. Gordon's only concession to working in the dust of the basement was to remove his coat and tie and undo the top button of his shirt. His clothing remained immaculate, creases were still in the pant legs, the shirt was still a crisp white, even the cuffs at his wrists were white with no signs of having been anywhere near the dirt of the basement. There were some tiny scars along his jawline and brow ridge, but otherwise, his neutral expression was smooth and unlined as he carried the pitcher to the table with only a slight limp of his right leg.

***

"We tried our best. Those bank investment records just aren't here," I said. "They are not in the Chicago office. They are not in the Detroit office. They were not in the apartment either."

Frank asked, "Was there any place else that Jorgji frequented? Any place or anyone we might have forgotten? Did he stay or work at any other places that you knew of?"

"Not that I know of," I responded. "He hated hotels. Said they reminded him of the orphanages in Albania. After we moved to Detroit, he sometimes came to Chicago for business. He said he stayed here at the house, but he was in Chicago so much I thought he was having an affair here. If he had a mistress then maybe she kept his records. Just like my father had my aunt kept his lover's letters."

"I can assure you, Miss Imogene, your father must have had no idea your aunt kept those letters. If he had known, he would have destroyed them. It is not good for a marriage to keep reminders of old lovers," Gordon said, favoring his right leg heavily as he crossed the room to refill my drained glass from the fresh pitcher of lemonade. I should have told him to sit down and rest his leg, but I knew he wouldn't.

I gave a little laugh and told Gordon, "Gordon, you've never been married. How could you know what's good for a marriage or not?"

Gordon turned abruptly from me to walk to the refrigerator. He didn't say anything for several seconds. He had paused for a long time in front of the open refrigerator door before he sat the lemonade pitcher on the top glass shelf. Then, he remained in front of the open door, not closing it. I didn't think he was looking for anything in particular. He was just standing, maybe thinking of the road not traveled. *Maybe he had a Selena when he was a younger man?*

I hoped I hadn't hurt his feelings. I told him, "I think you would have made a wonderful husband and father, Gordon—if you had chosen to be married."

The refrigerator door finally swung closed. He turned and said, "I don't regret being here with you and your aunt. I had other opportunities. I didn't take them. This was my choice." A smile touched his face for a brief moment before the butler expressionless expression returned.

Gordon reassured me, "When your husband stayed here he was always busy with work. Always on the computer. He only looked upon me as the hired help, so we didn't converse much, but he did seem to have genuine affection for you. I don't know what he did at the office, but he never entertained lady guests at the house. Of that, I can assure you."

I wasn't so sure but had no idea of who the other woman could have been so I let the matter drop. I twirled my bracelet around on my wrist, trying to think of where else we could look for the records. *Was there another woman that no one knew about?* He could have met her somewhere other than there at the house.

"What made you think your husband was having an affair?" Frank asked me while Gordon wiped down the kitchen counter with a clean white cloth.

"All the classic signs. He became distant. He stayed late at the office. He went on 'business' trips a lot. He stopped talking to me. He started staying in the study in Detroit long hours with his Dell so he could do his business and make all his calls in private. It took some doing for me to even get access to the files on his computer. He always kept it with him and had it password protected," I explained.

"You had access to his computer?" Frank and Gordon both said in stereo unison as their heads swiveled in my direction.

"Not for very long. I didn't even have enough time to get everything downloaded. I had access just long enough for him to change his clothes," I told them. Seeing their astonished looks at me, I added more quietly, "after I spilled hot coffee on him."

Gordon walked the distance across the kitchen to me. His gentle fingers picked up my hand and searched my wrist for the clasp on the bracelet. He unsnapped it, took it off my wrist, held it up to confirm it had a USB port, handed it to Frank and said to him, "Miss Imogene, as the typist for Miss Warren's novels, always found interesting ways and places to store her aunt's manuscripts so the identity of the killer would not be known before the book went to press. I should have known her old hiding habits would not be so easily broken."

"Hey, that's my bracelet. You know I always keep that with me," I said reaching for my bracelet.

"I should have known, too," Frank said looking at the

USB connection that was out of sight when the bracelet was shut, and then looking at me in wonderment. "You are so clever at hiding right under a person's nose that I should have known you would be smart enough to get Jorgji's electronic records and find an ingenious way to hide them."

CHAPTER 23

Frank and I got dinner in a quiet, quaint restaurant, which he insisted had Italian food good enough to be his mother's. That seemed to be the yardstick by which he judged all Italian restaurants.

He told me, "Deputy Mayor Rhodes's name was all over Jorgji's records. He's now the prime suspect in your husband's murder."

I was trying to concentrate on what Frank was saying, but my mind kept wandering. I hoped we weren't going Dutch because I couldn't pay for my meal. My assets remained frozen, and I still didn't have the money Jorgji took from me. I only agreed to go to dinner with Frank so I could spend some time with him. If he didn't pay, I would have to do the dishes. *Oh, well.* At least I had some experience with that.

"Agent Stevens says Jorgji's laptop was probably where he held the bank information for where the money is being kept. If the laptop was smashed to smithereens in the apartment then, I either got there just before or just after he did the smashing because Jorgji had a hammer in his hand when he answered the door."

I shuddered. Jorgji hadn't seemed the violent type. He

was more the kind to charm someone out of their socks rather than take anything from them by force. I regretted I didn't have enough time to get all the records from Jorgji's laptop downloaded the day I spilled coffee on him. The records I did download had provided the FBI with Jorgji's laundry list of names, dates, and amounts of money that he took in for cleaning; there was just no hint of where the money ended up at. Those records remained missing. If the laptop was the only source for those records, they might be lost forever.

I breathed easier once the prosecutor had agreed to drop the charges against me pending the outcome of the FBI investigation. They were delving into the Deputy Mayor's involvement with Jorgji and the two Detroit police officers the mayor had fingered as his accomplices.

I smiled at Frank, who animatedly continued with his story. He appeared pleased that I was off the hook.

"When the deputy mayor was pulled into FBI headquarters and questioned he broke into a sweat, then he broke into a song and a dance, and then he just broke down. Seems his city paycheck wasn't enough to support his crack cocaine habits; he had worked out a deal with a few crooked narcotics officers. They held back some of the drugs from every bust. The drugs he got from them either got lost, or they stayed off the record books because they never got properly logged in as evidence."

Frank tore off a big chunk of garlic bread and chewed it a couple of times before he swallowed and continued. "The deputy mayor served as the inside man and tipped the dirty officers off whenever he learned there was an investigation pending." He took a quick gulp of foamy beer. "That was the investigation that you, as Penelope, helped me with."

I smiled, remembering. He smiled back before resuming. "The drug money they made from the sale of the stolen booty was given to Jorgji to be cleaned. He returned a large percentage of their ill-gotten gains back to them as 'investment' money and kept the rest as payment for his services."

This was where Frank's and my story intertwined. I smiled again.

"It was a smooth deal for everyone involved until Officer Miller got sick with cancer and was forced to take a medical retirement. The deputy mayor then had to scope out more officers willing to pocket some of the drug money in exchange for keeping silent. Some of the guys he approached weren't so willing to stay quiet. The mayor and chief of police decided to get the FBI involved when they got a hint of what was going on," said Frank.

"And that's where you and I came together," I said, remembering that night I had spent in his undercover car, his undercover house and how I'd wanted to be under his covers.

"Yeah, I never expected to run into Penelope Pembrook, or rather, Matilda Warren's niece, when I accepted that Detroit special undercover assignment, but I'm glad I did."

He didn't do anything more than look into my eyes, but I was so unnerved by that ripe-with-meaning look that a string of spaghetti slipped off my fork and down to the napkin in my lap. I was glad it missed the blouse. I had no idea what color soap was needed to clean a marina sauce stain off a white blouse.

"Didn't the deputy mayor know you were doing a sting?" I asked, folding the napkin so the wayward sauced string was trapped inside it.

"Not at first. But, when he caught wind of our probe he tried to get as much information as he could. He used his position in the mayor's office to force his way into meetings with Merle. The deputy mayor tried to learn every facet of our investigation so he could keep control of his drug business. Fortunately, the FBI doesn't share much information with outsiders until an investigation is over. That meant the deputy mayor was forced to slow up the drug thievery because he had no idea who was doing the investigating or where they were at in the investigation."

"Thank heavens your agency is clandestine," I said, knowing that Frank had been in terrible danger the whole time he was on assignment. One whiff of his FBI identity could have ended the investigation in tragedy.

"With the drug business effectively stopped, the mayor needed another source for money. He dipped into the city coffers to continue feeding his habit. Then, when Rhodes heard that the Secret Service requested an early audit of the city books to clear the president's visit, he panicked and grabbed a huge chunk of the city's money."

I twirled my pasta and marina sauce onto my fork and tried to get it into my mouth deftly and not on the blouse I'd borrowed from Janey. "How was taking even more money going to help him with the audit?" I asked. Pausing before stuffing the fork into my mouth, I added, "Wouldn't that only make it more obvious he was embezzling if more money was gone?"

"According to Rhodes, Jorgji said he could double his money. Rhodes figured that when the investment paid big, the skimmed funds could be returned to the city before the next routine audit. He could pay someone to alter the books to look like it was never gone and no one would be the wiser."

"Hadn't he ever heard: 'It takes one to know one'?" Guess I'm not the only one who fell for Jorgji's get rich quick Ponzi schemes," I said, but then quickly dropped the matter. The deputy mayor only fell for the scheme. I married the swindler. I had no room to talk.

"Rhodes hadn't counted on the audit being moved up. We, at the FBI, suspected that the police force had been compromised, but we didn't know who was involved. A compromised police force would put the president's November visit in danger from someone willing to do anything for a payoff. We were right, but no one expected the problem to go as high as the mayor's office."

"So that's how Jorgji ended up dead? The deputy

mayor was worried he'd be found out during the audit and was trying to get the investment money he'd been promised?"

"According to Rhodes, when he went to Jorgji demanding the money, Jorgji said the money was spread out in accounts all over the world, and it wouldn't be so easy to get it back; it would take some time to pull it all in. Rhodes told Jorgji he'd better find the money fast or something Jorgji valued a lot just might come up 'missing' until that money was returned."

I choked on a chunk of bread that got clogged in my throat and wouldn't swallow down. *Had I been the something intended to come up missing?*

"Are you all right?" Frank asked as he lifted my left arm over my head. I managed to stop coughing after a few seconds and thankfully completed my swallow, feeling that lump of bread the entire way down. I didn't want the next time Frank's arms are around me to be a Heimlich maneuver.

"Rhodes claims you weren't part of his plan," Frank continued after I drank some water to get my throat fully cleared. "He says he had no intentions of following through on the something-coming-up-missing threat. He was just going to have someone rough Jorgji up. Maybe cut off a finger or something. He only sent Miller and his buddy in to intimidate Jorgji into giving him his money back and to get the records that had his name on them. He swears he didn't know they killed him when they went to your apartment."

The meal and company were excellent, but as I looked at the little padded folder that had the bill inside, I was trying to figure out if I needed to pay for my share of the meal by digging out the loose bus fare change in the bottom of my diaper bag.

It was bad enough that I had no money and no courage, but I was also left wondering if Frank paid for my meal because he wanted that to be a date or because he knew I didn't have any money. *Was that lovely dinner a business dinner so he could close the investigation? Or a date?* I knew which it was for me, but after paying the bill, Frank was called away to a debriefing meeting in Merle Hartford's office, so I didn't get a chance to find out which type of dinner Frank intended it to be.

CHAPTER 24

Janey had to deflate her own air mattress after I made several failed attempts. I was sad to be leaving that small room with its adorable baby bed, dresser, and changing table, but I couldn't stay there forever, and I didn't want to stay at my apartment. I asked Keiko to start packing up my things there. Gordon was working on having the apartment sublet so I could move back to Illinois permanently. Not that it hadn't been fun in Detroit. It hadn't. But my lack of fun had nothing to do with the city and more to do with the blood stains that Keiko couldn't seem to remove from the apartment's tan carpet.

I pulled my Bentley into my Shelby Tower's underground parking spot and pulled out my English to Japanese dictionary so I could find the words to tell Keiko I wouldn't need her services after she finished up with the packing. Then a brilliant idea smacked me silly. I hurried to the elevators, in a rush to talk to Keiko about my plan to have her move back to Winnetka with me—as a full-time replacement for the household staff that had left.

Keiko could teach me Japanese, and I could teach her English. I also needed to tell her that she needed to pack

Jorgji's things separately because I had promised Karine she could have them.

Janey left that morning for Virginia to meet her husband's Navy ship. Frank was meeting with the U.S. Attorney's office regarding the deputy mayor's indictment. Gordon had promised he'd get the house ready for my return, complete with sugar cookies. Mandy had called me every day since the shooting incident, but I didn't bother to answer the phone. I hadn't seen her since Gordon rushed her and Martin off just after the shooting incident at my home. I wasn't going to call her; I needed time to adjust to what her mother did to my mother.

I left a voice mail message for Frank to let him know my apartment was no longer considered a crime scene, so I was packing up and returning home. I hoped he would call me back. I wanted to say goodbye in person before I left Detroit.

After angling my Bentley into my assigned parking spot, I cautiously opened the door. I hesitated to place my left foot on the cement of the underground parking floor, but only for a fraction of a second. I felt a little silly to be so nervous about coming back there. The dead body had been removed. The bad guys had all been incarcerated. I had nothing to fear, or so I thought.

I put both feet down on the hard concrete and stood up. The Bentley door slamming echoed in the underground parking, giving me a hollow feeling inside. The bulb in the socket nearest my parking spot was burned out again, but the lights by the elevator still worked.

I headed towards the light. I was not going to let my fears grip me. It was silly for me to be afraid. I had no reason to be afraid. My would-be killers had been arrested.

I knew it was silly to be fearful of a place just because someone once was killed there, or that someone tried to kill you there so I kept picking up one foot after another and putting them down in the direction of the light telling myself that I could do this apartment thing.

I didn't need help from anyone. Not Frank. Not Janey. Not Penelope. They weren't there anyway. Keiko was. Yes. Keiko was there. I wouldn't be alone in the apartment. Everything would be fine. I would be fine.

There was dead silence as I traversed the parking structure to the elevator. There was no hollow heel clicking echo as I walked; I had worn my Reeboks even though I didn't expect to have to run from anyone. Not anymore.

I waited nervously for the elevator doors to open. The longer I waited the nervous-er I got. I could have taken the stairs. But I didn't. Hired killers use stairwells.

I was running out of patience and nerve, so I turned away to go back to my car just as the elevator doors glided open.

Mrs. Grugel was tugging on a reluctant Miffy's leash. Both were wearing matching sweaters. Miffy's little plaid sweater had the word 'doggie' stitched to the side of it. Mrs. Grugel's didn't need a sign.

When Mrs. Grugel saw me, she grabbed Miffy up in her arms, protectively removing her from within my reach. I smiled sweetly and said, "Hello, Mrs. Grugel and hello little sweet pee." Miffy gave me a yappy bark when I reached to try to pet her. I wondered if dogs could detect sarcasm.

"How did you get down here so fast?" Mrs. Grugel asked me. She swept a wide berth around me as she stepped off the elevator and said to Miffy, "Come along, Miffy. We don't want a repeat of last time when that nice man was killed." Mrs. Grugel moved the fastest I had ever seen her go heading for her white Caddy.

I yelled at her, "It wasn't me last time, Mrs. Grugel. The prosecutor dropped the charges." But she was out of earshot and already closing her car door. I passed through the open doors and said to the empty elevator in a high, crackly, Wizard-of-Oz witchy voice, "I'll get you my pretty, and your little dog, too."

Let her think what she wanted. It didn't matter. I was free. I didn't have to see her again if I didn't want to. And I didn't want to.

The elevator went directly to the sixth floor. I stood outside the door of apartment 604 debating. *Should I ring the bell and have Keiko answer? Or should I screw up my courage and let myself in?* I pulled my key out and opened the door. A tear streaked Mandy rushed to greet me.

"Hello, Mandy. How did you get in here? Why are you so upset? Did you break a fingernail?" I asked, always suspicious of her tears. They were usually a mask for something else to come.

"Your housekeeper was nice enough to let me in to wait for you. I had to see you. I had to warn you. You need to get out of here. It's not safe."

"You don't need to worry, Mandy. I am leaving. I've only come back to see to the packing and have a word with Keiko."

"I don't mean move out. I mean leave. Now!" Mandy sobbed. "Before Martin gets here. He isn't bad. He gets like this when he drinks a little. I can't reason with him when he's like this. He isn't a bad person," she repeated again. "He just wants me to get my money."

"Martin? Why would he come here? And what money? What are you talking about?" I tried not to let my brain whirl to conclusions too fast. Martin would sooner eat rocks than be near me, which explained why he had to be drunk to show up at my apartment.

"My inherit-tince. I found out about ever'thing when Momma died. She told me on her deathbed, but made me swear to n'ver tell. I went to see your aunt Matilda. She tol' me it was all true. She'd been paying my momma money to keep quiet. Matilda said it was import'nt that I keep the secret, too. For all our sakes. She promised me I would be in her will if I kept quiet about ever-thing. Before I told Martin, I made him swear he wouldn't nev'r tell nobody so's you wouldn't get hurt. I didn't know that you already knew about me being your sister. Martin was mad that you had her change her will. I admit I was a little upset at you, too, but I never wanted you hurt for it. That's why I went to get him at your house after he left with the gun. Only I was too late. Luck'ly, he missed you. Now he's drinking again. That's why you've gotta get outta here before he shows up. He won't miss ag'in."

I listened, but I didn't understand. When I didn't move to leave, Mandy pushed my shoulders to spin me around. She shoved the center of my back, urging me towards the door.

"Inheritance? Who did you go see about an inheritance?" I didn't want to figure out what Mandy was saying. In the recesses of my mind, I think I had already begun to figure it out.

There was a violent pounding on the apartment door. Keiko didn't understand a word of Mandy's accented English screaming to not open the door, so she opened the door. Keiko must have thought Mandy was shouting *"Hurry. Let him in"* rather than *"Don't let him in."*

Martin stormed inside. He looked at me, eyes glaring with pure hatred. Then he looked at Mandy. She was wringing her hands and pleading, "No, Martin. Don't do this."

He said to her, "Mandy, you stay outta this. This is between me and Imogene." He looked back at me. The pupils in his eyes were dilated and seemed to strobe. Sweat had plastered his hair down to his head. He reeked of alcohol and sweat. His hands were balled into tight fists at his sides. All that was lacking was for me to be wearing red and him to lower his chin before he bull-charged at me.

Huffing he said, "When you changed that will you cheated my sister outta everything that should have been hers. I'm going to see she gets it one way or another."

Mandy rushed to my side. I was concerned because she was wearing red. I pushed her behind me. She leaned out from behind me to yell at Martin, "Killing her and your goin' to jail ain't gonna make sure I get the money."

"I've kept you out of it. You won't be charged with

anything, so they'll have to give it to you. You being next of kin and all," said Martin.

Mandy pushed her way out from behind me and stood between Martin and me. "Please don't hurt her. I don't care about the money anymore. Our daddy's dead. I don't want to lose my sister, too."

Martin wasn't listening, but I was. I knew Martin and Mandy's father was very much alive. It was my father that was dead. She had said our daddy's dead, and she didn't want to lose her sister, too.

I realized at that moment that Mandy was my sister. My half-sister. I was ashamed of my stomach retching at the thought. I was about to puke up all the bile that had risen into my throat.

Well, I might have done that, if not for Martin's fists around my neck keeping it from happening. He squeezed. The squeeze tightened.

Keiko screamed, "tasukete," over and over.

Mandy just screamed. I felt her nails digging into my skin as she worked to pry Martin's hands off my neck, but she couldn't stop him from squeezing tighter.

My vision was fading to black. I couldn't swallow. I was incapable of rational thought. I could only draw a sliver of air through the choke hold he had on me, like trying to drink tea through those little red coffee stir sticks. I was receiving just enough air to keep my heart thrashing in my rib cage, but not enough to feed my oxygen-deprived brain.

The air stopped moving in or out of my lungs when he tightened his grip even more. I was powerless to stop him.

I was being murdered.

The tightness mercifully released. I drew in harsh fire with one enormous hungry intake of breath. My hands instinctively came up to protect my bruised and scratched neck as I felt my brain fire back to life.

Fists were thudding. A broom was whopping. The air was punctuated with Japanese shrieking. I staggered to the couch, choking. Falling to the soft surface, I watched the ensuing ruckus.

Frank and Martin were fist fighting. Heavily engaged from what I could see. Keiko, broom in hand, was hitting Frank with the working end of the broom almost as many times as she connected with Martin. Finally, Keiko won out with a resounding broom blow to Martin's head, and he dropped to the floor with a thud.

Frank was close behind, on his knees, bent over Martin, breathing heavily, pounding Martin's bloody face. A valiant Keiko stood poised next to Frank, her bat-broom at the ready.

Mandy was torn between Martin and me. She stepped towards me, then faltered, turned, stepped towards Martin. Faltered again. Looked back at me, and then rushed away from me. She tried to seize Frank's fists to keep him from pounding the already unconscious Martin through the floor.

Frank was so intent on his actions that when Mandy got in his way, he swung back and aimed a fist at her. The fist stopped just short of connecting. Frank's eyes widened. He seemed to just become aware of the fact that it was Mandy he was going to hit. He looked down at Martin's bloody face and realized the fight was over as he leaned over to assure himself that Martin was still breathing, just unconscious. Satisfied, Frank rushed to my side.

"You sure have a lot of excitement in this apartment," he said softly to me as he knelt in front of me and gently pulled my hands away to check the damage to my neck. "Are you okay?"

I just nodded, unable to speak or even squeak. He turned to Keiko and said something in Japanese. She rushed off to do his bidding.

He knew Japanese?

Mandy sat in a plastic chair next to my emergency room gurney. We were awaiting the results of the neck scan done to assess the damage. She wasn't talking much, and I didn't know what to say. We had both lost so much in the fight for my life. She lost her brother to a jail cell. Long before that she lost her father to me. We have both lost years of sisterhood we should have had. I opened my mouth, drew in a big gulp of air and started to say something, but when my throat burned like fire, I hesitated and grabbed my neck.

"Don't," she said. "Don't even try to talk. You need to heal." She sat down heavily in the scoop chair the emergency staff placed beside my gurney when she had refused to leave my side. "I'm so sorry for all this." She continued, "I nev'r wanted you hurt. I had no idea Martin hir'd those goons to kill you until he got drunk one night and started to tell me how if you was dead I'd be the one to get Matilda's money. He was so mad those goons screwed up and gave him his money back. They said they didn't wan'a have anything to do with it anymore. He told me he was gonna do you in his-self. I was so reliev'd when he missed you at your house. I hid his gun, but I knew that wouldn't stop him. He had to rethink his plan when he saw you was always with that butler or your fella. Then he found out you were coming back to your apartment in Detroit, alone. I kept trying to call you to warn you not to go, but I couldn't get through."

It was a blessing that I was not expected to talk. I was ashamed of the way I had avoided Mandy's attempts to get in touch with me.

She said, "I tried to get you outta there before he show'd up. He nev'r would have done any of this if you hadn't changed the will. He was just so mad I'd been cheated outta ev'r'thing. But I'm not mad. Not anymore. I'm jus' glad you're okay."

I couldn't talk, or I would have told her I couldn't have changed something I knew nothing about. I didn't know what was in the will or why it was changed. I couldn't talk so I couldn't tell her I didn't know she was my half-sister until her half-brother choked half the life out of me.

***

Frank stuck around the emergency room long enough to be assured there was no permanent damage to Imogene's neck. When the doctor came out to give him the report, Frank thanked him, but he didn't ask to see her. He didn't want to see her. It was enough to know that she was all right. He had issues when it came to her. He almost beat a man to death. Good agents couldn't afford to lose control like that. Now that her case was closed he needed to back away. Good agents couldn't afford to fall in love. He couldn't afford to fall in love.

He swung his Jag into the underground parking at the McNamara building. He was going in to purge the files he had accumulated in Imogene's missing person case now that it was closed. Imogene was safe. She was going back to Illinois. He needed to get everything about her out of his life. He needed to move on. Brown eyes and smooth legs be damned.

He took the time to empty all his pockets and set his gun down on the conveyor to clear through security. No need for shortcuts. He was in no hurry.

Joe, the metal scanner guard, gave Frank a nod and a clap on the back and said as he gave Frank his possessions back, "Heard about you saving that writer's niece. Great Job."

Everyone congratulated Frank as he walked past them on his way to his office. Word of Frank's saving Imogene's life got around quickly. Everyone had heard it. What everyone didn't know was Frank was not feeling deserving of their praise because everyone hadn't heard that Frank came close to killing Martin Parker. That death would have been on Frank's conscience if Mandy hadn't intervened.

Johnny stopped Frank in the hall and asked to hear the details. Frank scowled, ignoring Johnny. Frank, in a hurry to get into his office, brushed past his buddy and closed the office door. Frank wasn't ready to talk about what had happened.

He grabbed the box that he had shoved in all the documents Marion gave him on Imogene's case. Flinging the lid over in a corner he hefted the records box over to the small shredder he was given when he first hired on. He could have just taken the documents back to Marion to shred in an industrial sized shredder, but he wanted to manually shred everything himself. It was better that way. It would be liberating to pick up the papers and feed them in and see them come out cross cut and unrecognizable. Just like his feelings. It was all for the best. He couldn't stay involved with her. Good agents didn't get involved.

He opened the first folder, picked out the first few pages and watched as those papers went through the shredder.

He was mindlessly feeding the papers in when the shredder jammed. *Damn.* The small office shredder he was allotted wasn't very efficient. It only took a few sheets at a time. He had fed too many papers through it at once. Frank hit the reverse button, and the wad of papers backed up out of the machine.

What he saw in its half shredded state reeled him right back into Imogene's case.

CHAPTER 25

I was too spooked to drive back to the Shelby Towers by myself, so I had accepted Gordon's offer to drop me off before he went to meet with a broker about subletting my apartment. I was anxious to be moved out. Most of my possessions had already been packed. Keiko was there working on the remainder. I had asked Karine to meet me at the apartment, so I could give her Jorgji's personal effects and tell her that I intended to see that the money Jorgji took was returned to his investors—just as soon as that money was found. It was a small consolation for the loss of her brother, but I hoped it would help give her some peace that his name would be cleared.

Gordon was concerned that I would not be able to handle the bad memories I would be facing at my apartment. He wanted to park underground and ride up the elevator to the apartment with me. I had already thought about how best to handle my return to the scene of the crime, so I had gotten Gordon to stop at the Icy Stone Creamery on our way there.

The French Toast ice cream was a cool solution to my sore throat, but it was also why Gordon was going to be late for his meeting with the broker. The unpredictability of the elevator would further delay Gordon's meeting, so I told him, "Just pull up and let me out at the front door of the Towers. Keiko is already at the apartment and Karine is meeting me there. I'll be fine. Plus, I have my French Toast ice cream to make this bearable." I held up the little dish to show him.

"If you need me, Miss Imogene, or want to leave earlier, just ring. I'll keep my phone on," Gordon said to me as he was opening my door and helping me and my scoop of ice cream out of the Rolls.

A light rain was starting, but luckily it only took a few steps to get to George, who was holding the glass doors open for me. I was fully aware that would be the last time George would smile at me and say, "Good evening. How are you feeling, Mrs. Dalmat?" I was going to miss George.

I wouldn't miss waiting for that old elevator. I waited, eating the melting French Toast ice cream from the cup that Susie had scooped it into for the last time. The elevator was taking its sweet time getting to the first floor, but I didn't mind. It was the last time I would have to wait for any fussy doggy stops.

Just like last time, both Mrs. Grugel and Miffy had dressed alike: wearing yellow rain slickers. Miffy's little coat looked better on her than Mrs. Grugel's did on her. Miffy goose-stepped off the elevator in her little yellow doggie rain boots. Mrs. Grugel accelerated her little yellow boots upon seeing me. She refused to look at me. They headed for the door that George was holding open for them.

I tried to yell after her, "It wasn't me last time, Mrs. Grugel. That was my sister you saw." But my throat was still in recovery, she was out of earshot, and George was already closing the front door.

I gave up on Mrs. Grugel and her doggie-walking; it was the last time I would have to be snubbed by her. I was just there to help Keiko and give Karine Jorgji's things.

I got a sense of déjà vu when I stepped into the apartment. Things were out of their packing boxes and scattered everywhere again. *Hadn't Keiko already packed everything?*

There was a muffled sound coming from the kitchen. Flashbacks of Jorgji stumbling down the hall, moaning in pain, filled me with a sense of dread. Goosebumps jumped up and down my arms. I didn't want to, but just like in the movies I had to go check out that noise.

Keiko was tied to one of the wooden kitchen chairs. She had a dish rag gag tied around her mouth. *Poor Keiko.* I knew burglars must have tied her up when she caught them in the act going through the packed boxes for valuables.

I loosened the gag and pulled it down. Even without a gag blocking her speech I couldn't understand what she was trying to tell me. I should have tried harder to finish that on-line Japanese program or at least had her learn English. Where was the FBI when you needed them?

"Missy Imagreen, dareka kokoni iru," she kept repeating over and over in Japanese. I got behind her to loosen the ties on her hands, but I stopped as I sensed someone had arrived in the room. I stood up, slowly looking beyond Keiko, afraid of what I would find.

It was only Karine. I blew out the air I had been holding. She must have arrived just before me and gotten a short bladed knife from the kitchen to cut Keiko out of her bonds.

"Oh, Karine. You scared me," I said relieved it was only her. "There has been a burglary. But you must already know that because you've found a knife to cut these ropes."

Keiko was going wild straining at her bonds. Her chair started to sway as she scuffed her feet on the floor trying to scoot away from Karine, away from the knife.

Of course, she was afraid of the knife, I thought. She had just been tied up by burglars. She had never met Karine, so she didn't know Karine was only trying to help. I was sure Keiko would be more trusting if I had the knife so I said to Karine, "She's scared because she doesn't know you. Why don't you give me the knife? I'll cut her loose while you go ask the doorman to summon the police." I reached for the knife that Karine was gripping in her hand.

Pain sliced through my palm and wrist. I pulled back in horror, oozing red. My blood immediately started spurting and dripping onto the floor. I looked down at the open gash, then at the floor. Another stain that wouldn't come out.

"Where you have put them?" Karine asked me.

I was so confused. The sight of the blood running from my throbbing hand and wrist was making me sick. I had no idea what she was referring to. "Put what?" I asked.

"Account numbers. I go to all accounts to get my share money. Everything moved. I break you safe and take all. It have papers and jewelry. No money. No bank papers. I come back. I search everywhere. Jorgji come. We fight. He say bank information hidden with you. He say he no want me. He want you. You only person he care for."

My face must have been registering incomprehension, or she just knew me to be dense from previous dealings. "You think I not know what you did to my Jorgji?" she asked me.

Martin had nothing over on her. She was blazing so hot you could fry an egg with just the look she was giving me. "I didn't do anything to him. I loved your brother," I responded.

Before I could say more Karine laughed a shrill, short laugh that pierced through my heart. Then she said, "No. He not my brother. He mine. He marry you only for money for us. He to get lots of money. You mess plan up. You make him love you."

"He never loved me. I thought he hired those men who came to kill me, but one of those men ended up killing him."

"Men not kill Jorgji. You make me kill Jorgji. You reason we fight, he try to kill me. You reason I stab him with shivia—with stick. I kill him because of you..." she pointed the knife in my direction. I could see my blood clinging to the blade, but I forced myself to stay upright.

Keiko was still tied. Keiko needed me. I couldn't faint.

"No. It was that policemen who killed him," I said.

"You," Karine said with renewed contempt and scorn. "You. You spoil everything. He not kill you like plan. He say he need more time. Always more time. I tell him I kill you if he not do killing. He say he kill your aunt. You get her money. He give that money to me so he not have to kill you. I read old lady will. You not get all money. Only half. Jorgji change will so you get all. He pay cook to lie about will. Then he kill old lady to buy me off."

I didn't know which was making me feel sickest. The loss of blood or the loss of love I didn't know was mine or my own inability to believe what she was saying about my husband. *Jorgji killed my aunt*? *He changed her will to exclude Mandy before the murder?* I couldn't fathom it. I grabbed hold of the chair that Keiko was still tied to trying to keep my consciousness conscious.

"He didn't kill my aunt," I said weakly, gripping the wooden back of the chair even harder with my un-bleeding hand. My phone started playing "The Lion Sleeps Tonight." It was a tune I had programmed for Frank's calls. I ignored it. "I thought you'd poisoned her with your cooking, but the medical examiner didn't find any evidence of wrong-doing in her death."

I didn't care that my blood was staining and pooling on the floor. I didn't care that my phone was beeping that I had a missed phone call. The pain in my hand was forgotten. It was nothing compared to the pain dripping from my heart.

There it was again. Her shrill, short laugh. "Jorgji smart. Jorgji good at killing. Jorgji know ways to kill without trace. He not so good at see his own death." Her mouth contorted into a hideous grimace as she came forward. "I kill him. You ring bell. I not know it you. I hide on balcony, in cold, till you go in other room and make safe for me go."

She stopped moving forward in favor of talking, taunting. Enjoying my physical and emotional pain. My phone rang again. I knew it was Frank, "The Lion Sleeps Tonight," but I couldn't answer it. I would be saying goodbye for real if I couldn't keep my distance from that knife. I circled around the chair away from Karine.

I was rapidly losing blood and didn't know how long I could play ring around Keiko.

Keiko struggled to free herself. Unsuccessfully. I moved as far away from Keiko as I could without getting closer to Karine. It was a small comfort, but a comfort never-the-less to know that Karine was focused on me. Not Keiko. At least Keiko was safe.

At least, she was until Karine stepped to Keiko's side.

"I want account and code numbers," Karine said. "Jorgji say he give with you for safe keeping. It not in safe. Not in boxes." Then for emphasis, like I didn't already believe her, she put the blade to Keiko's neck saying, "You want I kill her?"

My comfort level plummeted.

"There's no need to kill anyone," I said, urgently wanting to redirect Karine's attention back to me.

The floor was maroon with my blood. *How much blood does a body hold?*

I ignored the beeping of the phone that told me I'd another missed call. Karine felt justified in killing me. She had already killed Jorgji. I had no doubt of what she was capable of doing to Keiko. I had to get Keiko freed somehow, so I lied to Karine. "I can get you what you want. It's not here, but I can go get it. Let Keiko go. She doesn't have anything to do with this."

"She stay. She insurance. Like when Jorgji marry you."

I was doubled over in physical and emotional pain. To hear that Jorgji married me for my money was crippling me. I cradled my injured hand and tried to pull the cut, jagged edges together so I could staunch the flow of blood still running from the wound.

Karine couldn't resist. She continued, "When I hear you disappear I think Jorgji succeed in finish you off. I think he do right by me. I come to congratulate him getting his manhood back. He say it not him. He learn from crooked policeman someone take out contract for you. Jorgji want to take money we made. Buy contract. Cancel hit. He want you safe."

Karine's face was a bitter sneer of contempt. She removed the blade from its threatening spot near Keiko's neck and proceeded towards me.

I was not ignorant, no matter what anyone thought. I backed up and tried to angle myself towards the door leading to the dining room.

The going was not going so easily. The floor was slippery. My brain was dulled. I was slow and clumsy. It was like swimming in pancake syrup.

Karine had every advantage. Luckily, deranged Karine was so focused on doing a biting soliloquy about my treachery that she was not in any hurry to get to me. My emotional pain seemed to be making her happy. "He want me to hand over money to save you, sniveling, rich, pathetic American."

I was so close to fainting I couldn't think clearly. I couldn't have been hearing clearly.

"Jorgji lost to me. I want money. That my money, too. He smash laptop to keep money. He come at me. He going to kill me. I grab weapon that is like shiva. Thrust into chest. Like taught in Hayasdan. He fall. He die. Now you go to death."

Karine lunged at me. I saw only the knife as it loomed large in my sight. I had become too weak to move out of the way. When the knife was only a fraction away from my rib cage, it slammed out of my line of vision in a blur and clattered down into a pool of my blood. Slipping on the blood soaked floor, Karine went down hard and hit her head on the floor, unconscious.

I waivered as my knees buckled and soon there was going to be two of us in the same state.

Gordon dropped the umbrella he had used as a club and caught me as I pitched forward towards the floor.

He apologized, "I'm sorry to have interrupted such a

private conversation, Miss Imogene. You did not answer your phone, so Mr. Bachman called me."

Gordon, ever the consummate butler, called for medical assistance before he deftly tied Karine up with the cords he untied from Keiko. While we waited for the ambulance and police, Gordon wrapped a clean dish towel tightly around my injured hand and held it up high to slow the flow of blood.

My head was cradled in his lap as I lay on the floor, my feet propped up on a packing box Keiko found for that purpose. I could see the red and smell the blood. It had soaked into Gordon's starched white shirt and dark suit.

He was stroking my face and hair with his free hand as I wavered in and out of awareness.

I wasn't sure, and yet I was sure I could hear him croon in his calm voice, "Stay with me. You can't go. I can't let you go. Stay with me. Do you hear me, dear one? You have to hang in there. The ambulance will be here soon. I cannot lose you, too."

I guessed he was talking to Keiko, who continued to flutter and fume around a tied up, still unconscious Karine, sputtering something in Japanese that I'm glad none of us could understand.

Strong, handsome FBI agents couldn't be everywhere. That must be why God invented resourceful butlers.

CHAPTER 26

I woke up in the hospital to find Frank dozing on a chair beside my hospital bed. A plastic bag of red was dangling from a pole above me with a plastic line of red leading down to disappear into my arm, which was taped to a board. My free, unboarded hand wasn't free. It was wrapped in bandages half way to my elbow. I needed to scratch my nose because It itched so I brought my bandaged hand up and wiggled the fingers in the vicinity of my nose, then let my bandaged, useless hand drop down to the white spread. That would have to do. I was exhausted from the effort, and I was not waking up Frank to scratch any itch I had. Nose or otherwise.

I had a vague sense of Gordon in the room telling Frank to take a break; he would stay with me for a while. I wanted to open my eyes and thank Gordon for saving my life, but my lids were too heavy. I dozed again.

I heard a female voice whisper, "That's a bummer. Better have some tissues ready when you tell her that. She'll not take it too good. Never was a good loser. Always cried whenever Martin got the better of her. She was always a delicate little thing with fragile feelings." *Was that Mandy's voice?*

I tried to get my thoughts to swim to the surface of the haze that surrounded me so I could dispute her accusations of my being a poor loser. I thought Martin was the sore loser. I was a good sport.

Murky thoughts kept floating in the mist. Knives. Women in scrubs. Dripping blood. I finally stopped struggling and gave up to drift along where ever the murk took me.

The murk was replaced with a bright, brilliant light as someone clicked on the light above my bed.

"Time to check your fluid levels," said a cheerful young man dressed in a white lab coat carrying a tray of vials and other vile looking things.

I tried to orient myself. I couldn't stop blinking in the blinding light. Frank was still beside my bed. He blinked awake, too. He seemed to go from zero to full charge a lot faster than I did because he was already out of the chair and stretching. I rubbed my eyes with my bandaged hand and asked, "What time is it?"

"Time for me to take a walk," said Frank looking at the lab technician pulling out a tourniquet and a needle with a plastic connector. Frank grabbed his coat off the chair he was sleeping in and headed for the door.

"You're not afraid of needles are you, Frank?" I asked in a mocking tone as he scurried towards the door.

He turned at the door, smiled before he stepped out and said, "Not when it's you they're sticking. I'll be back as soon as he's gone."

Frank came back just as the lab rat got ready to leave. Great timing.

The phlebotomist picked up the wrapper from the band-aid he had just placed on my arm. Mr. Cheerful made sure all the labels were on all the vials and then walked out the door, whistling.

Frank's brow was showing worry lines. I wanted to

reach up and smooth the lines out, but I had an I.V. in one arm and a huge gauze bandage wrapped around the hand and wrist of the other, not to mention I was now sporting a little plastic bandage in the crook of my elbow.

"I don't know how they expect my hemoglobin levels to stay up when they take so many vials out of me," I jested, holding up my arm so Frank could see the new bandage.

"I'm sorry you have to go through all of this. If I'd done a better job of looking at all the documents I had from Marion's research, you wouldn't have ended up here."

"If you hadn't called Gordon, I wouldn't have ended up here; I'd be in the basement morgue. How did you know Karine was going to try to kill me?"

I saw the worry lines deepen and I knew the thing I was supposed to be fragile over was coming. I steeled myself mentally.

"I didn't know anything for sure, but it all fell into place when I saw the copy of Jorgji's and Karine's Albanian marriage license."

Not steeled enough, I closed my eyes, wishing I had a way to close my ears, too. "Karine told me Jorgji wasn't her brother. Why would he marry me if he were already married to her? Is it legal for him to do that?"

"No."

"She knew what he'd done. Why did she let him marry me knowing he was already married to her?"

"I think it was part of a plan they'd hatched up to get your money. Jorgji was raised in an orphanage. He ran away in his teens and hooked up with the Albanian mafia. He was smart. He married Karine and became part of her family's Ponzi investment fraud business. When their government cracked down, they made their way to America, land of the free and unaware. They managed to talk a lot of people out of a lot of money. You and your aunt were easy marks. You accepted his investment schemes without question. I think once they found out your net worth that's when he and Karine hatched up a more lucrative plan that went beyond getting your investment money. He married you intending to..."

Frank paused for several seconds. I think he was searching for the right words to protect me. I knew what he was going to say, but he didn't say it. "...get your money. I believe after he had married you he found he didn't want the money anymore. He wanted you. He was trying to find a way out of the arrangement he had with Karine. That's what got him killed."

"Karine said I ruined Jorgji. That I made him fall in love with me. She made it sound like I had some sort of spell over him. That I forced him to love me over her. I find it hard to believe that Jorgji would prefer me to a beautiful woman like Karine."

"I don't. Karine never stood a chance against you."

"Imogene, you sure you want to do this?" Mandy asked me as she helped me unpack my newly delivered boxes from Detroit. Those were the last of the items that Keiko packed from my apartment. I had delayed going through them. It wasn't because my hand was still bandaged. I was afraid of the memories the contents of these boxes would bring crashing down upon me. The man I thought I loved had killed my aunt. My cousin was trying to kill me for cutting the sister I didn't know I had out of a will I hadn't known about. I thought I was married, but he was already married, to a drop-dead-gorgeous woman who wanted me to drop dead.

The only good to come out of that whole mess was I had my very own sister.

In sisterly fashion, she agreed to open each packing box and tell me the contents before I looked at them; that way I could leave the room if it was something I didn't want to see.

"I'm sure," I answered her question, nudging another box towards her to open. "I want you to have your entire share of the inheritance from our father and your share of the inheritance from Aunt Tilly. It's only fair. You know Aunt Tilly wanted it, too. You were always in her will. The will Jorgji hadn't altered."

Mandy gave a little squeal as she opened a box that contained the sweaters and neck scarves I had knitted while in Detroit. Holding up a pink cashmere, she rubbed it against her cheek. "You won't mind looking in this box. Everything is keen."

No longer feeling like knitting, I gave the whole box to Mandy. She was delighted with it, more delighted than I was. I told her, "Once all this is sorted out I'll see that you get what should have been yours before my husband stole it and you can buy all the cashmere sweaters you want."

"Are you sure? You haven't even recover'd the money stolen by that rat who married you to get your money. If you give me my half, you won't even have enough to live on proper." She twisted her mouth into a frown. She had on a rhinestone studded baby blue tee shirt that had plastered across the front 'Big Sister.' It didn't come down to her navel, so I was sure she bought it in the children's section.

She looked so genuinely distressed at my financial situation that I couldn't bring myself to tell her that after I gave her what should have been hers, and then divided what I had left among the people Jorgji bilked out of their investments I wouldn't have anything left to live on, proper or not.

"I can always cut back on buying yarn," I joked as I handed her the next box to open. She opened the box, and joking threw one of the balls of yarn from inside at me. It hurt when it hit my arm. I picked up the cashmere-silk blend blue yarn that I had bought for Jorgji's socks. "Now where did this come from? I've been wondering where this got off to."

"I found it under the couch when the movers picked that thing up to load it on the truck. Keiko put it in one of the boxes with some of the stuff you'd knitted." Mandy said.

"It's pretty yarn and soft as all get out, but it does seem to have this little hard thing in the middle of it."

I furiously unwound the ball, letting all the yarn pile up into a wad on the floor, until I got to a small rectangle piece of techno-plastic that had been wound into the center of the ball. It was a data storage chip.

Frank was right about finding chips in the weirdest places.

CHAPTER 27

Janey was in the kitchen making dinner. Her husband was in the living room reading Lamaze pamphlets in preparation for their big day. Agent Stevens was at the dining room table with Frank busy explaining how the yarn-hidden files showed the pattern of how all the money was moved around to avoid detection. I was pacing from the living room to the dining room to the kitchen. Feeling left out and wanting to do something useful, I offered to assist Janie with fixing dinner.

"If you feel up to it, you can wash and peel the potatoes," Janey said to me.

When I reached under the sink, she rapidly changed her mind and decided she would wash them herself. She needn't of worried. I was only reaching to get that bottle of green stuff to clean the bowl to put the potatoes in, I wasn't going to use dish soap to wash potatoes. I was smart enough to know I'd have to use vegetable soap for vegetables.

"How does this thing work?" I asked as I picked up the handle of the kitchen implement she handed me and peered at the loopy end that had the blades in the center of it. It had to be for the potatoes because Janey had set that inside-out knife near the bowl of potatoes she had just washed, without soap of any kind. Go figure.

"It's a potato peeler."

When I looked confused, Janey said, "Here. You use it like this." She took the peeler and in one swift motion shoved the blade flat against the potato, and a curl of brown peel came out the center of the blade.

I took the peeler back from her and gouged at the potato. No peels magically came out the center of the peeler. I tried again. The bandages that were still on my Karine-cut hand made it difficult to use the peeler. I was not aiming for my thumb, but it kept getting in the way so I tried a different hold so I wouldn't peel my thumb better than the potato.

"Never mind," said Janey, promptly removing the blade from my clumsy hands. "Since your hand is not fully healed we'll have baked potatoes instead. Have you ever wrapped a potato in foil?"

"No. But I remove the foil before I eat one. Does that count?"

"Hmm. How 'bout you take this wrapping foil and pretend these potatoes are irregular-sized gift packages you need to wrap?"

Now gift wrapping was something I could relate to, and the tape I found to use didn't even burn much in the oven.

We were almost through the steak, salad, and baked potato dinner and I was disappointed that no one had yet complimented me on my fluffy, tender, expertly-done baked potatoes. Frank and Agent Stevens were engrossed in talking about the significance of this latest find of decoded records. Janey was showing the father-to-be all the ultrasound pictures and baby naming books she had amassed since he was at sea. He put his hand on her belly waiting for the baby to kick it. I guess a great baked potato just couldn't compare to impending parenthood or getting investor's back their almost unrecoverable money.

Janey caught my downcast look and said out of the blue, in a voice just loud enough to carry to Frank, "Imogene baked the potatoes. Weren't they fabulous?"

"She did?" Frank looked up at me, smiled and said, "Did you use your magic blink, Genie? They were delicious."

Janey was going to be a great mom.

***

Mandy used a chunk of her inheritance to post bail for Martin and hire him a good defense attorney. He needed one. Scuffy was singing like a terminal cancer-coughing canary. He had sung a long string of tales of deceit and deception that extended from the mayor's office to the police department to the killer-for-hire business Scuffy started with Tappy for extra cancer-cure cash when the drug money was stopped pending the audit and FBI investigation.

Gordon was helping Keiko get settled into the house in Winnetka. I was planning on asking Mandy if she'd like to move in, too. I didn't know which one Gordon would have more trouble understanding: Keiko with her lack of English or Mandy with her lack of proper English.

I still found it hard to believe that the man I was sort of married to was already married to Karine. Now that Jorgji's second set of records were recovered and Karine jailed, I wanted to put my debacle of a marriage behind me. As near as anyone could discern Jorgji never divorced Karine before he married me. My lawyer told me that he could get me free of Jorgji, legally at least.

Not much of the money had been found, but I was assured by the FBI they would recover as much as they could. I didn't know where that would put me, but after having survived new-found sisterhood, guns, knives, fake husbands and knitting needle death accusations, I had been strengthened into forged steel. Like the new set of crochet hooks I was learning to use—I was giving up knitting for a while. It was too dangerous.

I was going to have to give up a lot of things if I was going to survive with no money, but I was confident I could figure it all out without anyone's help.

My first figuring-it-all-out step was to have a talk with "Undercover Fan." Frank had been asked to cut his leave short, probably to do dangerous undercover work in life-threatening cases known only to him and Merle. Frank had worked out an agreement with Merle to delay going back to work one more night so he and I could go to another little good-as-mom's cooking Italian restaurant where he had reserved one of the private booths in the back. This time he left no doubt. It was a date.

Frank's eyes had that smoldery look I had come to know, and this time the smolder was not from anger. He took hold of my uninjured hand and looked at me with an intensity I couldn't bear, so I looked away and focused my attention on the gondola scene painted on the back wall. The ferns and flowers dripped off iron trellis's attached to brick structures, all alfresco without the inconvenience of being outside. When I didn't turn back to face him, Frank's other hand came up and gently turned my face so that I was facing him again.

"Tell me this isn't the end of us," he said with just the slightest bit of pleading in his voice that set my heart to beating erratically. "I think I love you and I know you feel something for me."

My heart began to go wild. I was glad he had waited until after I'd finished eating to broach the subject of us, but just in case he didn't, I had worn a red dress and asked the waiter for two napkins.

"I don't know what I feel," I began, choosing my words carefully, knowing, now that it was happening, that it was too soon for me. I had so much confusion to work through. "All my life I wanted someone to love and someone to love me. I wanted to be someone's wife and someday a mother. I sat home quietly knitting, reading, responding to my aunt's e-mails, waiting for the love of my life to show up. Then, one day there was Jorgji, tall, handsome and charming. I thought Jorgji was the someone I'd been waiting for. I thought he loved me. Looking back on it all, I think he really did want my love more than my money. He just couldn't untangle himself from the web of deceit he'd been woven into. Then, when my life was in danger, I was quick to disbelieve that love and label him a fraud. I thought I loved him, but I didn't really. I'm a bigger fraud than Jorgji. I was only in love with the idea of being in love."

Frank started to say something, but I put the fingers from my bandaged hand to his lips to shush him. "I do feel something for you, but I don't know if what I'm feeling is real love or just my soaring to new heights, finding out I'm stronger than I thought I was. Finding out life is more than just sitting at home knitting while your butler brings you tea and cookies. I've learned that life isn't going to come to me. I have to go get it. I have to find a way to get it. I need time. I need time to find me first, to be happy with me first before I can be happy with someone else."

"Please, if you love me, give me some time," I pleaded as I gazed unwaveringly into those intense brown, blue-flecked eyes. I held his gaze for as long as I could before I closed my eyes against the tears that threatened to start.

"My little yarn genie is out of the bottle." He pulled me closer to him and whispered against my ear as his lips nuzzled my ear lobe then they kissed my neck. "I love you— enough to let you go. For now. For a brief while. Go do what you need to. Find yourself. Get your life in order. Buy more yarns. I'll wait. But here's a little something to remind you to come back to me."

I felt his lips gently press against mine, the slightest of pressure, dry and warm. A little thrilling shudder went involuntarily through me as my lips pressed lightly back.

ZIG ZAG KNITTED SCARF

Materials:

8 ounces of worsted weight yarn
Size 6 straight knitting needles
Yarn needle

Gauge:

This scarf is done based on inches. The actual gauge is unimportant.

Abbreviations and Stitches:

K = Knit
P = Pearl
FO = finish off. Cut yarn leaving a tail for weaving in the ends securely.

Instructions

Cast on 28 stitches (for a wider or narrower piece use a number evenly divisible by 7).
Row 1: K 7, P7, K7, P7.
Row 2: K6, P7, K7, P7, K1.
Row 3: P 2, K7, P7, K7, P5.
Row 4: K4, P7, K7, P7, K3.
Row 5: P4, K7, P7, K7, P3.
Row 6: K2, P7, K7, P7, K5.
Row 7: P6, K7, P7, K7, P1.
Row 8: K7, P7, K7, P7, K7.
Row 9: P1, K7, P7, K7, P6.
Row 10: K5, P7, K7, P7, K2.
Row 11: P3, K7, P7, K7, P4.

Row 12: K3, P7, K7, P7, K4.
Row 13: P5, K7, P7, K7, P2.
Row 14: K1, P7, K7, P7, K6.
Row 15: P7, K7, P7, K7, P7

Subsequent Rows:

Repeat Rows 1 through 15 until the scarf is as long as you desire.
Bind Off [*working in pattern*]. Weave in ends.

Preview of
"Hooked Into Murder"
The second Yarn Genie Mystery

CHAPTER ONE

Tears stung my eyes as I watched Mr. Twerk grab an industrial-sized pair of scissors from his desk and reduce my credit cards to a colorful pile of plastic pieces. He used one unscathed card to gather all the little pieces up into a mound that he shoved off into a wastebasket at the edge of his desk. The bits all cascaded into the trash, making little plinking sounds as they hit the metal. All gone. Without my cards, how was I going to buy that lovely Christo yarn I'd been dying to try?

"Was that necessary?" I asked my financial advisor.

"Imogene Warren, you signed legal papers for me to negotiate your financial matters and get your bills in order. I've been trying to do just that, but since we've talked last, you have made sixteen more credit purchases. Your inheritance share of the royalties from your aunt's mystery series will just about cover the expenses for the colonial in Winnetka. However, her being dead, she can't very well write any new novels, can she? As time goes on, that revenue source will dry up. If you intend to keep her mansion, you have got to get your spending habits under control."

I reached into my pants pocket to finger the ball of Shesay yarn I'd secreted there, gray with little silver sparkles and metallic threads already woven in, a little stiff and scratchy. I should have brought the swatch of Cashmerino yarn I'd knitted up as a gauge for the scarf I made Frank. Frank is the undercover FBI agent who declared he loved me—just before I foolishly told him to leave me alone. That little knit square would have been much softer, more soothing to my nerves.

"Of course I want to keep the house," I told Mr. Twerk. "I've lived in that house with my Aunt Tilly since I was six years old. Now that she's dead, I miss her so much that I get distressed easily. I was only trying to brighten my spirits when I bought a few of the new Red Thread yarns. I didn't think it would hurt to make a few small purchases."

Mr. Twerk sighed a deep-down sigh. "Spending a hundred dollars ten times is the same as spending a thousand dollars. Even the small purchases add up. If you insist on keeping the mansion and its household staff, then I recommend you eliminate everything that isn't essential for your survival, cut your expenses to the bone, and sell all your other assets."

"Which assets are you referring to? My financial portfolio? That was only a fabrication made up by Jorgji to steal my wealth. My jewelry? That was all taken by Jorgji, too. The paintings and art collections? The house in the Cayman Islands? I had to sell that house, the paintings, and the art collections to give my half-sister her share of the inheritance from our aunt. All I have left, beside the mansion, are my clothes and my yarns."

"Too bad there aren't any additional manuscripts of your aunt's that you could sell. Those would fetch a mint now that she's dead."

I blew out a puff of air through pursed lips so my hair would blow away from my eyes and I could let off steam.

"You sound just like Rosenthal and Gildenstein."

Mr. Twerk raised his eyebrows at me. "Who?"

"Rosenthal and Gildenstein. They were my aunt's literary agent and publicist. If I have to tell them one more time that the last two manuscripts I have are unfinished and of no value to them, I'll scream."

The eyebrows went up farther before they settled back to their unemotional level above each beady eye. "You do still have the Bentley and the Rolls. They'd fetch a good price," he said, shifting in his chair. "Might keep the wolf from the door a few more months. It's a shame your husband was killed before the FBI could discover where he hid the billions he absconded with."

"He was not my husband!" I shot up out of my chair and began to pace the room. I didn't want to talk about Jorgji, the man who plotted with his wife, Karine, to get my money—and succeeded. "The lawyers have assured me that since he was already married in Albania, our marriage wasn't legal."

"Legal or no, until the FBI recovers your missing funds, you are without two dimes to rub together." Mr. Twerk tidied up the pencils, pens and other objects on his desk then slid the scissors back into the top drawer.

"They haven't recovered any of the money yet, have they?" he asked me, eyes averted to the stack of overdue household bills that I'd brought for him to deal with.

I stopped my pacing for a brief moment to glower at him. He continued to avoid my stare by shuffling the bills around a bit more before placing them in the file folder with my married name, Imogene Dalmat, neatly penciled on the tab.

"No. The electric company wouldn't be threatening to

shut off my lights, and I wouldn't be here talking to you if I had my money back. I've called the FBI Financial Crimes Investigation Unit every day, sometimes two or three times a day. Mr. Stevens, the agent assigned to my case, told me to stop calling him. He'll call me when he has news to share."

Mr. Twerk harrumphed. He slid the one lone unscathed credit card across the top of his desk towards me. "I'll contact the utility companies to negotiate delays in payment. I've already consolidated all your cards to this one account with the lowest interest rate. You'll have just one credit card bill to pay each month, but it'll be a whopper."

He took a pencil out of its wooden stand, stuck it in the electric pencil sharpener where it whirled around to sharpen its already sharp point. He removed the pencil to test the point against the tip of his index finger. Satisfied, he hunched over his desk and began making tiny sharp pencil notes in my file.

I paused my pacing to pick up the lone white rectangle with the holographic bird in the corner. I smiled a knowing smile. I was not alone. I still had my Select Rewards Visa. We headed towards the office door.

Mr. Twerk looked up from his folder scribbling in time to catch sight of my expression, the glint in my eye, and the tight grip I had on my credit card. He said to me, before he hunched back over his desk, "You won't be able to use the card for any more purchases. It was maxed out after I put my service fee on it."

Darn. I hadn't counted on my financial advisor charging me to cut up my cards.

A NOTE FROM THE AUTHOR

I am delighted you made it all the way through to the end of the second edition of *Knitting Up a Murder,* book one in the Yarn Genie Mystery Series. Changes were made to the point of view in the novel based on reader feedback. If you found this novel an enjoyable read or would like to provide feedback, please leave an on-line review at the location where you bought the book.

If you would like to follow the continuing story of the Yarn Genie and her exploits, please e-mail the publisher at islandcitypublishing@gmail.com.

All books go through several edits for content and grammar, but if you catch a spelling error or grammatical mistake, I would appreciate it if you would let the publisher know at islandcitypublishing@gmail.com.

Please note that while I strive to make the story realistic, everything in this book is a work of fiction. The places used in the story are sometimes based on real locations, but the use of them and the events surrounding them are purely fiction and should not be construed as factual or accurate.

Made in the USA
San Bernardino, CA
31 October 2018